GOOD GROUND

TRACY WINEGAR

OMNIFIC PUBLISHING

DALLAS

Omnific Publishing
10000 North Central Expressway, Dallas, TX 75231
www.omnificpublishing.com

First Omnific eBook edition, July 2013
First Omnific trade paperback edition, July 2013

The characters and events in this book are fictitious.
Any similarity to real persons, living or dead,
is coincidental and not intended by the author.

Library of Congress Cataloguing-in-Publication Data

Winegar, Tracy.
    Good Ground / Tracy Winegar – 1st ed.
    ISBN: 978-1-623420-33-8
    1. Love — Fiction. 2. 1930s — Fiction.
    3. Farming — Fiction. 4. Relationships — Fiction. I. Title

10 9 8 7 6 5 4 3 2 1

Cover Design by Micha Stone and Amy Brokaw
Interior Book Design by Coreen Montagna

Printed in the United States of America

Dedicated to my daddy and mom,
his daddy and mama, and to
Rosemary, Marlin, Minnie, DeAnna, and Lee.

*Train up a child
in the way he should go,
and when he is old
he will not depart from it.*

Proverbs 22:6

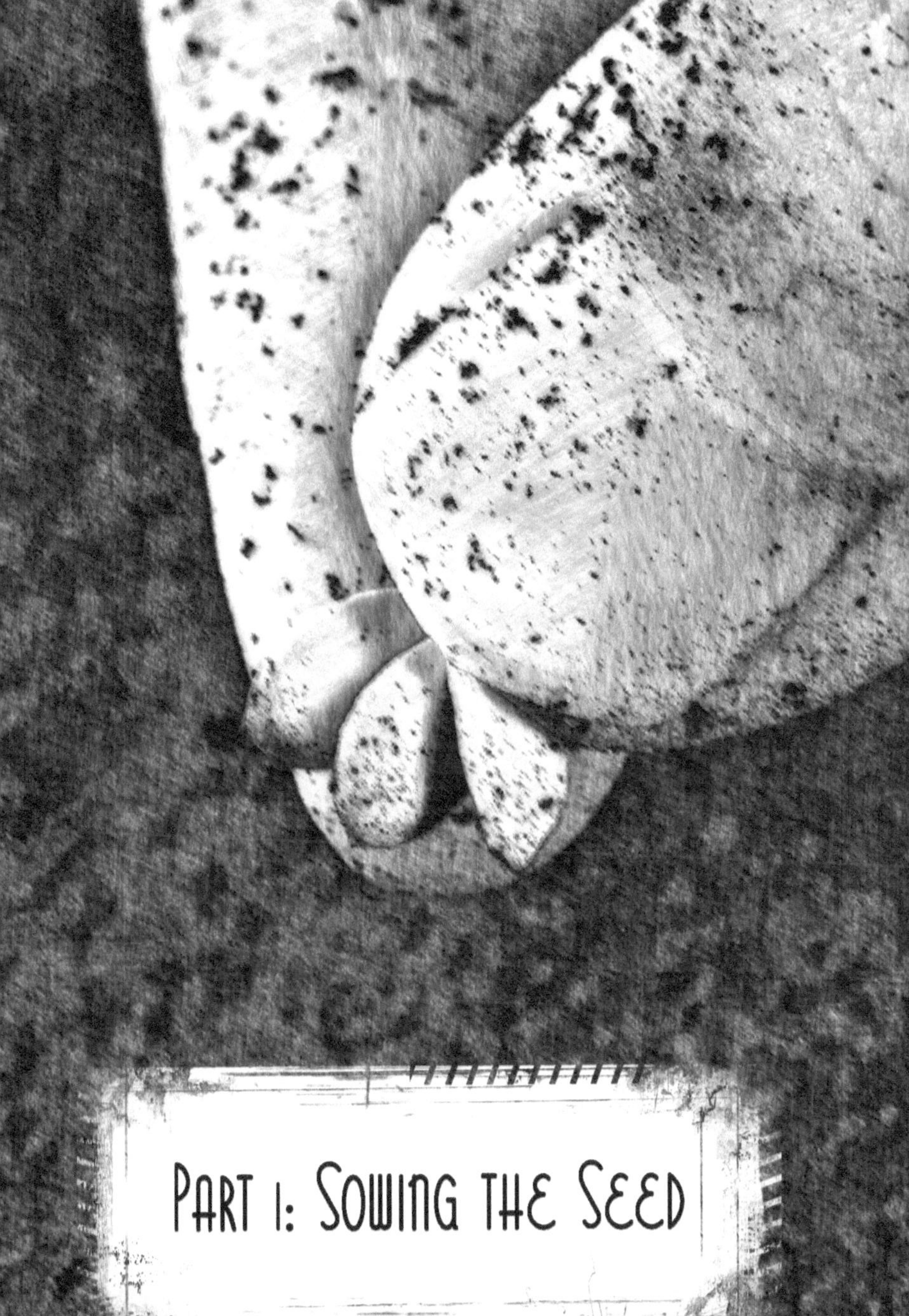
Part 1: Sowing the Seed

Chapter 1

Fall of 1908

im Hooper began walking on a Sunday, a day he generally set aside for worship. But Jim no longer had the desire to worship. The grieving had become so bad; he wondered if there really was a God in the heavens above, for surely no father could watch his child suffer so. His decline had been a steady and steep one. From the time he had covered her up in the ground two weeks ago to now, the fragile shell of his brain had succumbed to the pressure of his loss, and the cracks and fissures had begun to appear and spread like an egg being beaten against the side of a frying pan. So, on this Sabbath day, Jim was about other business.

He had always taken great pride in his land. The red earth neatly and precisely furrowed, worked up fine and soft. No clots. No weeds. Long, straight rows of hand-watered tobacco, fussed over much as a mother would fuss over a child. He had watched it grow with great affection. First had come the fuzzy leaves sprinkled with chartreuse flower buds, then the chest-high foliage, broad and thick and lush.

He was born to be a farmer. It was something that he was good at, something he knew well. He was a giver of life, an alchemist that worked in dirt, seed, and manure. Yet, as the days stretched by, he'd begun to question all that he thought he knew, even farming, that most fundamental part of himself. All else seemed to fall by the wayside. All that he had lived for — the very reasons he had gotten out of bed in the morning — had become unimportant, even trivial.

In the spring, he had planted the tobacco seeds in seed beds, protected with a canvas cover until they had grown strong enough to transplant to the fields. They had grown six to eight inches high, tall enough for Jim to see that they were ready to sink their roots into some real earth. Then he had done the setting, pulling them from the seed beds and putting them into the ground in the fields.

How he had fawned and fussed over them. But somewhere along the way, he had stopped caring. His heart was empty. She was gone, never to occupy the rocker, squinting in the light of the fire as she darned socks. He would never hear her hum a tune as she hung out the laundry, or watch her strain fresh milk through cheese cloth into a pail. There were so many small things that he had taken for granted when he had her. Jim now saw them for what they were: daily miracles of living.

Maybe he should have counted himself lucky that he'd had her at all, that for one brief moment she'd been his and they had known such complete joy. She had confided in him once that all it had taken was a good look at the back of his neck. She had said, with a sheepish smile, that she'd spotted him out back of Beaty's Grocery playing at horseshoes while she and her friends were having a grape soda pop, and just the sight of the back of his neck had convinced her that this was the man she would marry.

In all of his sad and difficult life, she had been the bright ray that had made it all seem worth the struggle. And what more could a man want from life than the companionship of a good and true woman? Edith had been that and more. So much more.

Two weeks had passed, and he had tried to keep up with the farm out of duty, out of routine, out of doing what he had always done. But gradually, as the days had slipped by, he had stopped toiling and struggling with it. To start with, Jim had wondered what might happen. He had the notion that the farm would go the way of his soul, a mirror image of the ruin he felt inside of himself. He imagined that if someone were to slice him open, he might very well resemble an apple that looked all shiny and golden by its exterior but once cut into was all decaying brown and rotten flesh, good for nothing. What did he care of the farm anyhow? Or, how could he care now that she was gone?

The place seemed to have a will stronger than his. Sure, it was worse for wear, but it still struggled on. God had seen fit to water his crop for him, and the tobacco had thrived on its own without Jim's loving attention, as if to flaunt its own abilities and confirm his lack of significance. And as the leaves grew stronger and paler, to a yellow-green hue, it was a painful reminder that life went on.

Now, the tobacco was ready to harvest, waiting to be cropped, managing, somehow, to have withstood the scorching heat of the merciless sun. Still, Jim ignored the signs he had so eagerly watched for in seasons past, and just as the cutting had been left undone, so had other things about the farm. By and by, he had fallen out of his usual habits and taken to sitting in a stupor of self-pity, letting the day fritter by with no productivity on his part as the evening shadows engulfed him. And his mind worked over what he could have done, what he should have done differently to save her. He, the man who had vowed to provide for her and protect her. He, the man who had failed her.

Out of mercy, Jim had finally given in and milked the cow that afternoon. It had been bawling so loudly that he just hadn't been able to ignore it any longer. How long had it been? Couldn't have been more than a day or two, he'd told himself. The old Guernsey was usually a gentle thing, but she had voiced her discomfort when he had finally come around to milk her, her teats leaking, her udder bulging and taut.

When Jim had finished the milking, he had gone into the house to have another drink. Though he was normally not a drinking man, he had taken up the pastime recently. He'd had an occasional glass of corn whiskey now and then but always for what he would have said were only "medicinal purposes." Never enough to get drunk.

Another exception to his usual conduct, he had gotten drunk. Very drunk. He'd let the devil have his way about it, giving into the thoughts that beset his weakened mind. *Have a drink*, the seductive voice had whispered. *It will surely take away the pain.* And, perhaps at first, Jim had attempted to resist. *It will take your burden from you*, it had insisted. *It will make you feel nothing. That is what you want, isn't it, to be numb, to feel nothing?*

The first several times he had gotten drunk, it had left him violently ill, for his system was not used to the ample flow of alcohol. But it had felt good to hurt so, to be so physically crippled, to inflict such punishment upon his body. He would drink until he vomited and then drink more. Eventually, he would pass out and later wake up in strange positions in various places about the house and yard. His mind was a splendid fog of confusion — long stretches of time gone and shameful behaviors Jim failed to remember. He could forget what had happened and live in the surreal hallucinations that haunted him.

When the drink began to leave his system, his limbs would shake and his body would break out in a cold sweat, his head throbbing cruelly. However, after several days of binging, he had grown to tolerate it. If he had not been so weak, so small and feeble, so pathetic, he might have had the guts to drink until he was dead. But he never brought himself to death — only the verge of it.

On this day, while he threw down one glass after another, his foggy brain had formulated a plan. His lips sucked the last of the amber liquid from his glass, and he slammed it back onto the table, angry that it was empty. Angry that he needed it. Angry that it hadn't taken away the pain and only seemed to magnify it. Angry that he had been driven to that point. Even angry enough that his plan seemed sane.

It made sense that someone should hurt as badly as he did, and since he couldn't punish God, he chose the next worthy candidate. The doctor had let her die. He had let her die, and there needed to be some retribution for someone, anyone…

She made his usual breakfast that day. Only it was not like every other day. It was the day his world would end. He didn't know that yet, and so he ate his bacon, eggs, biscuits, and gravy without enjoying them properly. His Edith knew how to please a man's stomach. She was far superior in that area to most women. He liked watching her at work as she kneaded the dough, scattering the flour across the surface of the table with her slender hands. How she stirred the pot slowly, deliberately, as if she were engaged in some form of worship, as if each meal were a work of art. She was so meticulous about her duties.

After finishing his breakfast, he kissed her and held her close, with her big belly pressed between them. He placed a little peck on her brow before putting his hat on his head and leaving to tend to his tobacco. After cleaning up breakfast and tending to things about the house, Edith eventually emerged to milk the cow, as she did every morning. He watched her with pleasure as she made her way to the barn, swinging the empty bucket in sync with her fast pace.

Jim thought it was funny that her stride was so broad and ambitious. Edith was such a tiny thing, but even he, with his long legs, struggled to keep up. She always wanted to get wherever she was going in such a hurry. Why was she so impatient?

The question lingered, but he did not have an answer for it, so he pushed the recollection aside, rubbed his whiskered chin, and let out a sour belch. Yes, Jim knew exactly what he would do.

He got up from the table, staggering a little, trying to steady himself on drunken legs, and went for the door, where his essentials were stowed on the pegs on the wall. He stuck his arms in his old coat, having some difficulty with it because of his state. He pulled his hat down tight on his head, went to the cupboard in the kitchen, and got his pistol. He headed out as the sun grew very low in the sky, lighting it up with fiery reds and oranges.

For the first time in two weeks, he had a purpose. He had a destination. He was going to town. He was going to have a visit with the doctor. If Jim hadn't been so drunk, he would have thought to take his horse.

With every step of the rutted road, his goal became clearer and sharper in his mind. First, it was an image focusing then blurring, growing dim and then bright. His pace grew faster as the memories flooded him. The more he walked, the more clarity came to him. He thought of her pain, her fear.

She went to the barn to do her milking, and he busied himself with checking the progress of his tobacco. He observed that it would be ready soon, ready to cut, ready to thread onto the tobacco spears that he would hang from the barn rafters to dry. He saw her come from the barn with the bucket filled to the rim with foaming milk. She dropped it.

Jim thought to himself that she was going to be good and mad for making that mistake and almost laughed, thinking on how she would scold herself thoroughly for such a blunder. But instead of stamping her foot and cursing, instead of bending to pick up the bucket, she remained hunched over, holding her swollen belly. He knew immediately that something was wrong, and he ran through the rows of tobacco, breaking the leaves of the plants in his haste, as he hurried to her. A dark fear rushed through him, starting in his throat and coursing through his gut, pushing him to increase his speed as he struggled to reach her.

He called to her. She said nothing, only looked up at him with eyes full of fear and panic, her mouth pressed in a grim line. She brought her hand up from between her legs and gasped when she saw it was wet. His arms around her, he carried her back to the house. Once inside, he lowered her onto the big iron bed.

Jim was sick at the thought of it. He gritted his teeth, and his long, calloused fingers curled tightly about the gun in his pocket, reassuring and comforting him, as each stride propelled him closer to his goal. Yes, he would go and call on the good doctor. He would go to his fine house, with all of his fine things, and he would pay him a little visit.

Chapter 2

It was fully dark by the time he hit town. Good and dark, the streets empty. The only trace of whiskey was the slightly queasy feeling in his stomach. His illness had left him, but his rage had not. The rage had replaced the drunkenness but felt even better. Now, rage drove him, not the drink, and he felt wonderfully lucid.

He hung back in the shadows of the trees that lined the street for a moment, watching the doctor's house for any signs of life within.

He had come here that day, once he had discovered how bad off she really was.

Edith was distraught. She told him that the baby was coming. But it wasn't time for the baby to come. It was too early. He told her he would fetch the doctor. He told her he would only be gone for a bit. He told her everything would be all right.

She agreed that would be the best thing to do, holding her belly and lying back on the bed. He didn't want to leave her. Fearful of what might happen with her there alone, he raced to harness the horse and hitch it to the wagon and then hollered the brown mare into a dead run out of the yard and onto the rutted dirt road. He took the curves too fast, nearly colliding with another wagon on the winding mountain road during the forty-five minute dash to town.

But when he reached Doctor Fielding's home, Gilda Fielding said the doctor was not there. He was off tending to someone else. Jim was panic-stricken, and Gilda could do nothing but sympathize with him.

"Please," he said. "I don't know nothin' to do for her. Please come on and hep her."

Gilda was in a difficult spot. She reasoned that if she left to go with him, the doctor wouldn't know to come. She said he wouldn't be much longer. She would tell him Edith needed help. She promised Jim that she would send the doctor out to the farm the second he returned. And she promised that she would come along too, to help.

Now, standing outside of that same home he had come to the day she had died, feeling his heart pound furiously within his rib cage and adrenaline pump through his veins, he wondered if he could do it. Could he kill another human being?

And then he thought of Edith. He thought of her thick brown hair, normally worn in a tight bun but which cascaded down to her shoulders when she would pull the pins and shake it loose. He pictured her tan cheeks and the freckles on her bronzed arms and remembered the milky white softness of the skin beneath her stockings and dress. He also remembered how her rounded belly had grown large and taut. His Edith, who had been so small, so fragile compared to his big, clumsy frame. She had been strong, could put in a day's work that was equal to a man's, but she had been slender and small-boned too.

The memories flooded his mind again, coming in a wave of remorse and regret.

He left the doctor's house that day without any doctor to show for it, pushing the tired horse back up the mountain road just as he had come, feeling an urgency he had never felt before. She was alone. She was afraid. She was his responsibility. It was his job to protect her, to take care of her, to see to it that nothing harmed her. She was relying upon him.

Leaving the winded mare to stand in the yard, he vaulted from the seat and sprinted into the house. He could hear Edith moaning before he reached their bedroom, and the sound made his stomach drop.

Relief flooded her face when she saw him again, glad that he had returned, desperate for help. She looked past him, expecting the doctor, but he wasn't following along behind.

She asked him where the doctor was. It was left to Jim to tell her the doctor was not coming. He saw the panic setting in and attempted to soothe her, reaching to smooth his frantic wife's hair.

It was torture to hear her groan, to see her suffering. And she told him how it hurt, how frightened she was, murmuring over and over that it was not time…It was not time. As she writhed in pain, Jim unlaced her dusty shoes and took them off her feet, setting them on the floor next to the bed neatly beside one another. He rolled her stockings down and pulled them off, placing them on the chest of drawers. He then followed her direction as she asked him to remove her soaked underwear and pulled her dress down to cover her legs.

Bewildered by his helplessness, he asked her what more he could do. Edith momentarily distracted him by requesting a drink of water. It gave him something to do, and he went quickly to the cistern in the kitchen and brought back a cup of water. Struggling to sit up, she drank it messily while he held the cup to her lips, sloshing much of it onto the front of her dress. When she signaled she'd had enough, Jim put the cup on the table next to the bed and helped ease her back onto the pillow. She whimpered a little, her knuckles white as she clenched her fists, a striking contrast to the colors of the quilt that her mama had made, one of the few things she had left to remember her by.

She could not keep from crying, the tears rolling down her cheeks as she bore the pain with pitiful whimpering. Gradually, the contractions eased, and she was still until they began again. Then, her body was wracked with another contraction, and she braced herself, her whole body tensing. Gritting her teeth, she held her breath, waiting for the pain to subside. Jim silently prayed for it to pass each time. Then, as the contraction slowly eased, she breathed deeply again with relief until she had to brace herself for another.

Jim tried coaxing her into relaxing. But even as he said it, he felt foolish. How could she relax in such a condition? He hated his inability to help her, to say or do anything that would take away her suffering. He was desperate to do anything that would bring her comfort. Why was he so useless? What was the point in saying something so obvious? She attempted to nod, to let him know that she was trying, but her half-hearted attempt ended before it began.

She grunted, writhed, gasped for breath, resisting the urge to push. As much as she fought to hold the baby, it seemed that the baby did not want to be held. He could barely make out her words as she cried out desperately that the baby was coming.

Jim lifted Edith's dress and watched in amazement as the baby slipped out onto the bed, miniature and blue. It was a girl. Her tiny head was about the size of a small apple, and her little arms weren't much longer than his fingers. The baby did not cry as he cradled her in his calloused hands.

Looking upon her, he understood that his daughter would not draw a breath, would not stir or open her delicate eyelids, laced with fine blue veins, so that he could even know the color of eyes that were hidden beneath them. She was as light as a feather, her skin wet and slippery. Her dark hair was plastered to her petite scalp, but he kissed it anyway, choking back the sorrow he felt.

Edith stirred, raised herself up onto her elbow. Upon seeing the lifeless little body he held, she let herself fall back onto the bed with a wail, not even trying to control her tears.

This recollection and the gun held tight in his grip gave him strength. Yes, with the thought of her fresh in his mind, he figured he could kill a man. Steeling himself with the bitter pangs of disappointment and her loss, he *could* kill a man. It was with determination that he stomped up onto the covered porch and beat loudly on the doctor's door.

All was dark and still inside the Cape Cod that was painted white with green shutters. The house sat on a corner lot surrounded by rose bushes and giant oak shade trees, the picture of tranquility and solitude, but the abrupt sound of Jim's banging broke the silence of the house within.

It was a very brief wait before the doctor pulled the door wide open so swiftly that Jim was slightly taken aback. He stood frozen, leaning heavily on the door jamb, meeting the doctor's startled expression with his own. The two men stood observing one another — one hazy from drink and rage, the other hazy from just coming out of a sound sleep — and for a moment the stillness returned again. As Jim looked at the doctor, he seemed oddly different in his nightshirt, out of his usual trousers and black jacket. No one in town dressed like the doctor did except for the banker. He looked very human standing there then without his best clothes on.

To see him with his hair tousled and his bare legs peeking out from his nightshirt threw Jim off. For a moment, he forgot why he was there.

"Jim Hooper?" the doctor finally got out. His eyebrows were knit together to match the confusion in his voice. Apparently Jim was the last person he had expected.

"Doctor Fielding," he said with a little nod, just as if they were exchanging a greeting under normal circumstances.

The doctor hesitated briefly before standing aside and motioning for him to come in. Jim stepped across the threshold, his hand firmly on the grip of the pistol in his coverall pocket. He stopped in the front hall and looked around.

Gilda Fielding had the finest parlor he had ever seen. He walked aimlessly about the moonlit room, gazing at the framed photos, the stitcheries, the lace doilies, the plump velvet settee, the rocking chair with its fat red cushion, a piano in the corner against the wall, and a fireplace all dandied up with molding and red brick. Yes, it was an elegant room, something proper that he would have liked to have been able to give to Edith.

Even as that thought came to him, he tossed it away. He could not imagine her there. She would have been out of her element in a room such as that. She had been of a much simpler mold.

Doctor Fielding lingered near the doorway, merely observing Jim as he satisfied his curiosity by prowling the parlor. When he saw that Jim had finished with his inspection, he said quietly, still mindful of his sleeping wife and daughters, "What did you come for, Mr. Hooper?" His voice was quiet and sympathetic.

Jim turned to look at him square in the eyes, not wanting to appear the coward. "I come to kill you, Doctor. I come to shoot you dead."

CHAPTER 3

The mantel clock ticked loudly in the darkened silence, and a thick tension hung in the air. Neither man moved. Neither spoke as they stood opposite one another, each trying to surmise what the other's thoughts might be. Jim felt as if time had stopped, as if the doctor hadn't heard or understood what he had said. Perhaps he had thought it a joke. Anyhow, the older man seemed unfazed by the threat.

"You hear me?" Jim forced out through clenched teeth.

"I heard you, but you'll do no such thing," the middle-aged man replied in a slow, even tone. There was no fear in those wise brown eyes. No panic of an impending end to his life. Only confidence that Jim was not capable.

"I brung my gun," Jim said, fumbling to pull it out of his pocket to prove it. "If I ain't gonna do it, then why'd I bring my gun for?"

"Don't be foolish. Put that thing away before it goes off by accident. You and I both know you couldn't hurt a fly."

"I'm not about to put this thing away. I aim to use it. You listenin'?"

"It won't do you any good, Jim. It won't change anything. You must know that."

"Maybe won't change nothin', but go a ways to makin' me feel better, anyhow."

"You been drinking?"

"A little," Jim admitted. He knew Edith wouldn't have liked that. She would have said only trash gets drunk. She would have scolded him for such an indulgence.

"How about you go into the other room there and sleep it off," the doctor offered.

"I'm of a sound mind! The drink is gone! And I didn't come to sleep. I come for you, Doctor."

"Jim, what could I have done?" he asked gently, as if he were speaking to a young child.

Standing in the gloom of the fancy townhome, Jim concentrated his hostile glare upon Doctor Fielding, who was watching him closely, waiting for what would come next. He felt nothing but hatred. If the doctor had only come when his wife had needed him, she would still be alive, still be with him. He didn't care that someone else had needed the doctor just as badly as Edith had. It only made him more angry to think the doctor had chosen to give someone else life over Edith. Edith, who had been so good and true. No amount of reasoning would convince him otherwise.

"What could I have done?" the doctor repeated, waiting for an answer.

"You coulda done plenty."

"Put the gun down and go on home."

Jim stepped closer to the older man and put the gun to the doctor's chest, pushing it hard against the striped flannel of his nightshirt. "I can't."

"You won't do it. You don't have it in you."

Jim raised his voice. "I don't, you say? I'll show you! I said I come to kill you, and I aim to do just that!" His bellow echoed in his own ears, ringing through the corridors of the doctor's silent home, as intrusive as if someone had raised their voice in the hush of a church house.

It was at that moment that a shrill little cry pierced the silence. Jim flinched, looking about wildly, thinking perhaps that he was being haunted by his own child. He pulled the gun away from the doctor's chest and dropped it as if it had burned him to the touch. The pistol clattered loudly on the hardwood floor. The doctor retrieved the gun and tossed it onto the settee.

"Darn it, you woke the house now," Doctor Fielding growled as the place came to life. He went through the parlor door into his examination room across the hallway as Gilda rushed down the stairs, braids bouncing.

Jim was frozen, his feet like lead where he stood in the parlor, watching the scene unfold with wonder, forgetting briefly what his errand in going there had been.

Doctor Fielding came back from his examination room, holding an infant over his shoulder, patting it gently on the back. He stopped before Gilda and grimaced a little. "Go back to bed, Mrs. Fielding. I'll take care of this one."

"You're sure?" she asked, sounding guilty, as if she wanted very much to go back to bed.

"Yes, I'm sure," the doctor told her. "I hope it didn't wake Millie and Rachel."

"I'll check in on them," she promised and then turned and headed back up the stairs, apparently unaware that they had a visitor in their parlor.

The doctor came back to where Jim was planted, a rather unpleasant expression on his face as he bounced and patted the bundle he carried. "You probably scared the poor thing half to death. For shame, Jim Hooper."

"What you got there?" he asked, craning his neck to get a better view.

"A baby, Jim. It's a baby," he said in exasperation.

"You and the wife don't got no baby. Your little 'uns is all big and growed now."

"It isn't ours. It's that Borden girl's."

The baby continued to wail plaintively, and the doctor switched his bundle to the other shoulder.

"Why isn't she takin' care of it?"

"Because she's dead," the doctor replied in an irritated tone of voice. "She was too young for having babies, and it killed her. Died on Saturday. The children's home down in Nashville can't come around until tomorrow afternoon to get this boy."

"Don't her kin wanna lay claim on him?"

"No one wants a thing to do with this little child. This one's mama wasn't one with a good reputation around here. No one can say for certain who the father is, and no one wants a bastard child. He's just another mouth to feed," Doctor Fielding explained. "Times are hard."

Jim stood there in his dirty overalls, with his unshaven countenance, and held out his rough hands, dirt caked beneath his nails and around his cuticles, wanting. "Can I have a look at him?"

The doctor hesitated, eyeing him suspiciously.

Jim knew the doctor was undecided and sought to sway him. He held his arms out a little further and gave him a pleading look. In spite of Jim's recent threats, the doctor reluctantly handed the baby over to him.

As Doctor Fielding lit a lamp, Jim carried the little babe with great care to the rocking chair and pulled the blankets back, inspecting the roundness of his cheeks, the dimples over each knuckle on his hands, his big belly, his naval—still a bloody stump—and fat thighs that tapered to fat calves and down to minute toes at the end of his long, slender feet. *He is a fine thing,* Jim thought. His body was solid, sturdy, and so very different from his little daughter's delicate physique.

The baby continued to wail. "Boy, don't he howl!" Jim mused with a chuckle, pleased with the baby's strong lungs. He glanced up at the doctor with a half grin and then back to the baby.

"Yes, he does howl," the man replied with a little less enthusiasm.

"This here is how my mama done it with her youngins," Jim said. Using his legs as a work space, he laid the baby's plump form along them as he tucked the baby's arms in next to his body and wrapped the blankets tight around him, barely giving him room to move. Then, holding the baby close to his chest, he began to rock, and the baby grew still and quiet. "He's a fine little feller." Jim cooed as he and the babe regarded one another. "Whowee," he said to the baby. "Whowee."

"You seem to have a knack with him," Doctor Fielding observed. He moved Jim's pistol aside and sat down heavily on the settee, watching the both of them.

Jim was quiet, somehow seeming settled and at peace as he rocked the baby, smelling his fuzzy scalp, patting his tiny bottom. At some point, Doctor Fielding drifted off, lulled to sleep by the pace of the rocker on the floor as it squeaked and creaked.

The baby in Jim's arms made him reflective. His mind settled on Edith, on the baby they had made together, the child that was their own that now lay in her mother's arms in the grave upon the hill. He would have done anything to stop Edith's tears that last day, to have given her some comfort.

Jim was painfully aware of the sorrow she was feeling. After a time, Edith stopped crying, wiping her cheeks with her work-worn hands. She told him then that she would have called the baby Ruby for her mother, and in a daze directed him to the crib in the corner where he could find a quilt she had pieced. Jim did not want to move, certain that if he held still long enough, he would find that it was all a dream, none of it real. But he couldn't ignore her request. He laid the little body on the bed next to Edith and did as she told him, going to the crib he had crafted with his own hands. Picking up the pieced quilt, he took it back to the bed and wrapped the baby in it then laid the tiny bundle against Edith's arm. As much as it hurt him to set the baby aside, his concern was for Edith now.

Her face was colorless; it seemed the bronze tone of her skin and the freckles had completely disappeared. She began to shake, and the trembling became so violent that her teeth chattered. The harder she strained to stop the tremors, the worse they became. Jim tucked a blanket around her, and she asked for another. He piled another on top of her, and after a time the shaking stopped. He sat on a stool next to the bed, clutching her hand. He supposed that Edith knew that he was worried over her, that he was frightened. As she hemorrhaged beneath the blankets, she murmured apologies to him. She was sorry. She was sorry.

Surrendering to his horror at the stillbirth of his daughter and the fear and helplessness he couldn't control, Jim began to weep. He doubted that he would ever manage to erase the horrific scene from his brain, ever dispel the picture of his daughter as he held the little, blue, premature body in his hands.

He let his head fall upon the bed beside Edith, beside the bundle that held their lifeless baby. She ran her fingers through his hair, soothed him, waited until he had calmed. He was quiet for a time with his eyes squeezed shut, trying to block out what he had just seen, what he was now feeling.

Edith's voice was unsteady and weak as she assured him that they would have another. That she would fill the house to the rafters with his children. She swore it to him. Why would she make such a promise?

There was something in her declaration that made him alarmed all over again. He asked her if she was all right. Barely able to whisper, her energy gone, she told him she was tired. Jim smoothed her hair away from her face and told her to rest for a time; the doctor would be along soon.

Nodding, her eyelids fluttered shut, and she fell asleep. That was the last time he had seen her blue eyes. He wondered if perhaps their little baby girl would have had eyes as blue.

Doctor Fielding finally arrived in his black Model T with Gilda in tow. Jim's eyes were dull and without expression as he let them in. Jim stayed in the front room, standing in the corner, swaying on his feet, wringing his hands, while Gilda tried to ask him questions, tried to get him to talk, as the doctor went into the bedroom. Finally, Jim broke away from her and drifted to the bedroom where the doctor had found Edith lying under a pile of quilts, her face slack, her body still. Jim knew she was dead. It hung heavy in the atmosphere, tickled the hairs on his neck. It had a particular sound and smell to it. All those things permeated the stale air in the room as he looked upon Edith's lifeless form. When the doctor pulled back the blankets, he saw the baby, swaddled in a new quilt, the umbilical cord still attached to the placenta. The older man cut the cord and covered the baby's face and then pulled a quilt over Edith's sallow features as well.

Then he looked up at Jim with a sort of horrified expression, which only further confirmed the truth of it. While Jim knew, he couldn't reconcile himself to the fact that they were gone. It didn't look like her, therefore, it could not be her.

"Let her rest a bit, and she'll be up and about in no time. See if she don't."

Jim buried Edith and their daughter, after Gilda had dressed and prepared the bodies, up on the hill in the old family cemetery surrounded by a sagging wooden fence, the dark green grass growing up around chalky stones carved with names and dates, overlooking the house and tobacco fields and barn. He dug the grave himself and laid the two in it. He knew that from up there, Edith would be able see out across the lush farmland to the creek as it ambled along its path and glimpse a spectacular vision of the sun as it went down behind the tree-covered hills beyond. That was a sight that she had always loved on the few occasions they had afforded themselves to laze on the porch swing in the evenings. It gave him some comfort that, if she'd been there to say, she would have chosen that very spot.

She was gone. Their baby too. Now, as he rocked this child, the one of flesh and bone, he realized that his memories had no substance. They were gone and done with. There was nothing tangible to them like the warm bundle he held onto now. He could feel the little one stir in his arms occasionally, could hear him softly sigh, and see a half smile curl his lip as a sweet dream drifted through his slumber. He was real, in the here and now.

Chapter 4

The next morning when Gilda came down, dressed properly for the day, she looked quite astounded to find her husband sleeping on the settee and Jim sitting in the rocking chair, still rocking away, the baby in his arms. Jim tried to smile shamefacedly, but it ended up being more of a puckered brow and a grimace instead. The baby squirmed in his arms, and he quickly began patting it, soothing it, and then the baby was still again.

"Mr. Hooper, whatever are you doing?" she asked.

Jim did not answer. He wasn't sure what to say. He supposed that he must have appeared very foolish indeed.

Doctor Fielding stirred, saw his wife standing at the door, and sat up fully awake. She gave him a questioning look, her eyes darting from him to Jim and the baby and then to the pistol lying next to her husband on the settee.

"Mrs. Fielding, would you fetch the baby a bottle?" he requested politely of his wife.

"Certainly, Doctor," she said, her curiosity seemingly unsatisfied. She left the parlor for the kitchen.

"Morning, Jim," he said cordially, as if the other man hadn't threatened to kill him the night before, as if they were old friends and had often shared such experiences.

Jim avoided looking at him, ashamed, now that his rage was gone, for what had transpired between them. "Mornin'," he replied.

"Mind if I go and get myself cleaned up?"

"Nope."

A few minutes later, Gilda returned with a glass bottle filled with warm milk and a brown rubber nipple rolled over the lip.

Jim hadn't moved from the rocker and reached for the bottle. "I'll feed the little beggar," he said.

The baby took to the bottle hungrily, sucking loudly, making smacking noises with his lips, fists balled and working furiously near his round cheeks, like a boxer feinting punches to the cadence of his swallowing. Jim grinned at the baby's enthusiasm. Gilda hovered nearby, observing.

The bottle was nearly empty when Doctor Fielding returned, freshly shaven, dressed in his usual professional clothing with his thinning hair combed back. When he came through the door, Gilda nodded ever so slightly and then disappeared. Whatever was going on there, it seemed she knew she was not a part of it. At least not yet.

"Well, look at that. He's got a powerful thirst."

Doctor Fielding hesitated before he said, "Jim, you'll have to go now. I've got work to do, and they'll be here for that baby this afternoon."

Jim stopped rocking and turned to the doctor, suddenly somber. His eyes dropped back to the baby, and he studied the boy thoughtfully. As he stared down at the tiny baby, Jim could sense apprehension in the doctor. It made sense, given what his purpose in going there had been. He knew that he should give the baby back, but he found himself holding tight to the little bundle, unable to do it.

"What's gonna happen to him?"

"They'll care for him down at the children's home, Jim. He won't go hungry. They'll feed him and clothe him."

"A little feller ortta have kin that'll raise him. You send him down there, and he ain't got a chance."

"He's got more of a chance down there than he's got with that Borden bunch. You ought to know that."

"Either way, ain't no good."

"What do you propose I do with him then?" The doctor looked at Jim's face and said, "Oh, no, you don't. Get that fool notion out of your head."

"I'll take him," Jim said. "I'll keep him on my farm."

"You can't do that, Jim. All by yourself, that's just crazy talk."

"Nobody else'll have him. I'll have him. I'd care for him. I'd keep him in clothes and feed him. I'd do right by him."

The doctor changed his approach, his stern façade replaced with a softer one. "Jim, you don't know what you're saying. You've been through something terrible…awful. So it's understandable that you feel sad, but you still have a life to live. You should be home tending to that crop of yours. That's where you should be."

"What good is that there terbacca to me? What good is it if ain't nobody to share it with?"

Doctor Fielding shifted uneasily, looked down at his shoes, and cleared his throat. "What will you do with a baby? You don't bring in that crop, and you'll lose everything, Jim. These days, there isn't any cushion to fall on. The bank'll take every blamed thing you own. What will you do with a baby then?"

"I'll care for him. I'll see to it that he's got what he needs. Don't you worry none 'bout that." It offended him that the doctor had insinuated that he wouldn't see to the necessities of this little one.

The baby finished the milk in the bottle but kept sucking, taking in air through the empty nipple. Doctor Fielding pulled the bottle out of his mouth. "Don't let him take that air in. He'll have some bellyache if you let him do that. Now hold him up and pat his back."

Jim did as he was told. He cradled the baby against his shoulder and began to thump his back.

"Not so hard."

Jim slowed down, and his patting grew softer.

Doctor Fielding looked doubtful when he said, "It isn't easy caring for a baby. It's downright difficult at times."

"Nothin' in this here life is easy."

The doctor waivered in uncertainty. "I don't know, Jim…" he began.

"Doctor Fielding, might I have a word with you please," Gilda piped up from where she lingered in the doorway of the parlor.

It was evident that Gilda Fielding did not share her husband's sentiments. She voiced her disapproval in the privacy of her kitchen, with Jim listening with rapt attention as he peered at them through the crack between the door and the wall. Gilda's eyes were wide in disbelief. The doctor's shoulders were rounded and defensive as they spoke in whispered tones.

"It would be folly to allow Jim Hooper to take a poor helpless baby off and subjecting it to who knows what," she said breathlessly.

"He doesn't have anyone and neither does that baby. Now they might both have each other at least. And besides," he said, "Jim Hooper's right about one thing: the state home is only slightly better than having that boy raised by animals."

"You think he knows how to care for a baby? You think he can do that on his own, with a farm to run and nobody to help him?"

The doctor shrugged. "Truthfully, I don't know. But I don't have it in my heart to say no to him. Chances are he'll have enough of the midnight feedings and constant attention that a newborn requires, and he'll come slinking back with his tail between his legs, asking us to take the baby off his hands before the week's out."

"You're soothing your conscience. That's what you're doing. It isn't your fault she's dead. I know he's had a hard time of it, but this won't fix anything."

"Yes, well, you may be right. I don't know. I just know that I feel that baby would be better off."

"Is he even capable of caring for that child? Do you even know if he's capable? Do you really even know that man at all? We know only what we've seen of him, and that isn't much."

"I suppose he is as good as they come. He always treated his wife with respect. She told me herself once that he was a good man. One of the best of them. She said that he found a mouse in the barn with a mess of babies at her teats. She said he didn't have the heart to kill it because it wouldn't flee to save its own life. It stayed to protect its babies. A man as tender-hearted as that must have some good in him. You know as well as I do he would have done anything for Edith. And he always kept his farm in good order. Those things ought to say something about a man."

"That is no indication as to whether he is capable of raising a child. And I believe there's a whole lot more going on here than you're telling me!" she accused.

The doctor paused, threw his hands in the air and said, "Well, then you go in there and tell him no."

She opened her mouth as if to say something. Jim could see her wringing her hands in dismay, and then she shut her mouth again with a huff. "I don't want to be the one to tell him no," she grumbled.

"Nor do I."

"Very well, then, you play God, and you choose that child's future for him, but if you think for one minute I will stay out of this, you're dead wrong, Doctor Fielding," she said. "I plan on going up there and checking on that poor child anytime I am of a mind to! It's my duty, and yours too, for that matter, you thick-headed mule, to see that no harm comes to that babe!"

She and the doctor returned to the parlor, doing their best to appear unruffled. The only telltale sign of their quarreling was Gilda's usually pale complexion which was now flushed.

With her strong conviction that the doctor's decision was dreadfully wrong, perhaps she might have told Jim no herself had he not looked into her eyes with a pleading that left her speechless. He knew that it was pity that held her tongue, but he didn't care. There was a flicker of life in him again, and he was willing to accept the gift of the child on such terms, if that was what it took.

Yes, she, too, did not have the strength to dash his hope. Whether she thought it a good idea or not, she would allow it. Gilda packed a flour sack with some of the essentials he would need, a few bottles and nipples, some canned milk, and some cloth diapers.

"Now, my Edith, she already done made some right purty little things for him to wear, and I got that there crib I done made and all. Don't need much more than what you got here." Jim didn't want her going to too much trouble.

It was at that point that she teared up, and her resistance completely crumbled. There was nothing to do but educate him. She explained to him that he shouldn't get the umbilical cord wet, that he should feed the baby every few hours, that he should burp the baby after every feeding, that he should keep him clean and change his diapers frequently, warning that his bottom would get sore otherwise. She showed him how to change a diaper, how to hold him if he grew colicky, and how to bathe him.

Jim sensed that she was concerned about her husband's decision to allow him to carry off a helpless infant. He could see that she had little confidence in him, for the misgivings were plain upon her face. He aimed to show her she was wrong.

"I will be up tomorrow to check in on him," she said, her tone like that of a strict school marm. "I'll bring along some more milk.

And if he isn't well and cared for, I'll be bringing him home with me. Am I being perfectly clear?"

Jim did not take his eyes from the baby, but he managed to answer, "Yes, ma'am."

Armed with this newfound knowledge, he carried the baby through town like a trophy. Those that did not know him thought nothing of it—just a man with a baby, nothing out of the ordinary. Those who did know him grew inquisitive, even outright stopping to watch. But Jim was oblivious. He had eyes only for the baby.

Chapter 5

By the time he got home, the little baby was squalling and fiercely red-faced, hungry and tired from the long walk. Jim heated some bottled milk on the stove, just as Gilda Fielding had told him to, and went to change the baby while he waited for it to warm up. He felt pretty proud of himself when he finished his task. He didn't see why they had made such a fuss over caring for this little one. It wasn't that difficult after all.

He went back to the kitchen to pull the bottle off of the stove. He picked it up out of the pot he had it in and let out a howl, dropping it on the floor. It was scalding hot. Though the glass didn't shatter, the milk spilled out across the floorboards, and he cursed at the mess at his feet. By this time, the baby was really putting up a fuss, his little face crumpled and distorted, red as a beet as he cried out, barely taking in air. Jim frantically set out to prepare another bottle.

He held the baby and bounced with him until the bottle was ready again, but the baby was in such a state that he wouldn't accept the nipple when Jim tried to give it to him. With the patience of Job, he ran the nipple over the infant's lips again and again. Finally, Jim took a bit of the milk on his pinky finger and ran it along the baby's gums. Once the little one got a taste of it, he took the nipple in his mouth and went at it furiously.

By the time he had finished the bottle, he was dozing contentedly in Jim's arms. Jim burped him and then went to the bedroom to lay him in the crib — the very crib that he had made with his own hands for his little daughter. It was an odd moment for him as he stood next to the crib, looking down on the newborn. He speculated as to what it would have been like if it had been his daughter, if Edith were in the other room getting dinner ready, if that day two weeks before had been nothing more than a bad dream. But the wonder of the moment wouldn't allow for him to be too somber.

"I'll call you Ellis after my daddy," he said softly, stroking the fine, fuzzy hairs on the baby's head. "You'd like that, wouldn't you? My daddy was an upright man. It'd be a good name for you. Ellis Hooper." He smiled a little to himself, pleased that he had thought of it.

Jim woke the next morning determined to bring in his tobacco crop. Bringing in the crop meant money, and he needed that money to pay on his mortgage, buy some necessities, and to get warm clothes and food for the baby come winter. He fashioned a sling out of an old blanket and carried the baby close to his chest as he went through his rows of tobacco plants to cut them down. Every few hours, he paused in what he was doing to go feed the little mite. Otherwise, the baby mostly slept, as newborns do, contented in his cocoon, swaying back and forth in a soothing motion that kept him dozing.

A baby was difficult to manage, with the frequent feedings and demanding schedule, but a busy toddler was nearly impossible. As Ellis grew, Jim felt it necessary to find inventive ways to care for him. During planting and harvesting, he'd lash little Ellis onto the back of his old mule so that he could keep an eye on him. He would sing to him a song about a pony and cart and a few other tunes he knew from his youth. Ellis begged for him to sing more when he was finished. Jim couldn't much carry a tune, but the little toddler didn't seem to notice, instead reacting as though it was the sweetest sound he'd ever heard.

True to her word, Gilda Fielding made infrequent visits to check in on things. Ellis was only four years old when she brought a stack of books for him. Jim and Ellis were caring for the animals when she drove up. Jim was amused that a woman had taken it upon herself to learn to drive and was out and about by herself with no man to accompany her. That was not a normal occurrence in Pickett County. But that was just the sort of pluck that Gilda possessed. She waved with her gloved hand as she parked the car in the front of the house and then waited for the two of them to come up from the barn.

"You go on and open the door for Mrs. Fielding now, Ellis. A feller always opens the door for a woman."

Gilda let a slow smile spread across her face. Ellis hurried before her and held the door open. She patted him on the head as she passed. "Thank you, Ellis. What a little gentleman."

His chest puffed with pride, and he ran his sleeve across his nose and sniffed modestly. "Ain't nothin' at all, Mrs. Fielding," he said.

"Heavens, I'm covered in dust!" Gilda patted at her face and chest.

Jim pulled a handkerchief from his pocket and offered it to her. She took it gratefully. "Thank you, Mr. Hooper. Take note, young Ellis, a gentleman always has a clean handkerchief to offer a lady."

Once she was sitting in the rocking chair by the fireplace, she pulled out the bundle of books wrapped in a cotton cloth so that Ellis could see them. The wait for the treasure was almost more than the boy could stand. Jim watched the scene with interest as Ellis's eyes filled with a look of pure desire. Gilda seemed thrilled with the response. She had probably forgotten what it was like to have a small child about, how they made the world seem such an extraordinary and miraculous place.

"Ellis, do you know what I have here for you?" she asked him in a conspiratorial tone.

He shook his head, leaning toward her. "Don't got no notion."

Jim stood in the doorway with a bit of curiosity as well. He, too, could not wait to see what she'd brought. She glanced up at him, their eyes locking as the two of them shared that brief moment. It only lasted a breath before she quickly dropped her eyes from his and turned her attention back to the boy.

Slowly, Gilda pulled back one corner of the cloth, and then another, and then another, until the stack of books was revealed. Ellis put out his hand so that it hovered over the copies of *Prudy Keeping House*, *McGuffy Spelling Primer*, and a book of children's poems. He looked to her, asking with his eyes if he might handle them. Gilda nodded, and he picked up *Prudy Keeping House*, flipping through the pages. He saw a picture of a man holding a basket of apples, a little girl who held one of the apples to her lips, and a woman with a long dress and apron, her head covered with a scarf.

"Who is it?" he asked.

"Well, you'll have to read it and discover that for yourself," she told him.

"Is it a mama and a daddy and their girl?"

"Why, Ellis, the story will tell you who it is."

He climbed upon her lap and wrapped his arms around her neck. For a moment, Gilda did not return the embrace. She chanced a glance at Jim, her eyes questioning. He attempted to suppress a grin. Slowly a smile spread across her lips as well, and she enfolded Ellis in her arms with a little sigh.

"My, but you are a handsome little man," she whispered, brushing his hair through her fingers. "I'm not used to little men. I've never had a boy before, only my girls."

"I never had no mama before neither," he replied. "Just my daddy. Maybe I could be your boy for you, and you could be my mama."

The smile left Gilda's face. Jim could guess at what she was thinking. She was not his mother, and to lead him along in the fantasy would be cruel.

"Why don't you take your books over to the table there so you can look through them," she suggested. He scooted off her lap and did as he was told. She and Jim watched Ellis turn each page and inspect it with fervent dedication.

"It was awful good of you," Jim said.

"My girls outgrew them long ago. I suppose now he'll find a use for them anyway," she said. "It's important that he learn to read."

Jim grew self-conscious as he broke his gaze with her and looked over at Ellis. "Well, now, I only got a bit know-how of it myself. Don't know if I'll be much use teachin' him."

"He's just a child, Mr. Hooper. I'm sure you know enough to teach him what he needs to start out with." She smiled reassuringly. "You plan on having him go to school, don't you?"

"'Course."

"Start him with the letters, and then teach him the sounds. And soon enough he'll be off to school where they'll be equipped to teach him more," she said.

"Hope he goes further with it than I done."

"If you let him know how important it is to you, he'll do just fine."

"I aim to raise him up good. I sure do."

"Well, you're doing a fine job of it, Mr. Hooper. He's healthy and happy, and he has all that he needs," Gilda reassured him.

"I ain't gonna let him make the same mistakes I done made. I'll see to that," he said fervently. "I'll teach him right, I will."

"I don't doubt it," she replied.

Jim cranked the Model T to life before Gilda climbed in to leave. He and Ellis waved goodbye from the porch as she gunned the automobile, leaving a cloud of dust in her wake. She headed down the drive, quickly becoming a small speck on the horizon, before disappearing completely.

Things changed when Ellis was old enough to begin school. Jim had not had the foresight to think much on how that would alter their lives. Up to then, they had lived in relative peace and comfort, isolated from the world around them on their own piece of mountain. Now he had to watch the boy go off alone each day to the schoolhouse. It nearly broke his heart to see him trudge away—a solitary figure against the morning sky—and know that his days of protecting the boy were over. Ellis would have to fend for himself from here on out. He would have to meet the cruel world alone during the hours he was away.

Jim was faced, for the first time, with what people were saying about him and his little son. No one dared say anything outright to Jim's or Ellis's faces, but the scandal plagued them still. Jim did his best to shield Ellis from all of it, which was a much easier task when he was just a little boy. Ellis appeared oblivious to it all, up to the point when he started his schooling. And perhaps the other children didn't know exactly what made him different either, only that their parents eluded to him being a misfit, or a no-good, or said things that only touched upon the not-so-long-ago scandal. He knew that children had a strange way of picking up on the pecking order without really having to be told about it. So the older generation would not forget, and the younger generation followed in the elder's footsteps, as tradition dictated.

Once, when Jim was laboring over a skillet of scrambled eggs for dinner, Ellis asked him, "Why don't I got a mama like all them other boys and girls?"

Jim paused, thoughtful. How was he supposed to answer a question like that so a six-year-old would understand? "Well, Ellis, it's 'cause Mama is with the good Lord in heaven. She done went on to live with them angels and such." He brought the skillet over to the table and shoveled the eggs on the two plates that had been set out for them.

"Didn't she love me?"

"Yeah, she loved you very much." Jim sat down at the table with Ellis, suddenly downhearted.

"Why'd she go and leave me, then?"

"Don't s'pose she woulda if she had a choice, Ellis. It's the good Lord that says what there is to say on it. And he done took her 'cause he needed her there."

"Didn't the good Lord think we needed her too?"

"Well, now, it ain't for us to know all there is to know. The good Lord, he knows it all, and someday we gonna understand why it gots to be this a-way. But your mama, she looks down on you, and she's a-watchin' over you, Ellis."

"What was she like, Daddy?"

"She was the purtiest girl I ever laid eyes on. Had brown hair, and she was a tiny woman. Just come up to my chest, just so." He held his hand up just below his breast to show Ellis how tall she had been. "And she was soft, and her voice was like buttermilk. She was always kind to everybody, even them that didn't deserve it. And she liked the color red. And, aw, I loved her so."

"Was she glad she's gonna have me?"

"Never was happier. If you was to be a girl, she'd a-called you Ruby after your grandmother. 'Course you was named for my daddy when you was a boy." He smiled to himself as a memory popped into his mind. "Why, she'd get to sewin' and makin' all them purty little things for you — a quilt and some dresses and such. One right after the other. And she woulda been a real good mama to you. She'd a rocked you and nussed you."

"Did she see me at all? Afore she died, I mean?"

Jim was getting in deeper than he intended, and he paused for a moment before saying, "Just for a bit. She held you, and she cried. She was so happy to see you. And she tole me to take care with you, to raise you right."

Ellis was a quiet child, but Jim knew that it was because his mind was always working. Jim could see it now, as the boy slowly ate his eggs with a puzzled expression.

He thought that perhaps he had addressed his son's concerns sufficiently, until a few days later when Ellis came home early from school with a note pinned to his bibs.

Jim saw the dried blood under his nose and his dirty clothes and was alarmed. He rushed to him. "What happened to you, boy?" he asked, taking the note from him.

Ellis shrugged, looking down at the dirt beneath their feet.

"Says here you got in a fight," Jim said.

Still, Ellis was silent.

"Well, what do you gotta say for yourself?"

"They was sayin' I don't got no mama," Ellis mumbled.

Jim's immediate reaction was outrage. He wanted to go thrash them himself. He knew that was not the answer, nor the fitting and proper thing to do. Instead, he took the opportunity to use it as a teaching moment. Instincts often led to trouble, and he wanted Ellis to be a master of himself, not a victim to others. He asked in a mildly disappointed tone, "So you beat on 'em?"

Again, the boy shrugged.

"You can't go on beatin' on somebody 'cause they say you ain't got no mama, Ellis. That ain't right." He bent down and swept Ellis's bruised hands into his. "These hands is for prayin', and workin', and playin', and writin', and…and doin' arithmetic. They ain't for hurtin' others."

"They work for defendin' yourself, too, Daddy."

"Defendin' yourself from what, son?" Jim persisted. He was doing his best to understand Ellis.

"Them boys."

"What'd them boys do to bring a beatin' on 'em? 'Cause this here note says you was after them. Not the other way."

"I tole 'em what you done said, Daddy, 'bout Mama and how she's with them angels up in heaven and all. Why, they just laughed at me," he said, his face burning with shame.

"Still ain't no reason to beat on 'em," Jim repeated.

"Well, now they circled me up, and they'd push a feller in to hit on me. And I'd beat on him back, and then they'd put another 'un in after me when I got that a-one. So I just kep on a-fightin' 'em till the teacher come 'cause they wouldn't let me be."

"You tell it to the teacher?"

"Sure I did."

"And what'd she tell you?"

"Teacher tole me I's nothin' but trouble since the day I's born," Ellis answered.

The direct way he said it seemed almost comical coming out of a child that was no taller than his thigh. Jim would have laughed if it hadn't been for the nature of what he had said.

"Don't matter what I's to say, she wouldn't believe me, Daddy. She says I's a natural-born liar."

"That ain't so," Jim said as he pursed his lips. "You ain't never been a moment's trouble, child. And you sure ain't no liar. No, sir. Not my boy. You a Hooper, and Hoopers don't tell no false tales."

"Well, I ain't a-goin' back there. You can't make me," Ellis told his father as he gritted his teeth with resolve.

Jim put his hands on Ellis's shoulders. "Now, Ellis, what she done weren't right. And I sure do wish you didn't have to go on back there, but, son, you gotta get your learnin'."

"But, Daddy…" Ellis began.

"Times like these, sometimes a man gotta swaller his pride and do what needs to be done, Ellis, even if it ain't the easy thing to do. I'll go on and have a talk with her, but no matter, you gotta go and get your learnin'. Understand?"

"Yes, Daddy," he agreed with his head bowed.

His submission filled Jim with guilt. The last thing he wanted was for his child to have to go back and face those tormenters.

Jim squatted down so he could look Ellis in the eyes, so that he was at his level. "You're a good boy, no matter what nobody says, Ellis. None of 'em knows you like I do. And someday with your learnin', you gonna be a fine man. Just you wait." He tried not to grow emotional as he told Ellis, "Just 'cause a body says somethin' don't make it so. You know who you are, and they can't change that no matter what them cacklin' hens is to say." He tapped him on the chest. "What matters is what's in here, son. Not a soul can take that away from you."

A man of his word, Jim went with him to school. "You wait out here, Ellis. I'll only be but a minute." He left the boy sitting on the bottom step with his chin between his fists then he let himself into the schoolroom and approached Miss Frank with his hat in his hands. He was decent about it when he quietly suggested to Miss Frank that she was not exempt from having a past. He gently reminded her that he knew for a fact that she had been caught in a compromising situation with Merle Carter's son only a few years previously in an elopement gone awry. He reminded her that not many people knew about the minor scandal, and it really would be too bad if it ever got out, her being the teacher and all. He left the school feeling as though he might be struck dead on the spot for extortion, but then, if saving Ellis meant he had to go to hell, it was a sacrifice he was willing to make.

Just to be sure that all was well, Jim stood outside of the schoolhouse at a distance, waiting and watching. He sat there within the recess of the woods, torturously idle, going over all of the work that was waiting for him back home. Finally, he saw the children file out and watched them take up playing. He spotted Ellis, so small and vulnerable, hanging back with his hands in his pockets, squinting his eyes against the sun. He stood apart from all of the other children, who were laughing and running and busy at amusing themselves. Occasionally the ball would roll over Ellis's way, and he would kick it back out to the crowd that was playing with it.

Once, a few of the boys who were several years older than Ellis approached him. He kept his head down and did not respond to them. Miss Frank was sitting on the steps at the front door. She saw them begin to surround Ellis and sat there observing at first. Her casual manner made Jim angry as he watched.

He wasn't sure that she would do anything, and he was determined that Ellis would not suffer through another bullying session. It had been his intent to stay out of it, but he could not tolerate watching while his poor child took another beating. He came out from behind the trees and drew close to the edge of the woods, prepared to intervene.

His mounting anger set his blood pressure pounding in his temples. "Try and lay a hand to him," he muttered beneath his breath.

Just as he was ready to step out into the sun, Miss Frank slowly got up, taking her time. She walked over to the group of boys and spoke softly to them. Whatever she said was effective. The boys surrounding Ellis broke up and moved away. Miss Frank went back and sat down on her perch, and Ellis remained alone, standing by himself as he had been before. Jim relaxed a bit and stepped back into the trees. Maybe his threat had paid off after all.

When the school day was over, he came out to collect Ellis and walk him home. Ellis put his little hand into Jim's big one, and they started off down the road toward home.

When they had gotten out of sight of the schoolhouse, Ellis looked up at Jim with a puzzled expression and asked, "Why you walking me home, Daddy? You never done it before."

"Figured you might could use some company is all," Jim answered.

He looked as if he were thinking this over. "And what was you doin' out by the woods today?"

Jim stopped short, his eyebrows drawn together and a look of surprise on his face. "What do you mean?"

"You was a-standin' over yonder in them trees over by the school," Ellis said.

Jim thought for a moment and then replied, "You saw that, huh? Had some business in town and was just happenin' by is all."

"Oh," Ellis said, taking Jim's hand again and continuing to walk in rhythm with him. "I thought you was there lookin' after me."

Jim looked down at Ellis's wide and innocent eyes and burst out laughing.

The boy looked utterly confused. "What got you so tickled, Daddy?"

"Don't let nobody never tell you you ain't got a brain in that there head of yours."

"I won't never, Daddy," Ellis replied, the true meaning of Jim's words lost to his youth.

Chapter 6

Jim hung his long underwear up with clothespins on the line that was spread between two pine trees. He had a difficult time keeping up with the farm and the woman's work too. He often put the laundering off for too long, but something had to give, he reasoned.

Ellis came tearing around the corner of the house with Lobo, his pup, right at his heels. He held his hands up before him, holding something up for Jim to see. "Daddy!" he cried. "Daddy!"

Sensing his urgency, Jim dropped the clothespins into the basket and rushed to Ellis. Held carefully in the palm of his hand was a rabbit, a small rabbit, its fur as fine as the fluff of cotton. It was just big enough to fit within Ellis's boy-sized hands.

"What is it?" Jim asked.

"Oh, Daddy, he's a-tremblin' so!" Ellis lamented. "I found him out yonder in them bushes. That ole cat was a-prowlin' 'bout, and I could see he's up to no good. So's I come up on him and shooed him off, and I found this little feller hid up. He's hurt bad, Daddy."

Jim inspected the baby rabbit and found the work of the cat upon his body. The rabbit had no chance of surviving the attack. His front paw was torn up, and as Jim looked him over, he realized that the rabbit had probably been hurt at least a day or more. The maggots had already found him. Jim could see the white worms darting their heads out now and again as he examined the poor animal.

"Yeah, son. He's hurt bad."

"We gotta hep him, Daddy."

Jim's heart hurt. He looked upon Ellis, with his big eyes fervent and full of faith, and he didn't want to crush the child's tender feelings. He looked back to the rabbit, a swell of pity rising within his chest.

"Ellis," he began. "There ain't nothin' can be done for him. He's soon to meet the maker."

The boy grew outraged and at the same time began to cry. "We gotta hep him, Daddy! There's somethin' we can do! There's somethin'!" he insisted.

"Ellis, he's hurt too bad."

Ellis shook his head. "Feel him. He's shakin' so. He must be awful afeared. He can't hep hisself. If we don't heal him, he can't do it hisself. There must be somethin'. Can't we take him on up to the doctor? I bet you he could save him, Daddy."

"Son, this rabbit is gonna die. Sometimes there's no savin'. Sometimes there's only lettin' go. The kind thing to do for this here animal is the lettin' go."

As Jim spoke, Ellis shook his head violently and whispered, "No, Daddy! No! You gotta fix him!"

"Ellis, dyin' is part of livin'. And it's this rabbit's time to die. It'd be nothin' but cruel to draw out his sufferin'. Some things can't be fixed."

"Oh, no!" He wept bitterly. "He never done no harm to nobody. Why'd that cat go on and do him this a-way?"

"That cat don't know no better. That's what a cat does. They chase after whatever will be chased. It's born in 'em. It ain't nobody's fault. It's just the way of it," Jim consoled. "Now go on and put that rabbit down and leave it."

Ellis pulled the rabbit up to his chest and held it close. "I can't, Daddy."

"He's hurtin', Ellis. Leave him be. Let him go on. Put him down; leave him in peace now."

"I can't leave him to die alone," Ellis whimpered. "Not alone." He trudged dejectedly over to the porch and sat upon the steps, holding the baby rabbit in his cupped hands, shedding tears.

Jim watched him for a while and then went and sat next to him. By and by, the rabbit died.

"He's in a better place, son."

He and Ellis took a shovel and dug a hole out by the barn and placed the little creature in it. They covered it with dirt and stood quietly side by side for a time.

The boy woke Jim up sometime in the wee morning hours. It was still dark out, and Jim did his best to fight the bleary disillusionment that confused his brain as he was pulled from a deep sleep. He rolled over and sat up on the edge of the bed, rubbing his face briskly. "What is it, son?"

Ellis leaned into Jim, pressing himself against his chest. "Daddy, I don't feel so good," he said, and then he promptly threw up down the front of Jim's long underwear and the side of the bed.

Jim refrained from cursing, although that was his first inclination. He jumped up, trying to figure out what he should do. His reactions were delayed, and he couldn't seem to formulate a plan of any kind. Finally, he took Ellis by the hand, led him into the main room, and sat him in the rocking chair. He stoked the fire and went about getting water in the basin so that he might wash Ellis's face.

"Keep this here so's if you get sick again," he said, placing a bowl on Ellis's lap. Then he went about cleaning himself up and proceeded to change the bedding in the bedroom.

When he came back to Ellis, the little boy was drooping, his mouth slightly open, his eyes betraying how bad off he really was. Jim wrapped him in a quilt and sat him on his lap as he rocked through the night. It was just as he had done nearly eight years before. Ellis was no longer a baby, but he was still small enough to curl up comfortably on Jim's lap.

He rocked him and sang to him. "Oh by baby. Oh by baby. Oh by baby by oh baby…" he sang softly.

After a while, Ellis asked for a drink, and as soon as he sipped it down, it came right back up again.

Jim touched his brow and felt an instant panic spread through him. "You're burnin' up."

He swabbed his face, neck, and chest with a cool cloth, holding him tight as he tried to figure on what he should do. As he rocked the boy, he began to pray. "Lord, don't take him from me. Please, Lord, don't take this child from me."

The recollection of the dying rabbit from the previous day spooked him. He recalled the words he had said to Ellis of how dying was part of living. Thoughts of Edith played with his senses. Jim had held her with delicate care just like Ellis had held that rabbit as its life slipped away. He thought of losing Ellis too and was nearly in a panic. He could not lose Ellis! The thought was too terrible. This boy was his only salvation, his only reason for living.

When the sun came up, he left Ellis long enough to feed the animals and milk the cow. Then he took him, still bundled in a quilt, into his arms again. Laying him down in the bed and making him as comfortable as possible, Jim lay down next to him and watched him sleep. Now and again, he would place his open palm on the boy's back to reassure himself that Ellis was indeed still breathing.

"I learnt my lesson, Lord. I learnt it good. Don't go and make me learn it again," he mumbled. "I can't stand to lose him. I can't stand for it, hear?"

He was so filled with dread and fear that he contemplated whether he should take Ellis into town to Doctor Fielding's place. Was it scarlet fever? Perhaps typhoid? He didn't even want to consider polio. And just like that, this child that he had grown to love, this little son of his, could be taken away. How fragile, how fleeting this mortal existence was.

In an attempt to appease God, he began to make bargains. *If only you will spare him, let me keep him, I will be a better man. I will make up for the mistakes I have made. I will raise him right. I will help him turn out better than I did. Yes, he will be a better man. I will see to it.*

Physically exhausted and worried half out of his mind, Jim somehow managed to calm his frazzled brain enough to drift off to sleep for a short while, his arm over Ellis's small frame. When he woke, he was alone in the bed.

He rolled off the side of the mattress and sat up, trying to get his bearings all over again. "Ellis?" he called out. He got up and went into the other room, but still no child. He called out again, "Ellis?" He went to the front door and opened it, looking out over the yard. And there was Ellis, chasing the dog and laughing out in delight.

"Ellis," Jim said, trying to get his attention.

"Daddy, ole Lobo got a squirrel!" he said, proud as could be.

"Ellis, I thought you was sick."

"I ain't feelin' so bad now, Daddy."

"You ain't sick no more?"

"Not a bit," Ellis confirmed. "Fact is, I'm awful hungry."

"Well, come on in then, and let's get you somethin' to eat on."

It must have been nothing more than a twenty-four-hour bug. In his panic, Jim had feared the very worst: losing Ellis. To have him die as his wife and daughter had, to be alone again. He never wanted to be alone again. The push and pull—one minute the world was ending, the next everything was as it should be—there was no accounting for it. He was given more time with his boy, more time for him to turn nine, and then ten, and then eleven.

Chapter 7

As Jim watched with pride, Ellis grew into a man. One day he was a child, innocent and curious about the world around him. The next day he was fifteen, and he needed to be shown how to shave because he was growing facial hair. Gone were the days of rough play and the unconditional adoration of a little one. Jim now had a man to guide. He felt what all parents felt: a strange mixture of regret and a longing to keep him small and dependent, along with a pride in his progress and a desire to help him along so that someday he might be independent and able to care for his own needs.

Horse-drawn wagons were beginning to fade from the streets of town, and Jim, through sacrifice and saving, acquired a truck the summer that Ellis turned fifteen. A nice, nearly new, 1922 Red Baby service truck that ran well and was a useful addition to the farm. Jim held out longer than some, but had finally managed to save up enough for the coveted machine.

In order to teach Ellis how to drive, he took him out to a wide open field to let him practice. As they were bouncing along in the tall grass in a steady downhill descent, he decided that it was a good time to talk to his son about the inevitable interest in girls. Because just as dying was a part of living, so too was procreation.

For a time now, Jim had thought that he should bring the matter up, but he'd been reluctant and had put it off and put it off. Confronting the issue and discussing it with Ellis would be shedding the innocence of childhood for good. Couldn't he keep him young for just a little longer? But then he had noticed Ellis making eyes at Callie Roberts in church on Sunday, and he realized that he would rather talk about it now before it was too late.

So he cleared his throat and did his best to keep his voice from shaking, not wanting Ellis to sense his nervousness about the topic at hand. "Ellis, there's somethin' I wanna talk over with you."

Ellis kept his eyes forward, completely focused on the task of driving. "Yeah, Daddy?" he said absently.

"Well, now, you're growin' to be a fine young man," he began, thinking back frantically to what his own father had told him on the issue. But it wasn't much, certainly not enough to draw from in order to broach the subject with his own son. "And now that you got ole enough to understand it, I wanted to talk to you 'bout…well, 'bout what a young man needs knowin'." He put his hand on the wheel and steered it gently back on course. "Keep it steady now."

"Yeah, Daddy?"

"Now, when a boy gets to be that age, it's only natural and right he starts to thinkin' 'bout what it means to settle down and have a family. And, well, I know you prob'ly figured there ain't no cabbage patch where babies come from no more."

Ellis still seemed unaware of his father's intent. He was rotating the wheel this way and that, weaving his way down the hill in happy ignorance. "Don't suppose they do."

"Now, son, here's what I got to say on it. Every boy wants to know what all goes on 'tween a man and a woman. Only natural. But now, it's a serious thing. Somethin' you don't take light, you hear?" he said, trying to keep the nervous edge from his voice.

Ellis turned his attention from the windshield and passing scenery to his father, his face full of concern. "What you tryin' to say, Daddy?"

"I'm sayin' you treat a girl right, and you treat her with respect. A girl ain't no object to have for your pleasure. And a decent 'un don't want no boy takin' liberties when it ain't his right. A girl needs to be treated good, and talked to nice, and given no cursin' nor rough treatment to, hear?"

He looked up and saw Ellis was headed straight for a tree near the edge of the clearing. "Look out!" he called.

Ellis stamped the brakes and came to a screeching stop. They sat in silence for a time, both shaken.

Jim took a deep breath and tried again. "What I'm tryin' to say is—"

"I know, Daddy," he said in exasperation, attempting to end the conversation.

"You don't, son," Jim said firmly but gently. "And it's my duty to tell it 'cause I do know." He paused for a time, trying to find the right words for saying what needed to be said. "A feller don't got business foolin' round with a girl 'less he's done right by her and took her to be his wife before God and a preacher. The good Lord done made us better'n them animals. You don't take a girl 'cause you got an itch to like a dog do. You take her 'cause you love her. That's the way it's done. Understand?"

Ellis nodded dumbly, his fingers clenching the steering wheel in a death grip.

"It's a serious thing to take a power of creatin' into your hands. A serious thing. Can be life or death even."

"Like Mama?"

"Well, yeah, like Mama. But a baby is a life. A life you answer for if you was the one that done the doin'. And don't you go takin' that on till you're ready to 'count for a child and for carin' for a family and a woman, see?"

Again, Ellis nodded, his Adam's apple bobbing as he swallowed hard, looking as though he had been waylaid by the turn of events. He finally managed to get out the words, "Yes, Daddy."

As an afterthought, Jim added, "And now, don't go runnin' with any of them whores and such. Nothin' good'll come of it."

The two of them sat listening to the engine idle for a time. And then Jim, having said his piece, broke the silence again. "Swing her round and take us on back home."

Ellis turned the wheel, pulling the truck around in a semi-circle as he headed back toward the house.

"That's it," Jim encouraged. "Now you're gettin' it."

Part II: Germination

Chapter 8

Early Fall of 1934

The fiddle and the banjo rose together in a pleasing whine that lit the place on fire with excitement. Ellis recognized some of the songs that the Carter Family, Blue Sky Boys, and Clinch Mountain Boys were known for. A makeshift stage, comprised of bales of hay, towered above the crowd. A young girl, maybe sixteen or seventeen, stood on the stage, played a guitar, and took turns singing with a middle-aged man. Their voices sometimes mingled in the tight harmony of a duet. The mood was infectious. Ellis could hardly contain himself and was barely able to keep his feet from jigging as he walked into the barn.

He was a man now. Not an overly tall man, but there was something in his character and stance that made him seem as though he had more height when he walked into a room. His jaw was square, as was his chin. His eyes were a deep brown and seemed to perceive many unspoken things. The quiet of them could make others uncomfortable, as his thoughts weren't always clear or obvious. Those eyes now gazed around the room as he took in the scene before him.

He saw Clifton Davies and Forster Montgomery right off. They were hard to miss with their loud laughter and rowdy behavior. The two of them were shoving one another, bumping into people who were crowded into the tight space. Clifton tapped a man on the shoulder who was in the midst of dancing. Judging from the reaction on the man's face, he seemed very annoyed, and then Clifton burst out laughing as he moved on along to his next victim. Ellis wasn't sure if he cared to join them. They tended to help themselves to the home brew that the older men kept in a crock jug out of general view. They made good corn liquor, coaxed to life in a still, seasoned in wooden barrels, hidden somewhere in the woods.

Clifton and Forster were the boys that were closest to his age, and there they were, still a trio of bachelors. It was embarrassing to be lumped together with them. They never took anything seriously. They were perfectly fine with fooling around and shirking responsibility. As much as he liked them, he didn't want to be one of them. It hurt his pride. There were plenty of people packed into the space for Ellis to choose from, but Forster and Clifton were the boys he was most comfortable with, the boys he had grown up with.

Then he saw Fergus Bayard hanging back by the wall, brooding and sullen. He didn't reckon he wanted to hang out with him, either. Fergus was skinny and slight of frame and was always looking for an excuse to mope, it seemed. Despite the music and laughter and throng of folks in a joyous mood, tonight was no exception. Fergus stood, as always, with the top button of his collar buttoned to just below his chin, with his hat drawn low on his brow, and his face displaying a look of inconsolable sadness.

It looked as if the whole county had shown up: young children, old married folk, some he recognized, some he didn't. He laughed a little to himself when he saw Purvis Little dancing with some young thing half his age. Purvis was a widower who was on the prowl for a woman to raise his brood of seven. Ellis felt a bit sorry for the girl. She looked awfully uncomfortable in the arms of a man old enough to be her father.

Purvis had some acreage next to Ellis's daddy's place. Not as big as his daddy's place, but then Purvis wasn't very good at caring for what he had. He was the sort of man who let his children run wild over the hills unsupervised and basically left to raise themselves. He was the sort of man whose crops never did well because he never tended them properly. He was the sort of man who left his tools lying about in the yard to rust and ruin. Yes, Purvis didn't own much land because he couldn't handle much land.

Ellis quickly lost interest and turned his attention from foolish Purvis to the rest of the crowd. His eyes fell upon Dulcie Mae

Prewitt, and with some annoyance, he saw her looking at him. Ellis was startled. He felt a shock run through him as their eyes met. But Dulcie Mae, with her deep green eyes, stared back unashamed. Her face was carefully neutral, although those green eyes held a curiosity that was barely perceptible. But Ellis saw it. He knew her well enough to detect it. He turned his gaze from her quickly, unwilling to let it linger there, somewhat ashamed that she had caught him watching her. He hated himself for getting caught but hated her more for being there in the first place.

Even as that thought popped into his head, he knew it wasn't true. He had, at one time, wanted her. Oh, how he had wanted her. Truth be told, he still wanted her.

Seeing her now brought a rush of fragmented memories. He recalled a stolen kiss in the afternoon sun as they were returning from the well with a bucket full of water. She had sloshed water onto the front of his britches, making it look suspiciously as if he had wet himself. Her laughter had trailed behind her as she ran, giving him many a backward glance to see if he might pursue. He remembered the brush of her hand against his and the tingling sensation it had left on his skin. The way her touch awakened his senses and made his body feel alive was the thing he missed most of all.

He recalled another time with her. She had been wearing a white dress, her honey hair fanned out on the grass as they picnicked next to the creek. Dulcie Mae had lied to her mama and told her that she was visiting a sick friend. Ellis had lain next to her upon that perfectly green grass, sucking her delicate earlobe, caressing her face with his hands, delighting in the soft feminine curves of her cheeks and lips. He'd nearly been unable to concentrate on the words she whispered with a moist, pleasant tickle against his skin as she ran her fingers along his neck, through his hair.

Ellis allowed himself these memories as small indulgences before he chastened himself for letting his thoughts go too far. She was a married woman now. She was wife to Homer Pond, the son of a wealthy tobacco broker, and she had been for the past three years. Yet every time he saw or thought about her, he felt bitterness well up within him, felt the inevitable reaction of his pride colliding with his anguish. He had seen her only a couple of times since she had gotten married and moved away. Ellis had asked her to marry him. She had said no. Her mama and daddy didn't approve of him, something he never quite understood. She refused to go against them—a good daughter who would not question them.

He told himself that it was her parents that had been their undoing. He wanted to believe that she had loved him as he had loved her. It hurt less that way.

He felt oddly out of place because young men his age were usually settling down, getting on with their lives. By twenty-three, his own daddy had gotten himself a farm and a woman, and they'd been expecting their first child. And here he was, twenty-six, empty handed and alone, a man who longed for a woman who belonged to another man. She would never be his, and he still felt the sting.

Yet, Dulcie Mae's rejection had been positive in that he had gotten determined about things. He had taken the money his daddy had set aside for him and had put a down payment on a fine piece of land not far from where he had grown up. While it was rough around the edges, still needing a lot of clearing, he was proud of it because it was his. The house he and his daddy had built there was a crude thing—one large room that served as the kitchen and sitting area, one bedroom off of that—but it had a nice covered porch that ran the length of the front of the house, a place where he could sit and just be. Eventually, if he wanted or needed to, he could add on and make more room for a growing family someday.

He figured his getting a farm and showing signs of becoming responsible would make him more respectable in others' eyes, prove his worth, but it hadn't entirely done so. While Ellis never understood other people's aversion to him, he suffered from it nonetheless. They were mistrustful of him. They had no respect for him, and he felt it, maybe even knew deep down inside that something was amiss, but he had grown up being treated in such a manner; it was normal to him.

He ran his fingers through his thick, dark hair in annoyance and moved away from the door as he was nudged by others trying to come through, and out of spite, he asked the first girl he saw to dance. He hoped that Dulcie Mae might be watching him. He wanted her to know that he was good and over her, that she held nothing over him. The girl with him seemed pleased to dance, but she kept jabbering and laughing loudly. It was messing up his rhythm. He couldn't concentrate on the music. He wouldn't ask her to dance again.

The next song, he picked a new partner, one who was pretty good. He knew her a little. It was Arlene Lee's little sister. Her name was something like Agnes or Alma; he couldn't recall for sure. All of the children in that family had names that began with the letter A. She smiled at him pleasantly. He didn't want someone to smile at him. He didn't want to flirt or talk or meet new people. He just wanted to dance.

"Y'all havin' a nice time?" she said, having to raise her voice to be heard over the music.

He shrugged. "Nice enough, I s'pose," he shouted back.

She didn't make any more attempts at small talk; he had let her know he was clearly not interested in that. They held hands loosely as they moved their feet in a dance that was known locally as flatfooting. Nice thing about flatfooting was that anyone could do a basic step and add a little personality of their own to it. It could still be done with a partner and look good. It could be done alone as well, like the fellow who was dancing mad near the fiddle player. He was too drunk to realize they weren't playing the music solely for him. There were no restrictions with flatfooting.

Just like the songs and ballads that had been circulating through the mountains, no one really knew where flatfooting had come from, but it had been passed around for generations. Ellis was better than most at it, although his daddy had taught him not to brag. He enjoyed music in general, and the songs seemed to be a part of his soul. He also had a good voice and used it often when he was in the fields following his mule, setting the tobacco to an old mountain melody. He thought it amusing that his daddy couldn't carry a tune to save his life. Ellis figured he must have gotten the gift from his mother.

It was often the music that had consoled him or lifted him during his trying times. It was the music that had made up his life. The gospel words and mountain tunes managed to fit together like the pieces of a crazy quilt. It all combined to make a beautiful piece. For any given circumstance he had experienced, there was a song to match it.

At the end of the dance, Ellis smiled and nodded his thanks to his partner. When the next song began, he headed for the door to get a breath. There was a bucket and a dipper set out, and he went and took a good long drink of water. As he took in the cool evening air, Fergus Bayard sidled up next to him with his fists deep in his overall pockets.

"How do, there, Ferg?"

"How do?" Fergus said, a little petulant in his tone.

"Enjoyin' yourself?"

"Them boys is always up to no good."

"Who?"

"You know who," Fergus accused, but decided to humor Ellis anyhow. "Clifton and Forster. Why they gotta be that a-way for?"

"What'd they go and do now?" Ellis asked, not able to hide his amusement.

That only made Fergus more out of sorts. "They don't take nothin' serious. I went and was goin' to ask one of them gals to dance, and they done tripped me up and made me fall, right there in front a-her. Boy, they saw I's plenty mad 'bout it, and they done took off. They got outta there afore I whooped 'em, them mules."

"You ortta knowed they'd be up to no good, Fergus. They's nothin' but a bunch of fools, the whole lot." Ellis laughed.

"Now it ain't funny, insultin' a man that a-way, and in front of a girl. They just better steer clear of me, is all. 'Cause I'll show 'em. I'll knock their blocks off."

Ellis took another sip from the ladle before he let it drop back into the bucket of water. He knew that Fergus was all talk. That boy couldn't do harm to anyone. He was small, whiny, and awkward for a man. He was his mama's only boy in a passel of girls. Ellis never did like him much. But it wasn't in Ellis's disposition to treat anyone unkindly, no matter how distasteful they were, and so he tolerated the man. As his daddy had always said, "There's never no cause for bad behavior."

Ellis felt sorry that Fergus had just never had a father to teach him any better. "You just pay 'em no mind, Ferg."

Fergus shrugged and kicked the dirt with the toe of his boot. The two of them stood, watching the shadows and forms of others littering the yard. Some were lovers who shied from the light, attempting to steal kisses. Some were drunk and ornery, looking for a fight. Some, like Ellis, wanted a breath of fresh air.

"Even afore they gone and done that, I's done good and heated," he complained.

Ellis could see that Fergus was waiting for him to ask why, but he didn't feel up to humoring him. He honestly didn't care.

So Fergus went on without being prodded. "My girl says she's a-comin' to meet me here, and I ain't seen hide nor hair of her."

"Your girl?" Ellis said, raising an eyebrow in surprise.

"Ain't you heard? Elvira Little and me is a-goin' together," Fergus bragged with a smile of satisfaction.

"Purvis's daughter?"

"What other Elvira Little be there?"

"Well, now, she's a right purty little gal."

"Sure she is." Fergus gave an enthusiastic nod of his head. "I done kissed her too," he confided in a low laugh.

"Ain't that somethin'?" Ellis replied, feeling his stomach turn over at Fergus's kissing the sweet fifteen-year-old girl with ebony hair and a woman's body. Why, if he was Purvis, he'd keep a tight rein on that one. But Purvis was too darn ignorant to trouble himself over it.

"How 'bout you, Ellis? You got yourself a woman yet?"

Ellis shook his head, his lip slightly curled. "Don't reckon I do."

As if they had conjured her with their talk, Elvira came loping across the yard, her eyes alight and eager as she approached Fergus. "That's where you been keepin' yourself!" she squealed as she jumped at Fergus, looping her arm through his.

"Where you been? I done looked everywheres for you," Fergus said, as standoffish as he could muster.

"Why, I's just a-lookin' for you," she told him, losing a bit of her bubble. "Now, you ort not to be cross with me, Fergus. I ain't had a bit of fun when I was a-tryin' to get to you."

"I'll be, you look awful good," he admired, letting his eyes roam over her.

She giggled. "He do say purty things."

Ellis vaguely recalled her as a little girl. She'd been a young kid, nothing special then. Seeing her now, he was surprised that she hadn't gone after bigger game than Fergus Bayard. To Ellis, she seemed like a huntress—too cunningly sultry, slightly manipulative in her manner.

"He talks so sweet and fine. His sweet talkin' likes to make me tickled all the way to my toes," Elvira cooed, batting her eyelashes.

"Go on, gal. Get back in there, and I'll be in direc'ly," Fergus instructed, giving her a swat on the bottom. "You and me is goin' to have a dance."

She gave him a quick smile and headed back to the barn.

"I done tole you, didn't I?" Fergus asked.

"For sure you did."

As they stood talking, Ellis's eyes fell upon a woman who was alone, making no attempt to conceal the intense gaze she focused upon him. He didn't know how long she had been observing them. It was impossible to tell how old she was. She looked to be middle-aged, pale, and perplexed as she eyed him. Ellis figured that she wore that forlorn look often, gauging by the deep wrinkles in her furrowed brow and the frown lines that marked either side of her mouth. Hers was as sad and bewildered an expression as he had ever seen.

He stared back for a moment, and then the spell was broken as she strode toward him, now seemingly angry. The woman took his chin roughly between her thumb and forefinger, turning his face this way and that, scrutinizing his features as she might an object she was looking to buy. He dumbly allowed it, unsure of what he should do.

"I done seen a ghost," she whispered. "Who do you belong to?" she asked, sounding angry and distressed all at the same time.

Ellis knew she was asking who his father was, but he didn't understand why. "My daddy's Jim Hooper, ma'am."

"Jim Hooper!" The woman seemed to stew over this for a brief moment, and then she looked him over again. "And your mama?"

"What's this about?" Ellis asked. He thought she had maybe helped herself to more moonshine than she could handle.

"Your mama?" she snapped.

"Edith Hooper. My mama's Edith Hooper."

"Edith Hooper? Like hell it is! Well, I ortta knowed it," she spat through clenched teeth. "I'll kill him!" She dropped her hand and stalked off with her fists in balls, like she was on her way to punch somebody's lights out.

Ellis watched her go in bewilderment. Fergus also seemed confused, and the two of them looked at each other in amazement, not knowing what to make of the woman's strange behavior.

"What was that for?"

"Beats me," Ellis replied. "I never laid eyes on that there woman afore this night."

Fergus chuckled nervously. "Law, you done made her good and mad! I never seen such a thing. I never did. She's a hellcat, for sure. What'd you do to cause her to go at you that a-way?"

Ellis shook his head in annoyance, unwilling to make any sort of reply, and then just walked away abruptly without another word, leaving Fergus to stand there alone.

That very night, a storm, the likes of which Ellis had never seen, blew in. The dark clouds gathered and then burst in sheets of heavy, pounding rain. The neighboring county was pummeled with hail and windstorms, laying waste to many a home and field.

Ellis felt his bad luck began after that night. He wondered in his mind if that woman had put a curse on him; if, in the instant she had touched his face, some ill-fortune had transferred to him from her. Though he could not figure why, he thought some deep-seated grudge had possessed him, marked him for a man destined to know nothing more than sorrow all his days.

Chapter 9

Lying in his bed alone, Ellis listened to the rain pound the corrugated tin roof of his cabin. Claps of thunder shook the little shack, rattling anything that wasn't fastened down. It made such a clamor he couldn't sleep. Restless and troubled, he finally pulled himself up and sat in his chair.

He whittled at a stick, listening to the fire sizzle and spit as the rain occasionally found its way down the rock chimney. His old dog, Trapper, lay at his feet, resting his head on his paws. He normally didn't allow the dog inside the house. Animals belonged outside.

Trapper had been one of Lobo's pups, the spitting image of his father, and just as faithful. Ellis had mourned the loss of Lobo, who had been like family to him, but Trapper had managed to fill the void. Trapper was getting along in years now too, though. He was an old man in dog years. His coat no longer had a shine to it. He couldn't run as fast. He slept more these days and did a little less chasing of vermin. But he was still a good dog, and Ellis felt pity for the poor animal as he watched him pace back and forth along the length of the front porch, his restlessness a product of the storm. And so they endured the long night together.

Dawn brought no relief. The sky was dark, blotting out any attempts the sun might have been making to shine. There was a heaviness to the clouds that was almost suffocating, as if they were pressing down, down to the ground. He could feel the weight on his skin. Lightning continued to flash, illuminating the darkness in jagged, bright forks, leaving an acrid smell to the falling rain. And when Ellis went to tend his mule and cow, he was soaked to the bone by the time he made it back to the porch. Trapper had followed him across the yard to the barn, back to the house, and now stood shaking, scattering a thousand drops of water in all directions.

The rains had subsided but somber mood continued through the afternoon, and about suppertime, Ellis noticed smoke in the distance. Great plumes rose above the far-off hills, and the odor drifted in through the open window, where the curtain fluttered on the wet breeze. He went outside and stood under the shelter of the porch. He eyed the smoke with unease, his hands in his pockets, thoughtfully pondering if he might investigate the cause of it. The dog paced to and fro, whining and seeming as anxious as his master.

Not in the mood to fix anything else, Ellis went back into the cabin and ate a stale biscuit and a cold chunk of beef left over from his dinner the night before. A short while later, over the din of the continuing rain, he heard a car coming up the graveled drive and stepped out on the porch. He watched as Purvis Little's beat-up old Ford pulled up in front of the house and skidded to a sudden stop.

Purvis immediately climbed out, obviously excited over something. "Grab your coat and hat, boy, and come on with me!" he yelled over the rain.

For some reason, Ellis didn't think to question him, didn't bother to ask why. The uneasy feeling creeping through his innards was enough to spur him to action. He reached in through the door and took his coat and hat off the peg just inside and hurried to put them on.

The closer they drew to his daddy's farm, the thicker and darker the sky grew with smoke, and a mix of ash and mist accumulated on the windshield. As they topped the ridge and exited the trees, Ellis immediately saw the smoldering ruins of the barn he had played in as a child. When they pulled up to the farmhouse, the stench was more than he could stand. It made him sick to his stomach, made him cover his nose and mouth with his arm to try to block the odor out.

That barn had been one of his favorite places. As a boy, he had lain on his back and watched the drying tobacco leaves flutter in the rafters above, collected eggs from the chickens' hidden nests, fed and milked the old cow, climbed through the empty stalls, wrestled with Lobo, and followed his daddy around as he went about his chores. Now, there was nothing left of the barn but the back corner of the rear and a side wall where they joined to form an L-shape. The ground was littered with smoldering debris and the dead, smoking carcasses of animals. That was the smell that had accosted him — scorched hair and burned flesh, the charred remains of living things.

"Where's my daddy, Purvis?" Ellis demanded with a quaking, panicked voice.

"We brung him to the house," Purvis told him softly, keeping his eyes straight ahead.

When Ellis saw his daddy laid out on the bed, he knew that his father's days of burden and care were coming to a close. His minutes were numbered. He breathed in shallow, ragged breaths, coughing weakly every now and again. The skin on his bare arms and face and head was charred and blistered, and his eyes were red and watering profusely.

He feebly tried to shift his body on the bed as he struggled to make his lungs work, laboring for a breath, but when he saw Ellis he became still. A few of the neighbors milled about the room, unable to help but unwilling to leave. They all parted to let Ellis through when he came to the door of the tiny room.

"He tried to save them there animals," Purvis said as he followed Ellis into the room, "but there wasn't nothin' could be done for it."

"Lord, Daddy, what've you gone and done?" Ellis said, dropping to his knees next to the bed.

"Ellis…Ellis," Jim whispered. "My boy, Ellis…" He stretched his charred fingers out, reaching for his son. "Death's on me, ain't it, Ellis?"

"It's gonna be all right, Daddy. I'm here now. And it's all gonna be all right," Ellis said, emotion choking his voice.

"Lightnin' hit that there barn and just lit it right up. Never seen nothin' like it," Purvis explained, turning his hat in his hands. "Me and some of the boys here, we done what we could. I come to get you, but Coy Struthers done gone to get the doctor."

Jim struggled again to speak. "Ellis, you been a good boy. You always been a comfort to me. You made me…you made me real…proud."

"Daddy, what'd you go and do?" Ellis asked again, shaking his head. He felt a sense of helplessness that was beyond anything he had ever experienced. There was nothing he could do and he knew it. "You gonna up and leave me now?"

Jim swallowed hard and said, "Ellis. I tried…to…to do…right by you. I tried…to make you a good man."

"You did, Daddy. You was the best daddy there ever was to a boy." He wanted to hold his father's hand, to touch him, but he was afraid to, afraid of the boils upon the blackened flesh.

"I only wanted…"

"What, Daddy?" Ellis prodded.

"All I done, I done 'cause I loved you, boy, 'cause I wanted… wanted you to be a better man than I was. Sorry…" He became troubled and emotional.

Ellis wasn't ready for Jim's time to be over so soon, but he listened lovingly as his father rambled on about the past. "I was holdin' you in my arms that day…walkin' that road home…" he said softly, almost inaudibly. "It was my choosin'. I thought I could make your life better. I thought…I thought I could do somethin' for you. But it was you…it was you what saved me," he murmured with tears in his eyes.

"Now, Daddy, you just take it easy. Don't upset yourself none. Just take it easy," Ellis insisted. "It's gonna be fine."

"Hear me, boy," Jim insisted, although it was near impossible for him to become too adamant in his weakened state. His fingers grasped at Ellis's shirt as he fiercely whispered, "All I done, I done 'cause I loved you. I don't want you never…never to doubt it." Then his charred fingers lost their grip on Ellis's shirt, and his hand fell limply to the bed. "Your mama, well, now…" He couldn't seem to finish his thought.

"I know, Daddy. I know," Ellis croaked. It was obvious that talking was a great effort for his father. He was attempting to ease his suffering.

"What's mine is yourn, Ellis. My boy…*my boy*…" The struggle to inhale and exhale was terrible to hear.

"Daddy, this farm don't mean nothin' without you. You can't go and leave me now. I got nobody but you. I got nobody," Ellis whispered, not knowing if he was talking to his daddy or to himself.

Jim continued to toil with his breathing until his lungs grew too tired from the effort and just stopped working. In that moment, a look of awe and rapture radiated from his face, and he soundlessly mouthed one final word, "Edith," and then was gone.

The room was quiet, everyone still in the wake of Jim Hooper's death. There was nothing but the rain, and that too had slowed to a reverent hush as the man silently slipped away.

The very night of his passing, Jim was laid in a pine box put out in his front room on the table. The neighbors kept a vigil through the night with Ellis, sleeping in the same room as the body, as was their custom. In the early morning hours as the sun began to stream through the window, it accented his daddy's profile and lit him up like a fiery angel sent to do God's justice.

Ellis couldn't tear his eyes from his father's face. He wondered if there was life after death, if Jim Hooper had really witnessed his Edith as he was passing over, or if it was just a dying man's prayer, falling from his lips in one last urgent plea.

The next day, Doctor Fielding helped Ellis dig a grave next to Edith Hooper's final resting place.

The rain had abated during the night. The day of the burial was sporadically sunny and overcast until evening, when it began to rain again. Gilda Fielding stood among all of the others with a black umbrella clutched in her hand, her face grim, her lips frowning. After the mourners had left, she lingered, cleaning the cabin, making a meal for Ellis. She had something to say to Ellis before she finally left.

She took him by the hand, looked him in the eyes, and waited for his full attention. "I don't know a soul that doesn't have their faults, Ellis. And your father wasn't exempt. But if there was one thing that he was perfect in, it was in loving you." And then she left him to himself.

With nothing to do but tend to the business at hand, Ellis busied himself in the gathering gloom, loading up some of his daddy's things that had managed to escape the fire. Any tools and equipment that had been worth anything had been in the barn. Ellis went through the house and put a few odds and ends in the bed of his daddy's old 1922 Red Baby truck: some household items, two quilts his mama had pieced, a few pots and pans, a pistol, and a rifle—things he figured would be handy to have about. Then he tied Edith's mama's rocking chair to the cab of the truck with some twine.

Jim had kept a few pigs too. They were set aside in a pen off in the cow's pasture and had survived the fire because they didn't live in the barn with the other animals. They were off to themselves in their own field.

Ellis borrowed some crates of rough wood from Purvis to transport them to his farm. He figured he would have to come back for the cooking stove anyhow, and he would return the crates to Purvis then. Climbing over the fence, he set to work catching the piglets first. They ran about wildly, voicing their resistance to being caught in high-pitched squeals. He caught the first by the hind legs and held fast as it struggled to break away from him. He dumped it into one of the crates and then went after the other squealer.

It was when he went after the sow that the real difficulty began. She appeared good and angry at the injustice done her piglets, and she was making quite a ruckus about it when the boar, with all of his one hundred and fifty pounds, came charging up the hill, his short legs carrying him with lightning speed to his lady's aid.

That boar was half wild, his snout long and ears short. All black with the eyes of a devil, wily and malicious. The boar's bristles were standing threateningly on end, the stumpy teeth on his upper jaw working against the one long tusk of his lower jaw. He cracked them together as he worked his saliva into a foaming lather. To add to his overall aggressive appearance, one tusk on his lower jaw was broken off, which had given him his name, Snaggletooth.

Jim had caught him roaming free in the woods several years before, and despite his best efforts had never managed to completely domesticate the angry beast. He was good for nothing but procreating. Ellis had long suspected the animal had a chip on his shoulder on account of his small size and was doing all he could to make up for it. He'd never liked the old hog, and the feeling was mutual on the hog's part, he supposed.

Snaggletooth put his head down and charged him at a full run, but Ellis managed to jump over the fence before he got it good from the boar's mean-looking tusk.

When he got up from the ground, he was fuming mad. "Well, I'll be, you son of a gun!" he yelled at the animal, picking his hat up and beating it against his leg to knock the dust from it before he put it back on his head.

It took him a good hour to get the two grown hogs trussed up and into the crates. By then, both he and the pigs were run ragged, filthy dirty, and drained of energy. He loaded them into the back of the truck by pushing them up a makeshift ramp fashioned from two wooden planks.

Just as he finished his work, he saw Coy Struthers coming up the drive with his eldest son, Cyril, sitting next to him in the car. Ellis waited for them to park the car and climb out to see what it was about.

Cyril leaned against the car with his foot perched on the running board, looking bored and resentful. It was likely his daddy had made him come along.

Coy smiled in a friendly sort of way and approached Ellis with his hand extended. "How do, Ellis, how is it with you?"

Ellis thought it was a ridiculous question, all things considered. How should he be? His father had just died. All the kin he had were now gone but for his aged great-aunt Sissy. And so he answered, "Just fine."

"Good to hear. Good to hear."

"I's just packin' up and headin' out," he explained, gesturing toward his daddy's loaded truck.

"Need any hep?"

Woulda been a fine offer when I was chasin' after them pigs, he thought. "Don't reckon so. I aim to come back for the stove, but I done got everythin' else."

"Well, I ort not to keep you, so's I'll get right to it," the middle-aged man stated. "I come to offer you a fair price for this here land." Just like that. No pleasantries, no condolences.

Ellis was surprised, taken off guard. It would make sense that Coy wanted the land; it butted up against his own property. He would have a mighty big piece if he were to get the farm. Ellis suspected that it was something he would pass onto Cyril, who apathetically watched the exchange with a detached demeanor, too young yet to know or appreciate what an immense favor his father was attempting to do for him.

Ellis hesitated. "Don't know that I aim to sell."

"Now, hear me out, Ellis. 'Tween this here place and your own, you couldn't care for it proper, and it's no good to you no how if you ain't usin' it for plantin'. 'Least this a-ways you'd have the money in your pocket."

"Don't know that my daddy woulda wanted me to sell it." Ellis pictured his father with a disapproving look on his face. This had been his land, his home, and he had worked his life away to make it prosper, to bring it to a thriving farm. His daddy had left it to him, just as Jim's father had passed it down to Jim, and Ellis just couldn't see that he would be pleased by the notion of selling out.

"Well, now, son, your daddy ain't here to tell you that you can't sell it. It's up to you now," Coy persuaded. "You're your own man now. It's for you to judge."

Ellis scratched his jaw line with a thoughtful frown, sorry to disappoint but resolved in his decision. "Sure it is, but I ain't in the mood to sell."

Coy roughly rubbed the back of his neck in irritation. He opened his mouth as if he might say something but then shut it again, looking over at Cyril who had climbed back into the car, ready to go. "If you don't wanna sell, you don't wanna sell. I can respect it. But now, if you change your mind, if you fix on gettin' rid of it, would you gimme first chance at buyin' it?"

"Fair enough. If I change my mind, you'll be the first to know it," Ellis agreed.

"I sure would be grateful for it."

"Yessir."

At that point, Coy probably didn't know what more to say so he held out his hand and they shook. "Take care, boy."

"Thank you," Ellis said with a nod of his head.

Coy turned back to his car, his shoulders slightly rounded with dissatisfaction. Ellis felt some empathy for the man, but he wasn't willing to get rid of the place. Money was not enough to convince him to give up his inheritance. Some things were simply not worth the almighty dollar.

Ellis paused to think about the happy childhood he'd had in this place before he shut the door to his boyhood home and headed back to his own place. Without his father there, it would never feel the same. Life would never be the same again. He felt a heaviness that he attributed to being alone in the world and realized that he had only himself to rely upon now.

As he drove away, he felt out of place in the red pickup—his daddy's truck. He recalled when his daddy had bought it eleven years before, how proud he had been when he'd driven it up to the house. It had made life considerably easier. Now Ellis would benefit from it; now it was his truck. That should have pleased him, but it only made his heart hurt worse.

Back at his place, he put the pigs in the barn, locking them in an empty stall for safekeeping, working in his mind as to how he would build them a proper pen and enclosure off the barn where they could wallow in the mud on a hot summer's day. He didn't fancy the notion that they should stay in his barn, smelling up the place, making a mess. Pigs didn't belong in a barn. No, just as soon as he could get to it, he would start on the new fencing and the small building that would house them.

He set about unloading the remaining items from the truck. When he put the rocking chair next to the fireplace, it seemed to belong there. He sat in it and rocked for a time, running his hands over the worn, smooth wood of the arms. Ellis leaned his head back to rest for a while, until he was forced to come back to his responsibilities and go out to feed his cow and mule, the chickens, and newly acquired pigs.

Thinking about the loss of his daddy created a steady ache in his chest. Struggling to lessen the pain, he told himself that death was part of life. He would keep his hands busy and his mind occupied, and the hurt, the emptiness, would become easier with time somehow.

Chapter 10

Ellis looked back on the summer with a certain sense of accomplishment. The long heated days wore into fall and turned the hardwood trees bright with patches of reds, yellows, and oranges on the mountainsides. One day blended into another as dispassionate in content and colorless in character as the next. It seemed as if they were all identical, as if it was the same day unending.

The work of building the pigpen and enclosure had kept him occupied. Along with that, he had set two wooden poles in the ground with a stout crossbeam for future pig slaughtering. He'd also brought in his and his father's abundant tobacco harvest and hung it up to dry in his barn. Then there had always been small projects and odds and ends he'd worked on. In truth, the busy work had kept him going; otherwise, he didn't know what he would have done with himself.

He didn't like admitting it to himself, but he was in a low place. With his daddy dying and his lonesome state, there were long stretches when he would get to feeling sorry for himself. He would linger there for a time, long enough to wonder why it was he continued going through the motions of living. Then he would scold himself mentally for allowing such self-indulgent behavior and would go on as he always had. With winter coming, there was plenty to do to prepare.

Somehow, the work and the monotony of repetitive tasks kept him from becoming swallowed by gloom. With his tobacco fields and his father's fields that had been set before his death, Ellis struggled to keep up. He traveled back and forth between his place and his daddy's, doing his best to care for both crops. As he worked, he tried to avoid looking at the burned-out shell of what had once been the barn. Memories would float through his mind, soft as cotton fluff spread by the wind.

Those were the fields he had worked with his father for so many years. The image of his father, solid and substantial, was what carried him along. It had not been merely his daddy's size that lent Ellis such recollections, but his strength of character, his unfailing steadfastness, his ability to strike at the heart of a problem with a minimal use of words. It left Ellis with a mixture of sorrow that he was gone and pride that he had been Jim Hooper's son. It gave him the desire to want to live up to his father. To try to be the man that his daddy had been.

Ellis brought in the last of the vegetables when the weather began to turn — carrots, squash, turnips, and potatoes — from his garden and arranged them carefully in crates. The crates were layered with fresh straw in between the vegetables and stored in a cellar he'd dug next to his house. He had lined the hole with fresh straw as well before lowering the vegetables in and covering them with a canvas to hopefully last through the winter.

He was sitting on the porch about noontime that day, eating an apple, when he saw a car coming up the drive. He stood, pitching the core into the yard, and leaned against one of the posts near the stairs, thinking at first it must be Purvis Little. It was Purvis's car, but to Ellis's surprise, Purvis was not driving.

As the car pulled around the last bend and over the final ridge, he saw who it was and had mixed emotions. He recognized that it was only Fergus driving the car and was disappointed because he would have preferred other company. But at least it was a visitor. It was Fergus and Elvira who had come to call. Despite Ellis's annoyance at the fellow, he supposed any company, even Fergus Bayard's, was better than no company at all. He hadn't gone anywhere for months, and no one had managed to drop by to see how he was faring.

Fergus and Elvira got out of the car and came up the steps, grinning as though they were up to mischief.

Ellis nodded a welcome to them. "I thought for sure you was Purvis. What're you drivin' his automobile for?"

"That there was a gift from my new pappy-in-law," Fergus boasted, his skinny chest puffed out as much as was humanly possible.

"Pappy-in-law?" Ellis asked incredulously.

"That's right. This here's my new bride," he said, indicating Elvira who was smiling bashfully and lowering her eyes.

Ellis looked at Fergus and Elvira and hoped that the surprise did not register on his face. He was amazed at the pairing of the two. While he had seen them at the dance, he figured that the young girl's interest in him would have evaporated long ago. Fergus was the butt of every joke as far back as Ellis could remember. He was a dyed-in-the-wool mama's boy. He had no prospects, no ambition, and no desire to ever cut the apron strings. And there he stood, with the most beautiful girl in the county.

Elvira had to be completely oblivious if she was not aware of these character flaws, yet Ellis did not sense any naivety in her. Although he couldn't put a finger on it, he was distrustful of her. Maybe it was her cat-like manner or the slightly devious look in her dark eyes; he wasn't sure. She was a strange combination of pouty girl and sultry woman, and in Elvira, the two didn't mix. She exuded femininity, a power that she likely didn't completely understand but wielded recklessly. What had she seen in Fergus? She could have had any one of a dozen other young men. Why him?

"Well, I'll be," Ellis replied with a pat on Fergus's back. "You gone and done it!"

He ushered them into his small front room, and they took chairs from around the table to sit by the fireplace. Elvira sat in the rocking chair, arching her back, running her fingers over the arms as she rocked. Her interested gaze roamed the room, as if taking mental notes of the place.

"Purvis done gave me that there automobile as a weddin' present. Said we'd need somethin' startin' out to get round in," Fergus bragged.

Elvira said, "We's livin' up yonder with Fergus's mama for now. But Fergus is goin' to get us a place right quick. Ain't you, Fergus? Ain't that what you said, that you's gonna get us a place right quick?"

"Certainly I am."

"And he says I's to have a garden right off the back door, a big 'un with enough to bottle so's I can fill the shelves all up, and it'd have a porch, and a sittin' room, and a wash room. Ain't that what you say, Fergus?"

"That's what I say," he concurred proudly.

"Oh, and I's to have a well real close, so's I ain't gotta carry the water far neither. A well with a proper pump and all. And he's goin' to make us a fine big bed. He done started it already. He's been in the barn a-workin' away at it with his tools and such."

"That sounds right nice," Ellis said. Fergus, with his incessant grin, was irritating him, and he kept telling himself that he shouldn't be so harsh with the man. After all, Fergus had reason to be in good spirits, and it wasn't his fault that Ellis was not.

"So we ain't goin' to be at his mama's place long. Just long enough to get us a place of our own. Not that you ain't got a real nice place here for yourself, Ellis, but we got plans for a bigger place. Somethin' real nice with lotsa room. Ain't that right, Fergus? Where we can spread out and have plenty of breathin' space and all."

"Now, hush up, woman. You're likely to put poor Ellis to sleep there for all your carryin' on."

He was obviously uncomfortable with her prattle. Perhaps he didn't want Ellis to know what the two of them had discussed in private; perhaps he thought she really was boring Ellis. On either account, her husband's mild reprimand made Elvira self-consciously gaze down at her clasped hands, avoiding the men's eyes. It was clear to Ellis she didn't like being put in her place like that.

"Well, I's just tellin' him what you done tole me," she said defensively.

Ellis felt sorry for Elvira, just a girl of fifteen and now a married woman. Because her family had lived on the adjacent property, Ellis had been privy to her past. Following the death of her mother, she had become a servant to her family. Someone was always underfoot, the younger children bawling and needing attention or to be fed or put to bed. She had never had time alone to herself. No one asked what she wanted. There were too many children to care for. The house was so small that they had all shared the second-floor dormer in her daddy's home, two or three to a bed. It couldn't contain them all, and they spilled out onto the porch and into the yard.

She must have had dreams of her own, desires left unfulfilled, moments where she wanted nothing more than to be still and know quiet. So much so that she had settled for marrying a man twelve years her elder to get what she wanted. Fergus, such as he was, was the means of seeing her dreams come to fruition.

"You don't gotta go and tell everybody what we done talked 'bout to ourselves," he scolded.

She pursed her lips and gave a quick nod. "Yes, Fergus, I s'pose you's right." She said very little after that, contenting herself to listen to what Fergus had to say.

"You ortta've seen Clifton Davies when he done found out 'bout Elvira and me. Oh, he don't like that I got the purtiest girl in town. No, he don't like that none at all. Just as sly as a snake waitin' in the grass to strike. I tell you he was downright covetous, lookin' at my woman. He nigh on didn't trust what I's a-sayin' to him 'cause she's so good to look at. He says to me, '*What, this little gal?*' And I says to him, '*Yessir.*' And he says, '*Did she get kicked in the head by a mule or somethin'?*' And I says, '*No, sir.*' And he says, '*Well, what be the matter with her then?*' Just like that. '*Well, what be the matter with her then?*'" Fergus railed.

Ellis thought that if he was a rooster he'd be crowing. Fergus was doing his best to mimic Clifton, and it tickled Ellis. He was pleased to see that for once, as unexceptional as Fergus was, he had the upper hand. He had something he could be genuinely proud of.

"You go on and laugh. I woulda liked to have socked him right in the noodler." Fergus continued, smacking his fist against the palm of his other hand. "You knowed I coulda too. I ortta taught him a lesson. That's what I ortta done."

"Clifton prob'ly don't mean nothin' by it," Ellis consoled.

"Clifton don't got no woman, and I do."

"For sure he don't."

Before their visit was over, Ellis was ready to be alone again. Fergus sure could carry on, and Ellis found it grating on his nerves. He showed them the new pen he'd constructed for the pigs and the tobacco drying from the rafters in the barn before they got into what was once Purvis Little's car and drove off. He waved to them as they left. Ellis was happy for Fergus but couldn't stop the nagging feeling that Elvira and he were all wrong for one another. He was relieved that they were gone and content in his solitude — cured of any loneliness he might have felt earlier.

A few weeks later, a man came around to buy his tobacco and haul it off. Ellis got a good price for both his and his daddy's harvest and was happy with the bulge of bills that he had stuck in his pocket. He would have enough to purchase feed for his animals to get them through the winter and enough to purchase seed come spring for his next crop. There was also a new plow he had his eye on too. The one he used now was second-hand and had seen better, more productive days. The prospects of what he could do with that money raised his spirits. It was pleasing to have goods to trade with, but there was nothing as liberating as having paper to buy what he wanted and needed. It was that green paper that prompted him to go to town on the day that his path crossed with an angry blizzard.

Part III: Taking Root

Chapter 11

Late Fall of 1934

Ellis was not in a mood to be at home. Bored by the lack of variety in his life, he was eager to go into town to get supplies before the weather turned. His same old routine had begun to feel like shackles. He was used to solitude and generally didn't mind being alone, but he missed visiting his daddy now and then. Ellis was truly alone now that his daddy had passed on. He still was able to get out and see his Aunt Sissy every now and again, but an old woman wasn't exactly stimulating conversation. There were days when he'd have gladly spoken to anyone just to hear words from another soul.

Too late for second thoughts, Ellis stood by his Red Baby truck, which he had parked outside of the general store, gazing into the gray sky above, questioning his own judgment. *I should have stayed on the farm and followed my instincts*, he thought. The clouds that had been threatening in the sky were breaking open, and soggy, wilting flakes were drifting down. The ground became wet and turned the dirt road into a slippery quagmire. He debated whether he should get back in the truck and head right back home then and there.

He ignored his instincts because snow storms were uncommon for the beginning of November, and he was down to the last bit of flour in his bin. He was worried that if he got snowed in until spring, he might be without necessities. Wintertime was a lean time. He reasoned also that the snow didn't seem in much of a hurry to get anywhere as it drifted gracefully to the ground.

On this day, Ellis walked into Forbes General Store with pleasure and ambled around, picking up things here and there as he went. He grabbed a new shovel and bucket, a ten-pound bag of sugar, two twenty-five pound sacks of flour, and a bag of beans—he couldn't live without beans. He got himself a nice slab of bacon too; it smelled fresh, and he thought it had been a while since he'd had fresh meat, except for the squirrels he regularly shot. The piglets were too small yet to slaughter, and the mother and old Snaggletooth were for breeding. As many times as he had thought to kill that mean old sire, he needed him, which left him strictly off limits.

He began stacking his selections up by the counter and went back to explore the shelves for more supplies. Ellis remembered the mystic allure, the magic he'd felt as a child when he had explored the odds and ends in this very store. Part of the fascination had been that he and his daddy hadn't had two nickels to rub together, like many of the other small-time farmers that did their best just to survive, and therefore much of what was carried in the store had been unattainable. He shook his head; it was a whole lot more rewarding when you came with a little money in your pocket.

Forbes carried just about everything: groceries, hardware, tools, knick-knacks of every description and use. It was a real country store with a hodgepodge selection to choose from. Closer to town, there were more specialty shops—grocery stores, feed stores, and such. In good weather, Ellis liked to spend time out behind the grocery. He could find plenty of fellows willing to try their hand at a game of horseshoes, while spectators sat in the shade of the porch, sipping at a soda pop or lemonade. It was a pleasant way to pass time. Right now, his main goal was just to get in, get what he needed, and get out. Maybe if the weather hadn't turned, he would have gone and had a look around town and seen what was going on.

A few old men loitered near the counter, arguing politics and commenting on the weather. If it had been nice out, they would have occupied the chairs on the front porch out by the wooden Indian, but on a snowy, wet day, they were content to mill around inside, looking for diversions to cut away the dead hours they had on their hands.

He could hear them talking like a bunch of women, gossiping about some scandal one of them had just gotten wind of. It made him smile. When he approached, they fell silent, eyeing him distrustfully. He paid for his things with his cash.

"Say, boy, where'd you get all that money from?" one of them asked. He was puffing on a pipe and let the smoke blow out the corner of his mouth, the cloud dispersing slowly toward the ceiling.

Ellis shrugged. "What d'you mean where'd I get it from?"

"You didn't steal it, now did you, boy?"

"No, sir. This here's the last of my terbaccer money." He faced the man. "Now why'd you go and think I stole it for, right off like that?"

"You's Jim Hooper's boy, ain't ya?"

"For sure I am," he affirmed proudly. "But my daddy never done a single dishonest thing all his life." His tone was firm and allowed for no disputations.

"I never said he did. No, Jim Hooper never a-stole. But it don't stand that his boy wouldn't."

Ellis could sense that his words had some sort of a double meaning, but he accepted his change, and with a nod of his head to the clerk, struggled to keep his anger in check. Before leaving, he turned to his accuser and said, "Well, sir, he done taught me right. I'd a-never stole no money neither. Like I tole you, this here's what's left of my terbaccer money." He pocketed it and left.

Ellis carried his purchases out onto the porch and began loading them into the back of his truck, carefully arranging it so that it would all fit in nice and snug. He covered the whole of it with a canvas tarp.

The snow was coming down harder, gaining momentum as the minutes slipped by. This gave him cause for concern. The winding mountain roads were not kind in bad weather. Ellis immediately altered his plans, and erring on the side of caution, decided that loitering about town would have to wait for another day. It was best to head home before it got too late.

Before getting into the driver's seat, he happened to glance up and see the foreboding scowl of the wooden Indian that stood watch next to the door of the general store. Bare-chested despite the inclement weather, arms crossed, feathers fanned out in an arc behind his head, he was glaring with piercing eyes at Ellis. It sent a chill through him, and he wasn't sure if it was from the cold or from the hostile eyes of the red man. With that stern image in his mind, Ellis got into the cab and headed home with dread of the long ride before him.

The closer he inched toward home, the heavier the snowfall became, blanketing the trees, the road, anything it settled on as it fell. As he drove, his uneasiness grew. The windshield wiper struggled to keep the glass clear, and the tires spun through the snow, churning up the mud below and causing the truck to lurch and slide as it forged ahead.

He made it about halfway home when he glimpsed someone walking on the side of the road, struggling to make headway against the blowing snow. As he drove by, he saw that it was a young woman.

She was leaning forward into the wind, wearing what appeared to be a man's coat, clenching the lapels together to keep it shut against the cold. Her stride was exaggerated as she lifted her knees high to compensate for the men's work boots that were too big for her feet. She was hatless, and her dark hair whipped violently around her face.

Ellis passed her by, loathing the idea of sharing his ride with a stranger, still in an ill mood after his exchange with the men from the store. But his conscience got the better of him. He knew his father would have stopped to help the unfortunate traveler, and he braked and put the truck in reverse. Once he pulled up next to her, he opened the driver's side door and stepped out onto the running board.

He shouted at her over the sweep of the wind, "Need a ride?"

She wore an expression of suspicious concern, as though trying to decide if she could trust him or not. "I just live up the road yonder there a-ways," she hollered to him, gesturing with her head.

"It ain't nothin' to me to drop you off up the road," he assured her. "I'm headed that a-way anyhow."

The girl hesitated. She turned back toward her destination, the snow pelting her face in stinging waves. He could see she was contemplating the overwhelming notion of continuing to brave the weather or take the ride.

Finally, she shrugged and faced him again. "I'd be grateful to you."

"The latch on that there door is busted," Ellis informed her as he pointed to the passenger side. He stepped off the running board to let her in. "You gotta get in through this here door."

She made her way around the front of the truck, got into the cab, and slid under the steering wheel and all the way over to the other side, hugging the other door to keep herself away from Ellis. He eyed her for a moment, in her worn penny cotton dress, faded red baggy wool leggings, the men's work boots, and oversized coat.

Even under that large coat, it was obvious she had a small, lean frame, and her cheeks were nearly gaunt yet rosy from the chill. He gave her a smile that he hoped was reassuring as he started back up the road. The rubber tires spun until they gained traction, spewing snow and mud behind them.

He noticed her wet face and her runny nose and reached into his pocket for a handkerchief. It was worn and gray now instead of white, but like her dress, it was clean.

"Looks like you might could use this," he observed, handing it to her.

"Obliged," she said, although she seemed reluctant to accept it. She blotted her face and then blew her nose. Wadding it up into a ball, she crushed it in her fist, stuffing it deep into her coat pocket.

They traveled in silence as the truck labored through the snow, which was now a good three to four inches deep in places. Ellis dared not push his speed past a few miles an hour, and they crept along at a painfully slow pace. Every now and then, the back of the truck would slide wildly back and forth, fishtailing on the slick surface of the road. He could almost feel the girl holding her breath. The road took a course that meandered around the mountain. At times, the wall of the mountain was to the inside of their path; other times, it was to the outside. Either way, there was always a steep incline or a sheer drop off that threatened their lives. One ill-planned maneuver, and the truck would simply fall off into oblivion.

Visibility was next to nothing, and it worried Ellis that he couldn't see what was coming, that he wouldn't be able to tell where the danger lurked, and the two of them might end up dead at the bottom of a drop somewhere. How long would it take for someone to discover the wreckage left behind? Or, perhaps no one would find them, and they would lay there undiscovered.

Whatever happened to Ellis Hooper? they would ask themselves. Their disappearance would be a mystery to all who might wonder over what had become of them. In truth, he hoped that the apprehension churning in the pit of his stomach was not showing on his face. He squinted and leaned in closer to the windshield, wiping the condensation building there away with the back of his hand.

"It sure is a-comin' down, ain't it?" he observed, more to himself than to her. "Maybe we ortta pull off to the side of the road and wait for it to clear up some."

His suggestion was met with seeming terror. "I gotta be gettin' home. My pa is liked to blow if I ain't back soon," she protested. "It's just up the road a-ways. Just a little further on up that a-way."

Ellis pushed on, getting stuck for a moment on the road at the bottom of a hill. He pumped the gas, listening to the engine roar ineffectually as the tires spun in the snow. He backed the truck up a bit and gunned it again. The tires got a grip on the road, and they were propelled upward until they crested the ridge and headed down again. He put his foot on the brake in vain as they catapulted downward, gaining speed and momentum. The tires skidded on the snow, and there was no stopping them. Blinded by a white fog of flakes, Ellis didn't know which direction to steer. He wasn't certain which side of the road was a ditch hugging the side of the mountain and which was the drop-off that would send them over the edge. He fought with the steering wheel as it rotated back and forth in his hands.

He heard the girl next to him let out a squeak that evolved into a full blown scream. Her hands grabbed for anything that might steady her as the truck lurched down the knoll and then came to an abrupt stop in a pile of snow off to the side of the road. The two of them were launched forward, and her head slammed into the thick windshield with a thud, leaving a crack where her forehead had collided with it. Sitting there stunned, hearts pounding, silent but for the hiss of the wind, all was still.

The girl shook her head, eyes wide, as if she were trying to shake off the confusion of what had just happened to them.

"You all right?" Ellis asked, his voice quivering ever so slightly.

"Bumped my head."

He leaned over and inspected it. "Looks like you got a knot a-comin' on," he observed, running his fingers over the bump on her forehead.

She shrank from his touch, nervous by the mere proximity of him.

"Let's try and see if we can't pull ourselves outta here," he said, easing the tension by diverting the subject. He put the truck in reverse and punched the gas, but the tires merely spun. No progress made. He tried again. Still nothing.

"I'm gonna get out and try and give her a push," he said. "You give it the gas when I say. Can you do that?"

She nodded her head solemnly.

Ellis forced the door open against the strength of the gale, and the girl scooted back over to where he had been sitting. The cold wind nearly took the breath right out of his lungs. He struggled to the front of the truck while blasts of air whipped his knitted scarf. The storm tugged violently at his hat and burned his eyes as it sent snowflakes to bombard him. He worked his shoulder into the front bumper and yelled above the bluster of the weather for her to give it gas.

The engine roared and he pushed with everything he had in him, but the truck remained stubbornly lodged even as he struggled to move it. She let up on the pedal to avoid flooding the engine. Ellis, now covered in a shroud of white, ran his hand along the side of the Red Baby. He was anchored only by the brush of his fingertips against the cold metal of his truck as the storm raged around him.

Every direction he looked, there was nothing but white; an invisible world loomed just beyond their perception. The implications of their predicament set in, and he knew that they were in a bad way. He climbed back into the truck, blowing into his hands to try to warm them.

"Settle in. We ain't goin' nowheres," he grumbled. "I'd go myself to get hep, but I can't see nothin'. Wouldn't make it far afore I'd be lost for good."

"But my daddy." It was barely more than a whisper.

"Your daddy's just gonna have to see we ain't got no choice in the matter here," Ellis consoled. "No point in lettin' the gas run out." He shut off the engine.

CHAPTER 12

Ellis woke, feeling frozen all through except for the parts that were warmed by her body pressed to his. He could see her even, crystallized breaths escaping in clouds of white condensation. He didn't move, worrying that he would wake her. The two had been forced to huddle together to try to keep from freezing all the long night. Ellis had given her his scarf, and she had covered her ears with it. At some point, they had drifted off to sleep, despite their fear of never waking again. The storm had calmed and then stopped during their slumber, leaving nothing but silence and a world baptized in shades of pure white.

As perilous as the storm had been, Ellis couldn't help but marvel at the beauty of it. The branches of the trees bowed heavily beneath their burden, laden with snowflake atop snowflake, resembling the fluff of a down feather. It was nearly a religious moment, solemn in the quiet of the morning. But then Ellis contemplated how mean this land could be to a man. How it could swallow a person up whole, leaving no trace of him. If it didn't kill him outright, it took its sweet time, stacking a load of burdens upon his back till it broke him down, made him old and weary. In the end, it would have him one way or the other. Yet he toiled over it. He sought to own it, wanted to bend it to his will, loved it, prayed over it, fretted for its welfare. And for what? To finally claim only enough of it for a grave. This red earth was a fickle thing that never reciprocated the feelings. He thought of his daddy buried beneath it now and how someday he would be too.

Ellis pondered these things. He wondered why people were willing to struggle so hard in this life when they all ended up in the grave anyhow. The answer was right there. He could feel it teasing him, darting in and out just at the edge of his mind. But the solution remained elusive. Struggle as he might, he could not figure it out. He did not settle upon the fact that a person's life was worth only the knowledge he had acquired and the relationships he had built. All else was left behind to rust. To ruin.

He was pulled away from his musings, jolted suddenly back to his present situation by the rap of a knuckle on the window next to him. He started, waking the girl, who guiltily sprang away from him as he opened the door. Immediately the cold seeped into his skin, and he shivered as he climbed out of the truck to talk to the stranger who had happened upon them. His legs and feet tingled from the lack of circulation.

"Dad gummit, my legs is dead," he complained, bending down to massage them as pricking of his nerves sent pain through his lower half.

"Looks like you done got yourselves in a real bad pickle," the stranger observed.

"Thank the Lord you come along. We been stuck here this whole night through. Nobody else happened by here but you, mister. And I'm obliged to you for stoppin'."

"It's a wonder you ain't froze to death," the man said, eyeing the girl and then Ellis.

She turned away under the stranger's scrutiny. Ellis could see that she was worried about what the man might be thinking.

"Lucky I seen you. Prob'ly wouldn't have if it wasn't on account of your truck bein' red and all."

"I come down that ridge and—" Ellis whistled and struck his hands together, showing with one of his hands how he had glided right off into the ditch "—run plumb off the road. Stuck good too."

"Well, let's see if we can't get you outta there," the stranger offered. "Will she start up?"

"Don't know. Ain't tried." Ellis got back in the truck and tried to get it running again. The first few attempts, the truck coughed, sputtered, and died out. But he persisted, and at last it roared to life. He put it in reverse and revved it, but it stayed stubbornly stuck where it was.

"Have your little gal there guide it, and you and me'll push," he suggested.

Ellis wanted to tell him that she was not his little gal. He thought better of it and kept his mouth shut. She, too, said nothing, only did as she was told. The two men pushed as she pumped the pedal. The results were the same. No luck, no progress.

"She's stuck good, all right," the stranger mused. "Tell you what. I got me a piece of rope up yonder. I can tie it up from your truck to my automobile and try and pull you out."

"I'd be grateful to you," Ellis said. He followed the stranger out of the ditch and to the road where his automobile was running idle. The two of them made fast work of it, tying one end of the rope to the truck, the other to the man's car. Ellis eased himself into the truck and gunned it while the man tried backing his car at the same time. The old Red Baby moved a few inches before progress was stalled. The man came back, removed his hat, and scratched his head.

"It ain't a-goin' to move."

"I got me a shovel in the back there. I maybe ortta dig myself out," Ellis told him, shuffling through his stash of goods in the bed of the truck. He pulled out his brand new shovel and went to work. He cleared the snow out the best he could from around the front tires and then moved to the back, making a path all the way up to the road. It took him a good twenty minutes of digging, leaving a trail of frozen dirt chunks and mounds of snow in his wake. All the while, the stranger waited patiently in his car until Ellis gave him a wave, threw the shovel haphazardly back into the truck, and got behind the wheel once again, with a prayer to God that it would work.

This time the truck did as it was directed and made its painfully slow way back onto the road. Ellis had never felt such relief in his life. The stranger came back and untied his rope.

"Can't tell you thank you enough," Ellis said, giving his arm a strong pump as he shook his hand.

"It wasn't nothin', neighbor. You be on the straight and narra again." The stranger pulled around them and disappeared into the distance.

"We's on our way now," Ellis told the girl as they headed along the road again.

Instead of looking relieved, she looked frightened half out of her mind. They drove for another few miles before she directed him toward a gravel road with a few fresh ruts imprinted into the snow.

"That there's the place you turn off up yonder," she told him.

Ellis turned off the main road and followed it until she told him to turn again along a narrow dirt road that ended down in a lonely hollow. A shabby house on stilts, no bigger than Ellis's own place, came into view, smoke belching from the crooked chimney. When they pulled up abreast the front porch, a swarm of half-naked little ones busted out the front door, clambering over the truck, whooping and carrying on like wild heathens.

Ellis had seen the likes before. There were some who lived like savages, like nothing much better than animals. They were scattered here and there through the hills — people who didn't know any better and some who didn't care. Ellis turned and studied the girl he had rescued and realized, from her sad and unkempt appearance, that this was her lot in life. He felt a bit of pity and regret that he would have to leave anybody to this base existence. He let her out of the truck. He could sense that she was ashamed by the way she hung her head and the way she avoided his eyes. One of the ragged boys was picking through the goods Ellis had tied down in the bed of the truck.

"Alfie, you get yourself down from there. That ain't for you," she scolded. "Go on! Get!"

He jumped down, barefoot in the snow, and seemed not to notice the cold. The boy looked sideways up at her. "Where you been?"

"That ain't none of your concern," she said firmly.

"Daddy's fit to be tied."

She tried to show a brave face. "Go on with you," she said halfheartedly, and he took off without further prodding. It was then that Ellis noticed a woman standing in the doorway, a bare-bottomed baby at her hip, watching the interaction.

The girl noticed her then too, her solemn face melting with relief. "Mama," she cried, running up the stairs and across the porch to wrap her arms around the woman. Ellis followed sheepishly behind.

"We was worried sick, girl," the mother said, returning her daughter's hug. She eyed Ellis over the girl's shoulder. "Your daddy's out a-lookin' for you. Been gone all mornin'. Where you been?" Her tone was soft and filled with concern. She seemed like a kind lady. She pulled away and inspected her daughter, running a gentle finger over the goose egg that had formed on the girl's brow.

"It was somethin' frightful, Mama. This here man, he offered me a lift home, and it was an awful storm. We was headed down that hill up yonder a-ways, and we went right off the road. Well, we done tried and tried everythin' to get us outta that there ditch, and we ended up stuck there all the night long. Why, I thought we was a-gonna die, Mama. But some feller come 'long in the mornin' and pulled us out. It was so cold, and we was so hungry."

"You been through it, ain't you?" her mother consoled, but Ellis could see that same worried expression on her face as her daughter was prone to wear. "I ain't got much, mister, but you welcome at my table anyhow," she said, nodding her head earnestly.

Ellis grew modest, dropping his gaze to his feet and shrugging. "Thank you much, ma'am. It's kind of you to offer, 'cause I didn't do much but get her stuck in this here weather all night, but I was hopin' I could just trouble you for somethin' to drink, and I'll be on my way."

"Clairey, you get our guest here somethin' to drink, will you?" her mother said, stepping aside to let him in.

The interior of their little cabin was dimly lit, the primary source of light being the fireplace. The warmth in the room enveloped him. He noticed the sparse furnishings and the shabby appearance of the place. A middle-aged woman sat by the fire in a rocker, holding a toddler, the floor boards creaking in time with her measure. She acted as if she weren't aware that anyone else was in the room with her, her expression carefully blank.

The girl named Clairey retrieved a mason jar filled with well water from a bucket sitting in the dry sink and brought it back to Ellis.

He drank it down in one gulp and held it out to her. "Can I trouble you for another? I got a powerful thirst."

She went and filled it up again and handed it over. Ellis was in the midst of finishing his second round when a large man in filthy overalls exploded through the door, his rifle clutched tight in his fist. Ellis jumped, taken completely off guard, the water he was consuming spewing out of his mouth and nose, all over the front of his coat and across the floor. He coughed and sputtered for a moment before he regained his composure and wiped his face with the sleeve of his coat. Ellis took a step back as he sized up the large man in front of him, with his wild beard that grew to the navel, his bald head, and broken and missing teeth.

"Where the hell you been, girl?" he bellowed.

The girl called Clairey let out a little whimper and took off at a run, retreating behind her mother, where she cowered in fear. It looked as if her mother would have done the same if there had been anyone else left to hide behind. The baby began to bawl, burying his eyes behind his dirty little fists.

"Now…now, Joe," the mother sputtered, "she be home safe and sound after a frightful night."

"Where?" he roared, obviously not appeased. "Where the hell's the dirty little tramp been?"

Ellis was horrified by the man's behavior. He felt a duty to intercede on the women's behalf. He thought that if he could just calmly explain the situation that Joe would cool off. He took a half-step forward, clearing his throat, and said with as much nerve as he could muster, "She was with me, sir." It came out matter-of-fact like, as if he were presenting to a judge and saying, "These are the facts as I know them."

Clairey's father turned his attention from the two cringing, trembling female figures to Ellis. His towering frame and hard eyes were deliberately meant to intimidate. "Well, damn it, boy, who're you? What's your business here?"

Ellis tried to stand firm, to appear as if he weren't rattled. "Name's Ellis Hooper, sir."

"I ortta kill you!" he yelled, flying at him in a fury, putting his face to Ellis's face. "What you mean havin' my girl out all ayers of the night!"

"Now, Joe, it weren't nothin' like that. This here boy was tryin' to do good. He was bringin' our girl home in that there storm, and his truck come off the road. They's stuck till this mornin'," Clairey's mother tried to explain, but her voice was shaking and timid. It sounded unconvincing even to Ellis's ears. "Look here at the knock she got in the head. She's in bad shape."

"That the truth?" he asked Ellis, leaning in closer to him. "That what happened? Or was you out on *other* business?" His meaning was clear. Ellis didn't care for the implications, and he didn't care for the man's threatening tone.

"Daddy, it weren't nothin' bad. He's just givin' me a ride, Daddy," Clairey cried, still safe behind the protection of her mother.

"No, sir. No. It's like they done said. She's a walkin' in the snow, and I was goin' to give her a ride. We was on our way and went off the road up yonder ways and was stuck. Some feller come 'long this mornin' and pulled us outta there. I brung her home straight a-ways. That's all there was to it. I swear it, mister. That's all that happened."

Joe paused for a moment, as if he were mulling their story over, and then snarled, "It don't matter!"

"It don't *matter?*" Ellis repeated, perplexed by his reaction. A warning began to sound in his head, and the hammering of his heart was telling him to get out, to run and get away from that place.

"I ortta bust you up, draggin' her in after a night of carousin'!"

"Carousin'? We done no such thing," Ellis replied, indignant at what the man was suggesting.

"You done ruint her!" Joe accused. "You done ruint her just the same."

"I didn't do nothin', mister," Ellis responded, now fearful about where the man was going with his accusations.

"What man'll have her now? She been out all night, alone with some boy. Why, nobody'll have the tramp. They'll take her for used up."

"How'd they know one way or the other? Nothin' happened and nobody knows no different!" Ellis protested.

"She ain't no good to me now. Not now that no man'll have her," Joe insisted. "She's ruint, I say. You done ruint her." His voice grew deafening with his conviction.

Ellis looked around, sure that everyone else would be just as shocked as he at what the man was charging. The woman in the rocking chair continued to rock, stroking her child's hair, remaining carefully neutral, while Clairey and her mother seemed too frightened to protest what was happening.

"Nobody else'll have her, so you gonna have her, boy," Joe continued, his presence becoming more and more threatening as he pressed the tip of his finger into Ellis's chest.

"Now, now you tryin' to skin me!" Ellis retorted, outraged by what was transpiring. "I'll not have her!"

"You say you won't have her? *You won't have her?* I say you will," he growled.

"Daddy, please…" Clairey begged, gathering enough courage to venture out from behind her mother. She tugged on his cuff.

He flung her off, not breaking eye contact with Ellis.

"Daddy, he didn't do nothin'. He's just tryin' to give me a ride—"

Joe turned on her with uncontrolled fury. "Shut it!" he roared, raising his hand as if he would strike her. She shrunk away from him. With her out of the way, he turned his attention back to Ellis.

"I ortta kill you. That's what I ortta do. Take a man's daughter, keep her out all night, and don't do right by her?"

"I's just givin' her a lift. We didn't do nothin' wrong. You tryin' to skin me, and I won't have it!"

"You won't have it?" He looked as if it were taking all of his energy to control his rage. Then he pointed a quaking finger to the door and roared, "Get out!"

Ellis was confused. He looked from Clairey's father to Clairey to her mother. It was as if everyone were frozen, afraid to move, afraid to breathe, afraid of what Joe might do next. Ellis slammed the jar down on the table and bolted for the door in a rush to get away from that place. He had nearly made it to the freedom of the outdoors when he heard Joe's heavy steps behind him. He turned to see the big man following with his hand clutching Clairey by the hair, dragging her.

"Daddy, no! No!" she yelped, trying unsuccessfully to plant her feet. But her frantic attempts to free herself were futile against his bulky strength, and she was hauled along easily despite her desperate resistance.

Her mother rushed forward and begged, "No, Joe. Please stop!"

She tugged on Clairey in the other direction, and Clairey all the while was yelping in pain as her hair and arm were pulled back and forth between the two of them. Joe gave his wife a vicious backhand that sent her and the baby sprawling. She lay there stunned, pressing her fingers to her mouth to stop herself from crying aloud.

Ellis spun around, on alert, ready to either bolt or defend himself. "I done said I won't have her!" he shouted, sweeping his hands in an arc in front of him in an effort to show that he meant it.

"She ain't no good to me no more. Not now that no man'll have her, so the dogs'll have her! It's all you're fit for is the dogs!" He sent her spinning past Ellis with a powerful thrust of his hand, out through the door and into a heap on the front porch.

"What in the—" Ellis stammered. He backed out of the doorway, stumbling over the threshold, nearly losing his footing. He turned and ran for the truck as the door shut with the sound of thunder. He scrambled behind the wheel, ready to speed away from the place, until he caught sight of Clairey on her knees, banging pathetically on the door.

"Daddy, please," she begged. "Please, Daddy. I didn't do nothin'!" She was weeping and hysterical, and it moved him.

How could he leave her there like that? How could he drive away, knowing she had been turned out in the cold? He simply could not abandon her. Slowly, he got out of the truck and walked back up the steps, standing over her for a minute or two, unsure of what he should do.

"Daddy, please!" she continued to wail.

Ellis squatted down next to her and put his hand gently on her shoulder. "Clairey…" Her name sounded strange on his lips for the first time.

She ignored him, pounding more desperately, raising her voice in a fevered pitch. "I'm sorry, Daddy! Please! Please!"

"Clairey," Ellis said softly, "you come on with me now."

She turned to look at him. "He won't open the door to me," she told him with a moan, as if he didn't know.

"You come on with me now," Ellis repeated, taking her by the arm and helping her up.

She followed him reluctantly to the truck with her shoulders sagging. She appeared to shrink before his very eyes as the weight of the moment bore down upon her. Ellis watched as she debated whether to get back into the truck. He could only imagine the struggle that must have raged within her. She had no choices. For what could a girl on her own do to earn her keep? Without her father, she was as good as dead. He watched as she resigned herself to a fate that was no longer in her hands. She climbed into the truck and watched out the window as he drove away, leaving her childhood home to disappear into the distance.

At the end of the lane, Ellis sat indecisively at the crossroad, thoroughly overwhelmed, unsure of himself and of what he should do. He knew that it was his choice, his responsibility to do what was right. He knew what his father would have expected of him; above all else, he would have wanted Ellis to do the honorable thing. There was only one option left in his mind. He pulled onto the main road, heading back toward town again.

Chapter 13

It was near dark when Ellis pulled into the yard in front of his cabin. Trapper greeted them on the porch with an eager wag of his tail. He was hungry after his two days of neglect.

When Ellis hauled himself through the front door, he was more than a little relieved to be home. Indeed, he wondered why he had ever wanted to leave in the first place. Clairey was worse off than he, barely having enough energy to ascend the steps. She had been crying for the better part of the day, and with her eyes puffy and swollen, her hair a tangled mess, and the knot on her forehead now a deep purple color, she was an unsightly wreck. Every time he thought she was through with it, she would begin anew with fresh tears and stifled sobs. He had at first felt sorry for her, but now he was thoroughly annoyed.

Ellis's first plan of action was heating the place up. He headed for the hearth in the darkness, accustomed to the place enough to know where everything was, and with his cold fingers, worked to start a fire. Then, he went to the iron cook stove and lit a fire in the firebox and put an old pot of beans on to warm. He also lit a coal oil lantern, and as he worked, Clairey stood near the door, surveying the little house as a stranger, as an unwilling guest. When the flames had caught in the fireplace and a small fire was burning, he fed it some heftier logs.

Consumed with his tasks, he had ignored the girl, waiting and unsure, until he turned away from the fireplace and saw her like a spirit, her shadow hovering on the wall behind her, her face all pale and solemn. As much as he wanted to empathize with her, all he could think was that she was the source of all of his troubles at the moment. He struggled not to be angry at her.

"Take off your coat. Take a look round if you wanna," he offered indifferently.

She didn't appear to want to look around, but Ellis could see she did not want to be displeasing to him either, so she took a few tentative steps further into the little house, her wide-eyed gaze falling on the wood burning cooking stove. She admired its oiled black surface then moved over to the table and stood there waiting, watching him as he went to wash his hands in a tin basin sitting on a small cupboard against the wall, a round mirror hanging above it, a leather strap for sharpening his razor blade dangling next to it.

The water was cold, and he rubbed it vigorously all over his face and onto the back of his neck before he grabbed a towel hanging from the nail on the wall and dried himself. The pot of beans took a little while to warm, and they waited without conversing until he dished them out into mugs and set them on the table along with spoons. He sat down and motioned for her to do the same. She did as he directed and picked the mug up, first savoring the taste slowly then shoveling the beans into her mouth nearly all at once. She seemed ravenous, hungry enough that she evidently didn't care what she must have looked like as she finished them off greedily. Ellis watched her as he chewed more carefully, distracted by the sight of her consuming the beans. He thought she resembled a wild animal devouring the carcass of its prey. It was disconcerting to him. He watched with disgust as she wiped her mouth with her fingers and then wiped her fingers onto the skirt of her dress.

She hadn't taken the old coat off. Maybe she was still cold. Maybe she was too uneasy with her new surroundings to feel that she could remove it; he didn't know.

He finished his beans and got up from the chair. "I gotta get the truck unloaded and tend to them animals," he explained, shrugging back into his coat. He went out to the truck and brought the food goods in, setting them in a pile at the end of the table. Ellis went back for another load, leaving the other items stacked neatly on the floor next to the door. He went out to the barn to see to the livestock, feeding and watering them, before he saw to the cow, who desperately needed a milking. When he finished, he latched the barn door, checking about the yard to make sure all was secure, then went back into the house with reluctance.

"Well, I'm beat," he informed the girl when he came through the door, trying to avoid looking at her. "I'm gonna turn in." He stretched his arms above his head and yawned loudly. "I can put it away proper tomarra."

She just sat there as if she hadn't heard him, her hands clasped in her lap, her eyes darting between her hands to the empty mug before her, careful not to meet his gaze either.

He walked past her to the only other room in the house—the bedroom. It was frigid in there, and once he had removed his boots and clothes, he climbed under the pile of quilts, waiting for his body heat to warm the bed, settling in with the blankets pulled in tight around him.

After a while, she came to the doorway of the bedroom and gazed at him under the quilts. Ellis opened his eyes and looked at her. The firelight from the main room was behind her. She had removed the heavy coat, and her slight figure was silhouetted against the flickering firelight which danced in random patterns across the floor and walls.

Ellis watched as she stepped tentatively forward and then stood quietly next to the bed. She took off the clunky boots first, kicking them clumsily off and pushing them away with her toes. He watched with amazement as she unbuttoned her dress with shaking fingers, frightened half to death, and it slipped off her shoulders into a pool at her feet. She stood there in a pair of men's long underwear—once red but now a faded dark pink—and her slouching socks. She waited for his invitation, visibly trembling, dreading what would come next.

Ellis wore an expression of surprised revulsion, his eyebrows knit together and his lips drawn down at the corners as he understood what she was doing—that she was offering herself to him. He cleared his throat before he said calculatedly, "You ortta get some sleep. It's been a long day," and rolled over so that his back was to her.

A few moments passed before Ellis felt her lift the covers and slip quickly into the bed, her back to his.

They lay like that, woodenly, without moving, until he heard her muffled crying again. He wasn't sure if he should try to comfort her; he didn't want to. Not like this. Not while they lay in the same bed. It was uncomfortable. The whole darn mess was. He did the only thing he felt he could do and tried to go to sleep.

Ellis woke in the middle of the night to throw some more logs on the fire before it burned out completely. The coals were red hot, but they were giving off very little heat until he stoked the fire and added fuel to it. When he padded barefoot back to bed, she was sleeping soundly, her face relaxed, her breathing even.

He studied her with interest for the first time since they had met, really able to look her over with a clear head and the absence of distractions. Her dark, wavy hair fanned out against the pillow. Her thick, apricot-colored lips parted just slightly in restful repose. A light sprinkling of freckles crossed the bridge of her tolerably broad nose. On the whole, her looks were agreeable. He estimated her age to be somewhere around twenty. It wasn't that she was unattractive; no, it wasn't that. Though he'd seen more beautiful women in his day, she wasn't unpleasant to look upon. Her face was pretty enough, but her overall disheveled appearance detracted greatly from that natural beauty. Looking at her now, he had never felt so much fear, so much dread. She was his responsibility now, his burden, his wife.

This was not what he had pictured when he had imagined his wedding day. A quick wedding in town performed by a justice of the peace in his front room while the bride wept through the ceremony had not exactly been his ideal. Ellis had always thought it would be Dulcie Mae beside him in the church with a minister to perform the rights, proper and right before the Lord. Now he lay on his marriage bed, cold and miserable, wondering if he had done the right thing. Wondering if his sense of duty had doomed him. What he had wanted was to marry the girl of his dreams, to hold her in his arms and make her his. What he had gotten was an unfamiliar stranger because it was the right thing to do.

When he woke, it was to the smell of eggs, biscuits, and fried apples, the sound of sizzling bacon in the skillet. He lay there, unwilling to open his eyes, just relishing the aromas and the warmth of the quilts that piled on him in a cozy nest. Ellis had never known the tender hand of a woman, the comfort of a feminine presence. His mother had died at his birth, and he and his father had been the inadequate cooks of their household. He had never experienced the true pleasure of food prepared by someone who really knew how to elevate a biscuit from a thick, dry bit of flour to a light, fluffy, melt-in-your-mouth delight.

Clairey used buttermilk, kneading the dough with her own gentle hand, mixing it just enough to blend it, taking care not to overdo. When he sat down to the table and slathered homemade butter over it, watching it melt into the dimples of the baked dough, then taking a tentative bite and savoring the flavor that teased his taste buds, he had a brief glimpse of what heaven must be like. Clairey poured him a cup of milk from a pitcher and set the pitcher down within his reach before she moved to the stove to gather up the cast iron skillet and baking pan. She dumped them into one of the two galvanized tubs in the dry sink, scrubbing them before she dried them with a towel and put them away in the Hoosier style cupboard.

"How…how'd you do that?" he asked, holding a biscuit up and shaking it slightly at her.

She shrugged. "Flour and fat and buttermilk," she said.

Ellis tried the apples and rolled his eyes with a groan, jabbing at his plate with his spoon. "Them's the best apples I ever ate."

Perhaps not used to being complimented, she stood there dumbly, with a look of bewilderment on her face, as if she wasn't sure if he was poking fun at her or if his remark was sincere. Unable to decide which was his intention, she did not reply but turned back to her task.

"You done gone and milked the cow already?" he asked, eyeing the pitcher of milk she had left behind.

She nodded her head in reply.

Ellis could not recall the last time he hadn't had to milk a cow in the morning. As a child, it had been his job, and being the only child there was no one else but him to do it. "That was awful good of you. I been milkin' in the morin' since I was big enough to carry the bucket," he told her. "It's a treat. A real treat that I don't gotta do it this mornin'."

"It weren't nothin'," she replied.

"I don't mind you a-milkin' the cow, but you keep clear of that there pig pen. That ole boar, he's a nasty sort, and he'll run you through just as soon as look at you. He's good for nothin'. So I'll be the one to feed 'em," he told her.

"Yessir."

"Now, don't go on and call me sir. I's just tellin' you so's you don't get hurt or nothin'."

"I'm awful sorry. I didn't mean nothin' by it. I aim to stay away from them pigs, just like you tole me," she promised.

"You're to call me Ellis. It's only right and fittin' you call me by my given name. It's only right and fittin'."

"'Course," she agreed in her small voice. "I'm to call you Ellis, and you're to call me Clairey, if you'd like."

"I got me some fencing to do," he told her, pushing his chair back when he was finished with his breakfast. "I aim to prove up that field up yonder, clear out some of them there trees, stumps and all, but it'll be a real fine piece of land once I got it all done. Keep a dozen or more beef cows on it to start with. Now I'll have to barra against 'em till they fetch a price."

Ellis surprised himself, divulging his plans to someone he'd only just met, but it seemed natural for some odd reason he couldn't name, to share these specifics with her. Or perhaps it was his nerves manifesting themselves through mindless chatter. He couldn't say for sure.

He wandered over to the cupboard, took out a towel, and helped himself to some biscuits and bacon, folding them neatly inside before he went to leave. He paused at the door to shrug into his coat and then added, "Got two sets of hands now. Might barra for more seed for spring plantin' too." With that, he slipped outside and let the cabin door bang behind him.

Ellis headed to the barn, his breath a white fog, his senses enlivened as the cold assaulted him. He stopped to collect the mule, his flatbed wagon loaded with fence posts, and his tools for the day's work. When he emerged again, he noted the girl watching from the porch, shivering in her immense coat. Ellis chose to ignore her and went on about his business. He took Katie the mule past the house, on past the garden — barren now that growing season was over — and to the hill beyond, leaving a trail in the snow as he went.

He didn't notice her at first, noiseless and furtive as she followed along at a distance, her feet treading softly on the white carpet left upon the grass by the storm. But then he sensed her eyes on him and the slightest movements just behind him. He turned and spotted her several yards away, a sore thumb sticking out against the colorless landscape. When he looked at her, she stopped and was still. Ellis thought that would be enough to get the girl to go away. He continued with Katie up the hill. Clairey resumed her pace as well.

Ellis was aware, then, that she had continued to tag along after him. He turned and shooed her away with his hand. "Go on!" he scolded. "Get."

She came to rest beneath a tree, her head lowered, and it seemed as if she hadn't heard him.

Ellis again proceeded toward the pastureland he was intent upon clearing. The ground was cold but not completely frozen. Still, the frosted earth would make the job more difficult. He was just beginning to work at a stump when he noticed her again. She was hanging back, watching him, looking timid and pathetically weak. For some reason he couldn't put a finger to, it made him angry.

Ellis turned and confronted her. "What do you want?" he asked.

She ducked her head down and gave him a shrug. "Don't know."

He couldn't figure her out. What was she pestering him for? What was her purpose in following him? He had things to do, and he didn't want her keeping him from it.

He tried to ignore her and went on with his work. She must have grown tired because at some point, she squatted down, covering her legs with the skirt of her dress to stay warm as she continued to keep a vigil. He thought it was his imagination at first, but then it became clear that she was slowly moving in closer to him. Perhaps wanting to help but unsure if her assistance would be welcomed, she remained slightly aloof, her face red and chapped from the cold.

Meal time came, and Ellis took the biscuits and bacon wrapped in the towel and sat down on the flatbed to eat. It had been his intent to disregard her completely, just pretend that he didn't know she was there. So he took a bite and then another. With his cheeks bulging, he chanced a glance, and there she was, her wary eyes upon him. He groaned to himself with the knowledge that he had lost the battle. How could he eat with her gawking? How could he enjoy his lunch knowing she would be staring all the while? He refused to look at her straight on as he held out his hand with a biscuit in it.

Tentatively, she approached. Careful and distrustful, she snatched it from his hand, turned her back to him, and shoved it into her mouth as if she were afraid he might take it back from her. When she faced him again, her jaws were so filled that she gagged a few times before swallowing.

When he went back to work, doing his best to leverage the great stump from the ground, the girl finally grew bold enough to come up next to him and assist him in his task. Ellis wasn't sure if he was grateful or bothered by her help.

She spent the rest of the day toiling with him as he removed that stubborn stump. They managed to work up a sweat despite the cold. He was surprised by her tenacity and strength. Clairey left only to go ahead of him and prepare supper.

From then on, although their relationship was mostly built on silence or awkward exchanges, they tolerated one another, even took some unspoken pleasure in their togetherness. In the evenings, he would read from the Good Book to her. That was when he discovered that Clairey couldn't read, that she had never had any proper schooling to speak of, although she said she "knew of them letters and such." He himself had not had much learning past the sixth grade, but he took what he did know and shared that knowledge with her.

Ellis provided her with the few books he owned, treasures from his childhood. When he gave her *Prudy Keeping House,* she ran her fingers along the faded embossing on the fabric cover in awe.

"Ain't Prudy a fine name?" she asked absently.

He remembered how Mrs. Fielding had opened up a whole world to him by giving him those same books so he could learn to read when he had been just a boy.

The other book he owned was the family Bible, impressively large and greatly worn. In the evening hours, Clairey would sit near the fire, brow wrinkled, struggling over the words of a verse for hours at a time before she would give up for the night and go to bed. But eventually, she began to catch on, and stammering and with great effort, she began to read the Good Book too. It gave him some insight into her persistence and willingness to work to have something she wanted. He admired her determination.

Though Ellis hadn't gotten the wife of his dreams, he did get a wonderful cook and farmhand out of the arrangement. Clairey was more than proficient at fried okra, with the breading thick and crisp, sweet potatoes generously slathered in butter and a bit of molasses, green beans with a hint of bacon grease for flavoring, thick slices of ham cooked to perfection and served with mashed potatoes, and batter bread that was moist and steaming hot when he broke a piece off. On rare occasions, she would bake up a batch of gingerbread dolloped with fresh whipped cream and sugar chilled outside in a mound of snow next to the front steps.

There was nothing to rival her biscuits with fried potatoes and milk gravy in the morning. She would cook the bacon up in the skillet then remove it to a dish, leaving the drippings behind. To that, she sprinkled in the flour and mixed it in with a fork until it bubbled and grew thick and pasty. Then she added fresh milk and stirred continuously, waiting for it to begin to boil till it was like pudding. She'd finish it off with salt and pepper to season it. It was the finest white gravy, with not a single lump in the whole batch.

Ellis would carefully break open a biscuit, laying the steaming halves side by side on his plate and generously bathing them with the gravy. Each bite was to be savored. Some nights, she would take an ear of corn, de-silked but still wrapped in its husk, and lay it in the coals on the hearth. When dinner came around, the corn was good and roasted, piping hot and full of flavor. She used this same trick for baking apples until their supply ran out about mid-winter.

Now and then, Ellis got the notion to put a chicken's neck to the block, and there was fresh poultry. Clairey could work her magic on that too, roasting it slow and long all the day, serving it up with potatoes and carrots from the root cellar. With what was left, she made chicken and noodles, where the noodles were cut from scratch, plump and slightly chewy. For lunch, Ellis liked nothing better than to break up a biscuit into rough, loose chunks, put the pieces in a bowl, and drown them in milk. It was simple fare but fast, easy, and so delicious.

Near the end of winter, he went hunting with his .22 and brought back two lean rabbits that he cleaned in the backyard. Clairey used the meat for a stew that she let simmer all day long. When he came in near dark from working, the aroma met him at the door. His mouth watered and his stomach growled. She dished it up for him, and what should have been gamey meat was so tender, so full of flavor, that it nearly dissolved in his mouth. There was no limit to her culinary abilities. But it was her dumplings that left him wanting more. Just the memory of them made his mouth water.

With the arrival of warmer weather, Clairey discovered a wild blackberry patch growing down close to the spring, and she picked the berries from it, carrying them back in the well of her upturned skirt. She made blackberry dumplings and served them along with dinner. From then on, Ellis couldn't wait until she served it up again.

His belly had never fared so well. He began to notice changes in Clairey as well—the benefits of a consistent diet. Her thin, undernourished frame began to fill out. This was not something someone might spot right off, what with the same stretched out, worn long underwear and sack-like dress she wore on a daily basis. When she needed to wash them in the large galvanized tubs, she would borrow a shirt and pair of overalls of his to wear around until she could put her dress back on after it had dried. But Ellis was a man, and his interest in her—how she moved, her habits and preferences—did not escape the scope of his awareness. He hated himself for it at times, but he couldn't deny to himself that he was intrigued by her and her femininity. When she took the dress off at night, he glimpsed a hint of her hips and bottom filling out the long underwear. The flesh of her cheeks grew rounded, and she was altogether curvier up top too. The bones that lay beneath her skin that had jutted out at unflattering angles had disappeared, and she was suddenly a woman.

However, Clairey's cooking and the second set of hands she lent were the only real benefits of their match. They may have shared the same bed, but that was where it ended. She was a constant presence by Ellis's side for the work, there to spread his table for meals, and that was the extent of it. Apart from that first night when she seemed to be offering herself to him, Clairey never made any movement toward intimacy, and Ellis was too backward with women to initiate anything on his own. As unlikely as it seemed, they lived as though they were brother and sister.

One reason was that Ellis was ashamed of how he had come to have Clairey. She wasn't someone he had desired and courted. She had instead been thrust onto him by her angry father like an unwanted dog. Again, he thought of her slinking after him that first day. A stray, that's what she was. It was an arrangement of convenience. Nothing more. She really had no place to go, and he would not be the man to turn her out.

Ellis was too vain to admit to himself that he was somewhat ashamed of Clairey. He felt aggravated with himself for it too, ashamed that he wasn't a better man, that he was so weak in his character. Clairey was a plain woman. If only she'd do something with herself. She didn't seem to want to be attractive. But then, maybe she just didn't know how. She had likely never been taught how to care for her hair or dress in a feminine way. And perhaps he was partly to blame for it too. He hadn't made any attempts at purchasing any clothing for her. She had no means of her own in acquiring a dress or fabric with which to make one. She relied solely upon him. Her wardrobe up to that point was limited to that single shabby dress, and Ellis would have been embarrassed for any of his friends to see her, let alone to introduce her as his wife.

Those were not the only complications surrounding their relationship. To Ellis, Clairey seemed skittish, afraid of men and what they were capable of. He knew her experience with her father had probably given her certain notions, that she most likely saw a woman as nothing more than a man's victim. Maybe that was something she did not want to be. She made no attempts to flirt with him, did not seem to show an interest in a romance. Perhaps she simply didn't want the inevitable hurt. So, both were held in check by the other.

There was also the issue of Dulcie Mae. Ellis would have liked to think he was over her. But whenever he allowed himself to do so, he would think back to that picnic they had shared, the feelings she had stirred in him, and the assumption he had made that they would marry. He had thought she shared the same feelings for him, and that was why it had been so painful when he'd learned she'd married Homer Pond. He could see now that it wasn't entirely her parents' opposition that had caused her to spurn him. She'd had a chance to make a better life for herself and had simply taken the opportunity when it was presented to her. Ellis could never have given her the kind of life Homer was capable of giving her. He would forever be nothing more than a simple farmer. When he thought about what might have been, he wondered if she ever regretted her decision.

Then, too, being raised without a mother, living in relative isolation with only his father, he'd never seen how a marriage worked. Oh, he knew plenty of the birds and the bees. He, after all, was raised on a farm and was not ignorant on that account, but understanding a complex woman was much more of a challenge than understanding how a male and a female came together to do more than mate.

In spite of the passage of time, he never got over a feeling that Clairey was a stranger to him, almost a hired hand merely to be tolerated and hidden away. The reclusion of winter and their inability to travel about freely did much to contribute to their confinement on the farm. Ellis thought it best. It gave him the time he needed to grow used to the idea of Clairey being his wife.

It took the snow thaw before he brought her to see his kin. On a pleasantly sunny day, winter on the verge of disappearing completely, the skies clear and the roads too, he drove her up to see his daddy's aunt. Clairey seemed pleased to be away from the farm as they drove along through the greening countryside. Even in the winter months, there was beauty to be seen in this land. The world around them looked like a subdued watercolor, all hazy with romantically indistinct lines and supple depth to its shades. Mornings, the frost was still thick on the grass, but they saw glimmers of spring peeking through during the day. Clairey had been put away all winter, and while she was apparently used to such a lot as this, she seemed to relish a change when one presented itself. And this was certainly a change for her.

"This here's my daddy's aunt, so's she's gettin' long in years," he explained. "Her man died nigh on six years ago, and she gets awful lonesome out here on her own."

He glanced over and observed Clairey absently twisting at the hem of her dress again. He had seen her do that often. It was a nervous habit of hers, the only thing that really gave away her true state of mind. Everything else about her was calm and still — her face, her voice — but he could see she was anxious.

"Don't go on and look at her too long when you first lay eyes on her. A dog got at her when she's just a child, and she got marks on her face still from it."

"That's awful sad," she murmured.

"She don't care none, I reckon. Had a time to get used to it. But she be terrible afraid of dogs. She won't have nothin' to do with 'em. Won't have one even to keep watch."

"Will she like me, you think?" Clairey asked.

"Don't know that Aunt Sissy ever met nobody she didn't like."

From the second Sissy opened the door, Ellis wanted out of there. He had warned Clairey about his aunt's face, had warned her not to be taken off guard. Sissy enthusiastically ushered them in, and instantly Clairey glued her eyes on the poor woman. She seated them in her small front room, where she had a large wood burning heater. The orange flames of the fire were glowing brightly through the slits in the small hinged door through which the wood was fed. The room seemed insufferably hot and stuffy, and Ellis immediately began to sweat.

Although distracted the entire time by Clairey's outright gawking, he was able to carry on a conversation. Sissy was a plump little lady with bowed legs and a round face. Her old skin sagged around the harsh white of the jagged lines. When she talked, only half her lower lip moved. The other half, unwilling to cooperate, drooped, paralyzed. She wore a threadbare black wig—far too dark for her coloring—that seemed to be on upside down, the weave that held the hair in place visible in some spots where it had worn through completely.

Clairey spoke hardly at all during the entire visit, just sat there staring. Sometimes she would try to look down at her hands in her lap, but then her eyes would slowly wander back to Aunt Sissy. Confusion would play out in Clairey's features; her brow would wrinkle as if she were working something out in her head. Ellis tried several times to get her attention, to motion to her to stop staring, but she never did look at him, only Sissy with her lopsided smile. It was like observing a small child who was unfamiliar with proper etiquette. No matter how discreetly one attempted to stop them, there was just no dignified way of doing it.

Sissy had them stay on for supper. In true Southern fashion, she fed them a midday meal, covering it with a cloth when they were finished, then pulled the cloth away at dinnertime so that they could eat at it again. Ellis left the two women alone briefly, reluctantly, to chop some wood for Aunt Sissy's pile. She was too old now to care for animals all on her own, so she had sold them all off after her husband died, living solely off of her garden. Ellis would bring her milk and eggs on a regular basis when the weather permitted, and he would make sure that she had enough to get her through the hard months.

CHAPTER 14

Once Ellis was gone, Aunt Sissy moved in closer to Clairey as if they were conspiring. "He's a dandy, that a-one," she said with a strange girlish giggle.

Clairey nodded absently, uncomfortable with being left alone with the old woman. She glanced several times to the door, as if she might bolt for it at any moment.

Aunt Sissy didn't seem to notice. "That boy is a blessing to me. Always was."

Clairey occupied herself by concentrating heavily at picking the hem of her dress to try to avoid looking at Aunt Sissy's ruined face. "Uh huh."

"I bore two of my own," Aunt Sissy confided. "One was a boy and the other 'un a girl."

"They close by to you?" Clairey asked politely.

"Just out yonder."

"That's real nice. Must be a comfort to you."

"They's buried up on the hill there."

It registered in Clairey's brain what Aunt Sissy was saying, and her face fell. She was ashamed that she had said something so thoughtless. "How sad," she whispered.

"My girl, Elsie, was born of 'em first. Oh, she come out cryin' and never did stop. Poor child. There was nothin' that could hep it. She wouldn't eat nothin', and she just cried and cried. Couldn't tell what was the matter with her." Aunt Sissy told her story in a casual manner, with the lack of emotion that distance of time allowed. "She died just a short piece after she's born.

"And then there was my Thermal. He cried an awful lot too. Pitiful little thing. He lasted longer. I had him for six months afore he died. He's layin' on the bed back yonder in the room, and he just rolled over, and there's blood coming from his mouth. And he's gone, jus' like that," she said, snapping her fingers. "Jus' like that."

Clairey could see a look of sadness, of pain, flash in the old woman's eyes. Strangely, it reminded her of a wounded animal. It was a brief moment of suffering, and then it was gone.

Aunt Sissy said matter-of-factly, "There wasn't no more after that. But Ellis, he come round and let me love on him, and I helt him on my lap and treated him like he's one of mine. And he don't mind that I fussed over him."

She smiled brightly, her eyes wandering over to the window, where the two of them could see Ellis as he chopped wood. "He come to the house and done things to make me laugh. Silly little things a child does, you know. Sometimes, he's a-bringin' flowers, other times a-bringin' a purty little somethin' he found here and there. And he's so bright. Looked like the sun had lit on his face. Took the hurt away some to have him round."

Clairey had been raised to be distrustful. All things were to be considered a threat. And anything said should be deciphered for its double meaning, for there could always be a hidden agenda of suffering and humiliation behind a person's seemingly innocent remarks. So, naturally she wondered if Aunt Sissy was trying to bond with her, or if she was giving warning that Ellis was hers and Clairey should keep her distance from him. But the old woman seemed guileless. Clairey suspected there were no ill motives. Whether malice or friendship was intended was not clear, but Clairey felt an empathy for the woman that left her feeling gloomy.

When Ellis came back to the house, Aunt Sissy was prattling away, and Clairey still had her big, deep-brown eyes glued directly on the disfigured woman. Ellis cursed her in his head, angry that she hadn't followed his directive not to stare.

Clairey just didn't seem all that smart to him. Why wouldn't she look away?

"Well, we ortta be gettin' back on home now, Aunt Sissy. We got them animals out yonder to tend to," he told her.

"Now, you-uns come round again soon, you hear? I do relish good company such as you."

"Sure we will," he promised. He motioned for Clairey to follow him.

She came out of the spell with a slight smile. "I thank you for havin' us," she said politely.

"An ole woman gets awful lonesome," Sissy replied, patting her hand softly. "It's good of you to come on by. Now you take care of that boy. He's a good 'un."

On the ride back, neither of them spoke. Ellis was afraid that if he said anything, he would just lay right into her with a whole string of scathing remarks over her ignoring his instructions not to stare at Sissy's deformity. Clairey didn't seem to have anything to say, either. She just sat there, dumbly picking at the hem of her dress again.

After a while, he finally found words. "What'd you mean a-lookin' at her that a-way? I done tole you afore we even come not to look on her face."

She seemed surprised. "I didn't look on her face."

"Why, 'course you did. I done watched you do it. Whole time we was there, you was a-lookin' and a-lookin'."

"I weren't lookin' at her face."

"What was you lookin' at then? 'Cause I sure thought you was. I mean, it seemed like you was to me. Seemed like you wouldn't take your eyes offen her."

As Ellis chastised her, Clairey was cringing, shrinking away from him. Like an animal that feared a ruthless master, she feared him.

"Go on and tell me," he prodded. "What was you a-lookin' at?"

Clairey watched him with her brown eyes full of fear, not daring to say anything.

"Well?" he pressed.

Her voice was small, timid, and strained. "I's lookin' at the hair of her head," she finally admitted.

Ellis thought about it briefly and then burst out laughing. "Her hair?" he repeated.

"It weren't right," Clairey replied.

Ellis saw her hesitate, as if she were wondering if she should laugh too or if he was on the verge of giving her an earful and this was the calm before the storm. It was something he could picture her father doing, laughing before he laid into her.

"Somethin' was off with it," she continued.

"That there was a wig," he explained.

"Do what?"

"A wig. A hair piece." He could see she was still lost. "Aunt Sissy went and sent away for it all the way to Atlanta."

"She done sent away for her hair?" Clairey asked.

"She says it's genuine real hair. But she had it for a long time now, and I s'pose it's seen better days."

"Now I'm awful sorry if I done made her feel bad. You think she thought I's lookin' on her face?" Clairey seemed genuinely horrified that she might have offended the old woman.

Instead of going with his gut and saying yes, he shrugged and gave her an evasive "Don't know."

"Well, now I'm real sorry for it. Didn't mean to spoil your visit. You think she feels I done her wrong?"

"Why, Aunt Sissy ain't the kind that'd hold it against you," he reassured her. "Don't worry no more on it. Just only next time, try and not do it again."

Ellis chuckled over her confusion with Aunt Sissy's hair. He was pleased that she was willing to try, at least, to behave properly. She had attempted to do her best to treat his old aunt well. Ellis liked that Clairey was kind. She seemed incapable of malice. He could see that she was making a genuine effort to pull her own weight, to fit in.

Even during the times when he was most exasperated with her, he could see that it was her simplicity and her lack of worldly experience—and not meanness or stupidity—that caused her to make mistakes. But it seemed that he was always catching her at awkward moments.

One morning, as she came back from milking, he was watching her from the porch when she suddenly dropped the pail and began a kind of frantic dance, waving her hands wildly about her head. He hurried toward her in the yard to investigate what was the matter. Not paying attention to where she was going in her frenzied state, she ran straight into him, bouncing backward and falling on her backside.

Ellis extended a hand, meaning to grab her arm and help her up. She cringed, as though expecting a blow. He shook his head in irritation. Did she really think he was that sort of man? It was offensive. Again, he pointedly offered his hand, his jaw set. This time, she reluctantly took it, standing up and brushing herself off.

"There's a wasp got after me," she explained defensively before he even asked.

"A wasp?" Ellis repeated. But then it registered with him that she seemed ashamed and so fearful only because that had been her long and vast experience in the past. He felt remorse wash over him and was unable to remain annoyed with her. He switched his approach to a gentler one. "You all right then?"

"Yeah," she affirmed, looking miserable.

"Why don't you go on up to the house, and I'll get the milk," he offered.

She gave him a nod and did as he said. He walked over to the pail and leaned to pick it up. Amazingly, she had managed to drop it straight on its bottom, not even spilling, which he thought was admirable, all things considered.

Reflecting on the torment that so often registered on her face, he wondered why he was always so hard on her. She was trying, after all. But it seemed that no matter what she did, he was frustrated by her attempts.

As he examined his motives for being unkind, he admitted that he resented her. Her being forced on him might not have been her doing, but he resented her just the same. As he walked back to the house, he told himself that he was in need of a change of mind-set. He was going to make a conscious effort to show her more kindness, to treat her with respect. He had seen the way her father treated her, and he certainly didn't want to resemble that man in any way. In spite of his resentment, she deserved better than that. So, Ellis vowed to try to be more understanding.

Chapter 15

The weather grew warmer still, and a gentle breeze played through the limbs of newly awakened trees where birds began to nest once more. Nature came around again to spring, and Ellis figured it was time to take his new bride to town to buy seed and replenish their food supply. The greening of the land renewed his own energy, and he resolved again to acquire a dozen head of cattle to put in the field he fenced. Now that he had Clairey to help with the chores and care for things in the house, he would plant twice as much tobacco as he had last season. Alone, it would have been a difficult, if not nearly an impossible endeavor to undertake. With her help, he was certain he could make enough profit to completely pay for his animal feed and seeds next spring. With luck, the year after that, he would be able to have the profit free and clear.

The idea thrilled him and put him in an overly pleasant mood. Clairey was watching the scenery pass by out her window but listening as he prattled. "I aim to plow up that whole field," he said, sweeping his hand out in a wide arc. "Plant two times what I planted last season. I barra against it now, and I can pay for it in cash come fall when I bring in the crop. And I aim to put some beef cattle in that pasture I done fenced." He rubbed his fingers along his jawbone. "Now, it's gonna take some doin', but I figure 'tween the both of us, we ortta manage it."

She listened attentively to his plan, nodding every now and then to let him know that she agreed with him.

"With the old plow I got and the new plow I bought myself in the fall, we'll be makin' faster work of it. We hit town, and I'll take care of all that, and you can get what you need."

"Plumb near outta everythin'," she answered.

Along the way, they passed the turnoff leading to the house where Clairey had lived and where she assumed her family still was. If Ellis recognized the place, he made no mention of it, and having found a new and better life, and recalling her father's cruelty, Clairey had no desire to go back there. She glanced at the rutted road leading through the trees but said nothing.

The town was a small one, a scattering of businesses lined up neatly on a paved main street. Not much to boast of, but it was better than nothing.

Ellis pulled the truck up next to the curb in front of the feed store and parked. "I got business with the feller over at the feed store. You go on get your groceries, and I'll be 'long shortly," he said and headed off.

Clairey had only been into town a handful of times in her youth, as she'd been mostly left at home with the younger children or not allowed to go for all the work needing to be done on their farm. What little that couldn't be provided for them by their farm was generally something that had been beyond their ability to afford anyhow. Besides, her daddy hadn't much cared to have a child tagging along with him when he did chance to go. The few times she had been allowed to come to town, it had been viewed from the backseat of the car, where she'd been told to stay. Town for her was a place that was full of forbidden things, things that inspired admiration and awe, things she didn't dare imagine might be hers.

She recognized the grocery store, but she couldn't recall ever having seen the inside before. It felt odd now, going into the store. She felt as though she were an outsider, wary of being discovered as an imposter, and so she entered nervously.

"Mornin'," the clerk called out as the bell jingled above the door. He was smiling pleasantly until he caught sight of her, and then his eyes grew suspicious and his broad smile diminished to a look of disdain.

By now, her dress was little more than threadbare fabric. It had been worn and washed so many times that traces of the floral pattern were hardly detectable. The clunky men's work boots she wore made a terrible clomping sound with every step she took, and the soles were worn through in places. Her face was clean and her hair combed, but the rest of her packaging was far from impressive.

"Can I help you?" he asked dryly.

"I just come to get a thing or two," she said as her eyes wandered over his selection.

Another woman was shopping with her young son, and she paused to watch as Clairey shyly picked up a can of beets. She took extra care in her inspection of it, admiring the bright red beets portrayed on the label, looking it over with wonder before she set it back on the shelf.

"Don't recall ever seein' you round these here parts," the clerk informed her. "Where is it you called home afore now?"

"Grew up just a piece from here," she said in a small voice.

"What be your name?" he asked. It was apparent the mystery of it would not let him give it up. He was intent upon placing her.

"Clairey Hooper, sir."

"Hooper? You kin to Jim Hooper then?"

"Yessir, I's Ellis Hooper's woman."

The other woman in the pale blue dress seemed to have forgotten her boy and her purpose in being there when she heard this. Her attention was fully given to Clairey. She piped up with an excited gasp, "Ellis Hooper done got murried?"

"Yes, ma'am'." Clairey picked up another can to examine.

"When did you-uns get murried?" she pressed.

Clairey guessed that the woman did not believe her. It was not surprising. She knew that Ellis was very capable of finding someone better. She figured the woman was unable to look past her poorly dressed state to see anything of worth.

"I never knowed he got murried."

"Durin' the winter," Clairey said simply.

"You said you's raised round these parts?" the clerk broke in with a puzzled expression. "I know most everybody, and girl, if you was speaking the truth I ortta know you too."

"Yessir."

"Don't recollect ever seein' you round. What was you afore you's a Hooper?"

"Davenport," she replied.

"Your daddy Joe Davenport?" the clerk asked, a hint of repugnance in his words. He had her summed up before she even had a chance to answer. It was always the same. Because he knew she was Joe Davenport's daughter, she was undeserving of consideration or respect. From then on, she felt his behavior was meant to intimidate and bully until she left his store. It didn't take much for her to realize he considered her trash and didn't want her hanging around.

"Yessir," she responded in a murmur that was hardly perceptible, with her eyes lowered as she picked at her nails.

"I'll tell you what I tole him: I ain't got no credit for liars and thieves." The storekeeper's summary of her daddy's character was meant to degrade her as well.

Clairey shrank under the hostile gaze of the clerk and the woman in the pale blue dress. Their open disapproval, their undisguised dislike for her, was demeaning, and it stung. They didn't even know her, didn't know anything about her or what kind of person she was. Clairey's expression didn't change. It was carefully blank from long years of practice. She knew to not leave a clue on her face as to what she might be thinking or feeling. Invisibility was a survival skill for her.

She was nothing. She was no one. This was how she had lived her life. This was what she had known from her earliest recollections. Her daddy had left his mark upon her. With her chin on her chest and her eyes scrutinizing the wooden floor, she walked to the door and went outside to wait for Ellis.

She didn't need to speculate about what they were thinking of her. As if the previous scene hadn't made it all crystal clear, their conversation floated through the open window, pouring like poison into her ears. She knew she shouldn't listen, should walk away, but her feet were glued to the spot, and she couldn't pull herself away from it.

"Did that gal say she's Ellis Hooper's woman?" the lady in the blue dress asked skeptically, as if she still didn't believe any of it.

"That's what she's claimin'," the clerk confirmed. "I know that Joe Davenport, and he's no good. No good, I tell you. Why, I got money owed to me by him, and I'll tell you right now I ain't never gonna see none of it. He's good for nothin'." His voice dropped as if he were telling her confidentially, "And then there's that woman's sister and the baby."

"What woman's sister?"

"Her mama," he enlightened. "Her mama's sister. Moved in and took up with Joe, and there's a baby outta it."

The mention of her mama hurt Clairey worse than anything else they might have said. Her mama, who took what was given her and didn't complain for fear of what would happen to her or her children if she did.

"Sounds like that's some match," the woman clucked. "That girl and Ellis Hooper."

"Nothin' good never come from the Bordens, and nothin' good never come from the Davenport clan, neither."

"Now, I was acquaintanced with Dilly Jane Borden. She was a right nice girl," the woman said pleasantly.

"How's she kin to Lottie Borden?"

"Second cousins maybe."

"I don't know no Dilly Jane Borden, but I done knowed Lottie Borden, and she weren't no good. Not no good at all. As good as a rotten apple spoilin' the whole bunch, she were."

"That Solomon Borden's girl?"

"She be the one," the clerk confirmed. "Died while birthin' that boy." And then for emphasis he added with a sad shake of his head, "No good." That seemed to be his favorite phrase for disparaging those he objected to.

"I heard tale of her," the woman said, and her voice was charged with implications, terrible insinuations that lingered unsaid between them.

"Don't know nobody that ain't heard tell of her. She's awful friendly with the men folk." The clerk sniggered. "And that caused the tongues to wag. Oh, Lordy, did it."

Clairey tried to make herself as small as possible as she leaned in closer to the window to try to catch the rest of the conversation. She couldn't help but consider what it all meant. Who was Lottie

Borden, and what did she have to do with Ellis? From the inferences being made, she couldn't help but speculate.

"What're you doin'?" Ellis questioned as he came up behind her.

She flinched violently, completely taken off guard by him and feeling as though she had been caught doing something wrong. "Nothin'," she gasped.

"Did you get what you come for?"

She said nothing, not quite sure what to say. Ellis waited for her to answer, but she still felt dazed by all that was happening around her. She stared at him blankly.

He repeated his question with impatience in his tone. "*Did you get what you needed?*"

"I…" she began.

"Have you been waitin' out here the whole time?" he asked disapprovingly.

"I went in," she defended quietly. "That man there done tole me I ain't welcome."

Ellis's eyebrows drew together, and he frowned. "What'd he say?"

"I s'pose he knowed my daddy," she explained. "And he don't want nothin' to do with his kin. He done tole me he didn't want no part of me and tole me to get. So I's waitin' for you."

He mulled the information over a moment. He seemed peeved, but she wasn't sure on what account, with her or with the clerk. "Well, you come on in with me," he ordered, putting his arm around her shoulder and guiding her toward the door with the pressure of his palm.

Her eyes widened as she took in a sharp breath and instinctively tried to back away from him. "I don't wanna go in there. You go on without me. I'll just wait on this here porch," she protested, trying to resist him, but he continued to prod her along, ignoring her objections.

"He ain't gonna say nothin'. You just see. Not one word'll come outta that feller's mouth." He practically spat the words out.

"Please, I don't wanna go in there. Can't you see I don't wanna?" Her voice cracked in panic.

His firm hand forced her through the door as she struggled against him. Once they crossed over the threshold, her resolve left, and she immediately grew still. Her shoulders slumped when she saw the woman and the clerk look up and eye her all over again. The woman looked from her to the clerk with an eyebrow raised, and the clerk pursed his lips and opened his mouth as if he would say something. But then he caught sight of Ellis.

Clairey could see the dangerous warning in Ellis's locked stare with the clerk, a muscle twitching and thrumming in his hard jaw line. "Good day to you," Ellis said, and the tone of his words was full of rage. It was a challenge, a call out.

The clerk appeared irritated, but his protest remained unvoiced as he seemed to weigh his options. She could imagine what he was thinking: should he speak out and risk Ellis's fury, or should he simply let them do their shopping?

The woman motioned to her young son. "Barnett, darlin', come on over here," she said. "We gotta be gettin' on home." Taking the boy by the hand, she slipped past Clairey and Ellis out the door, leaving no words of parting.

Now it was just the three of them—Ellis, Clairey, and the clerk—standing in uncomfortable silence.

"Clairey, you go on and get what you come for," he told her without breaking his gaze on the clerk.

Clairey stood there dumbly, too worried and afraid to do anything.

"Go on," Ellis barked.

She jumped and scrambled to do as he directed. She went down the aisles, trying desperately to remember what she needed, picking up two cans of lard, salt, sugar, some baking powder. She was frightened as she dumped her load on the counter and went back for more, aware of the glare the clerk alternated between her and Ellis. She picked up white corn meal, a bag of beans, and some molasses, adding them to her pile before she headed off again. When she had weaved her way in a semi-frantic state through the shelves and gotten all she thought she needed, she went back to the counter and stood behind Ellis's shoulder, seeking his protection.

"You need anythin' else?" he asked, still not looking at her.

She shook her head no.

Ellis stepped up to the clerk. She caught a glimpse of his side profile, every muscle in his face strained, his eyes filled with murder, and even she was afraid of him. "My wife's gonna need all this here boxed up for her," he spoke with an intensely quiet voice. "Next time she comes in, you'd do best to recall she ain't no Davenport no more. She's a Hooper now. And a Hooper's credit's always been good."

The clerk chose not to respond, the tension hanging heavy around them as they summed each other up. Evidently, he decided that the best course of action was to do what Ellis had asked. The scorching words of hatred in his throat remained unsaid. But his face said it all. He bent and picked up a few boxes from behind the counter and carelessly loaded the items Clairey had picked out into the cardboard containers and then shoved them roughly toward Ellis.

"Thank you, kindly," Ellis stated with his head cocked slightly, not wavering in his determination. He reached over and plucked a couple sticks of penny candy from the glass jars filled with colorful sweets that lined the edge of the clerk's counter. "I'll take these too." He held them up for the clerk to see and then scooped up one of the boxes. "Put all this here on my tab," he informed the clerk. "Clairey, you come on over and hep me with these boxes."

Clairey reluctantly obeyed. She took the other box and followed him as he left the store. It wasn't until they got to the truck that she felt she could breathe again, her churning stomach finally settled. She slid the boxed groceries into the bed of the truck, relief spreading through her insides. She caught Ellis looking at her, his anger not completely abated yet, but he, too, seemed to have relaxed a little.

"What'd you have done if he said no?"

"He never'd have said no." Ellis grunted and shook his head. "He's yella," he said in disgust.

"But what if he had?" she persisted.

"Don't matter what I'd a-done. He didn't say no, now, did he?" He handed her a stick of candy and popped the other like a cigar into his mouth. "I'm goin' to the hardware. You comin'?"

Every girl longs for a hero, perhaps even needs a hero, as the most fundamental of ideas, to make existence seem worthy and noble. Clairey never had anyone fill those shoes before now. No one had ever come charging in to save her, to rescue her from oppressors and abusers. Suddenly, she saw Ellis in a new way. There was something in her regard for him that shifted ever so slightly, that allowed room for an emotion that was new to her. Was it affection? Clairey wasn't sure because it was like nothing she had felt before—a warmth that seemed to penetrate her chilled heart, a lightness that made her want to smile, although she couldn't remember how just yet.

Chapter 16

Ellis took the seeds he had gotten from town and planted them carefully in a bed of soil near the tree line, safely protected by a canvas cover in the sun. The memory of his daddy doing the same thing came to mind. He couldn't have been more than four or five, just to his daddy's thigh, when he'd first tagged along. He remembered how his daddy had poked a hole with his pointer finger, dropped a few small seeds in, covered it with the displaced dirt, and gave it a generous watering with a bucket and ladle he carried with him before he moved on to the next one.

"Ellis," he said. "You're watchin' a miracle right under your nose." He gave a few of the seeds to Ellis and let him drop them into the hole he had already made. "In each of them little things, God put life. Now you take care with it, and you feed it with water and sunlight. And, most important of all of 'em, put it in good ground, and that life is gonna sprout right out."

"How, Daddy?"

"Don't know, son. Only the good Lord knows the secret to that. But that's how all livin' things is. You care for 'em and feed 'em and give to 'em, and they grow. Same with people, same with an animal, same with

*a terbacca plant. 'Cause the good Lord, he knowed what he's a-doin'.
He's smart that a-way."*

"What d'you mean, Daddy? Plants and people, they ain't the same."

*"Sure they is, boy. Sure they is. What happens if you don't give no
water to a plant?"*

"It's gonna die."

*"Yessir. And if you don't give somebody kind words and treat 'em
right, it's the same thing. They gonna die inside. All life, whether it be
seed or person, is sacred in the eyes of our Lord. You gotta respect it, you
see? You reap what you sow, boy. You sow good, you reap good. You sow
bad, and by and by, you gonna reap it too. Understand?"*

"No, Daddy," he complained. "It don't make no sense."

*Jim chuckled and gave his little son a pat on the back. "You'll see it
someday when you get to be a man."*

"We's plantin' terbaccer?"

"Yes, son."

"So's we gonna get good or bad?"

"We gonna get terbacca. Just terbacca. That's all." He laughed.

Ellis watched the seedlings vigilantly for signs that the little plants
were ready to be set in the ground in the main field, just as his daddy
had taught him. While he waited, he and Clairey planted a generous
garden in neat rows just off to the side of the house so it wouldn't
be far for her to go to tend to it, planting extra corn—nearly an
acre of it—to be dried and put away for the livestock come winter.
Likewise, Ellis planted several acres of hay to put away for the same
reason. Now that it was springtime, still cool but warm enough to
prepare for the crop, the two of them worked from dawn till dusk,
getting the earth ready for the year's yield.

Ellis and Clairey were in the field plowing when Forster Montgomery came around. They labored side by side, he with a plow
behind a mule and she removing rocks ahead of him, both working
to keep the furrow straight and stumbling over the red clods being
turned over. Occasionally Clairey would slip away to tend to other
chores and make preparations for their evening meal, but she'd return
to the field as soon as she could.

Making a turn at the end of a furrow, Ellis noticed Forster standing next to the rail fence, watching him and Clairey at their work.

He pulled the reins, halting the mule, took off his hat, and wiped his forehead with his handkerchief before he put his hat back on. It was late afternoon and already growing chilly, but he'd exerted himself enough to work up a good sweat.

"How is it with you, Ellis?" Forster called out.

"Well, I'll be. What you been up to, Forster?"

"Nothin' much."

Ellis grinned. "Sounds 'bout right."

Although Forster should have been offended by his comment, Ellis saw he was still his good-natured self. His friend couldn't resist joining in the laughter, knowing Ellis was poking fun at him.

Ellis looked over at Clairey who had stopped what she was doing and was watching the scene with interest. She did not know Forster, and therefore didn't know what a prankster he was known to be. She looked from him to Forster and then back to him again. He could see the curiosity in her eyes. She was probably surprised by his lighter side. For a fleeting moment, he was sorry that she hadn't seen it before, that he was always so serious around her.

"We'll knock off for the day," he called to her. "You go on up to the house, and I'll be up direc'ly."

She brushed her hands against themselves and then her dress to rid herself of loose earth. As she moved past Forster, she did her customary nod, and he tipped his hat ever so slightly to her. She had been working since before the sun went up, and it showed. Her face was weary, streaked with dirt and perspiration, the ever-worn dress needing a good washing after working in the furrows all day.

Ellis finished off the row he'd been working on, unhitching the mule from the plow once he'd reached the end of his straight and precise line. The mule's ears perked in anticipation of being fed and receiving a rest. Ellis clicked his tongue, goading the mule to move, heading for the barn. Forster fell into step next to him.

Ellis didn't speak; he waited. He knew that Forster had something to say, and he didn't want to spoil it for him. The wait was short.

"It's been goin' round town you done gone and got yourself a woman. Clifton said he heard tell you's murried. When he tole me, I thought it was a lie."

Ellis clicked his tongue again at the mule. "Come on, Katie girl." Without looking at Forster, he replied, "I reckon it weren't no lie."

"They say she's a Davenport."

"I reckon that's factual too."

"What you messin' round with them Davenports for?" Forster grilled as he stopped in his tracks to face Ellis with his disapproval head on.

Ellis ignored his dramatic stance and kept walking, and Forster, once he saw Ellis was not impressed, was forced to jog a step or two to catch up.

"Now I need your blessin' as to who I go a-courtin'?" Ellis said matter-of-factly. "Besides, she ain't no Davenport no more."

"I can't understand it," Forster said, looking genuinely perplexed. "Was you hopin' to gall Dulcie Mae, 'cause there be purtier girls what would have you. Hell, look at that gal Fergus Bayard done got hisself. She's a fine thing. It'd have got her better if you'd have got a purty 'un."

"Don't have nothin' to do with Dulcie Mae," Ellis said flatly. "Why you gotta go and bring her up for? I ain't talked of her in two years or more."

"Don't gotta say her name. A man can think it just the same, can't he?"

"Got nothin' to do with Dulcie Mae," Ellis said again.

"It don't make no sense. What for then?"

Embarrassed by Clairey's appearance and her family name, and galled by Forster's accusations, Ellis said, "Clairey's a real hard worker, and I could use two sets of hands round here. 'Sides, she can fix a spread better'n anythin' I ever tasted. And she don't complain none or ask for nothin'. She's a real easy gal to get along with. Just a real fine gal."

"So you done murried her 'cause she can work and cook?" Forster asked in disbelief.

Ellis yanked on the mule's halter and turned to face his friend. "Don't see how it's none of your concern. Not like you'd understand anyhow. I'm puttin' out twice as much as I did last year, and I got me some beef cattle in that pasture up yonder that I done got from Curtis Bowler, and you got nothin'."

Ellis could see that Forster was enjoying the show. He knew his friend was more than pleased by the fact that he had gotten under his skin.

Forster was grinning pleasantly as he said, "Ain't got no woman in my bed to keep it warm neither. You forgot that 'un."

"And you ain't got that 'cause your mama never taught you no manners, Forster. Gal's don't like crude talk. You ort not talk about a girl that a-way 'cause it ain't respectful." It irked him that if Forster knew the whole truth — that he and Clairey were married in name only — his friend would have poked some real fun at him.

They reached the barn, and Trapper, who was lying in the dirt, got up and came faithfully to Ellis as he led the animal into the barn. The old mule knew which stall was hers and didn't need to be prodded any further; she headed right for it. Ellis took the harness off and hung it from a wooden peg just outside the stall and then opened the swinging door to let the old mule in. He forked some hay into her manger and checked to see there was still water in her trough before coming back to Forster who was waiting for him.

"Now you knowed I's just messin' with you," Forster replied with a twinkle in his eyes.

"That's the trouble with you. You done messed round, and now you ain't got nothin' to show for yourself." Although his words were somewhat harsh, he was smiling when he said it, and the two of them laughed together again.

There was no use in pointing out Forster's shortcomings. Forster already knew them all and didn't particularly care one way or the other if he was successful or not. Everything was in good fun to him, and he could laugh as easily at himself as he could everyone else. "I ain't disputin' it. Ain't got the good sense God give me," he agreed.

After Ellis had tended to Clairey's mule, he said, "Come on up to the house. Share my meal with me, and then you can go on and get back to town and tell all them there cacklin' hens what you done found out."

"Awful generous of you. And I aim to take you up on that offer," Forster accepted, trailing along next to Ellis. "See just how fine her cookin' really is."

They came into the house just as Clairey was pulling a steaming cast iron pan from the stove, exchanging it with another pan filled with batter that she slipped back in its place to bake. She looked up as they came through the door. Ellis thought she eyed Forster uneasily; he knew she was probably distrustful of him, as was her nature.

She quickly returned to her tasks, turning the piping hot pan over and dumping the fresh batter bread onto a plate, the aroma wafting temptingly about the room. She gave the impression of being acutely self-conscious in the presence of the stranger Ellis called a friend, her hands in constant motion, fluttering nervously to her loose curls to try to smooth them and then down to her apron to pull it straight. Ellis noticed that she'd tried to make herself a little more presentable by washing her face and hands and running a comb through her hair.

"Forster's gonna stay for supper," Ellis informed her.

"We ain't got but two spoons," she reminded him gently.

"We just gonna have to share, is all." He went over to the wash basin, noticing that the water was fresh. Clairey must have dumped it and refilled it for him when she had finished with it herself. "Smells real good," he told her as he toweled off after washing his face and hands.

"It ain't much. Soup beans and bread," she said apologetically. "I had them beans on since this mornin', and I come up to start the bread an hour or so ago." She set the table, putting the pot of beans and bread in the center. Ellis and Forster sat down, good and ready for a meal, and Clairey chose the seat next to Ellis.

Ellis bowed his head and clasped his hands, and the others followed suit. He offered a blessing on the food, and in true farmer fashion, asked the good Lord to prosper his fields and crops. If anyone had sway over his sweet tobacco, surely it would be God, whose hand created all things. He always prayed, but his prayers were more fervent come planting time. He ended with an "amen," and Clairey and Forster copied him before the beans were dished out and the bread was broken into chunks of crispy-on-the-outside and soft-on-the-inside deliciousness.

The black beans floated in a thick broth that Ellis sopped up with his batter bread, eating it ravenously. It might have only been beans, but it was marvelous. When he caught sight of Forster, his expression said it all. He, too, was enjoying the meal, and Ellis felt a small swell of pride as he took his next bite of Clairey's batter bread.

"What Clifton be up to anyhow?" Ellis asked. "I ain't seen hide nor hair of him since…well, since my daddy died."

Clairey offered him the spoon, and he took it, digging out another full load of beans. He passed it back to her when he was finished so she could have a turn with it. Ellis was suddenly very aware of her hand brushing his as she took the spoon back.

"It's just Clifton. He ain't up to no good."

"Coulda guessed it, I s'pose. You boys ever gonna settle down, make yourselves respectable?"

He was finding it difficult to carry on a conversation, suddenly aware of a new emotion that plagued his consciousness. Clairey sat with him, as she had many times before, but this time seemed different somehow. He felt a measure of pride in her. In articulating to his friend her many qualities, Ellis had found, to his surprise, things about Clairey that he admired and liked. The act of defending her had invoked feelings of fondness he never knew he had for her. He'd never really thought about it before because there never was a need to.

She had always been nothing more than a shadow. He'd had no regard one way or another for her. She was just there, like hired help or a servant. But he began to see how significant her contributions were to him. Clairey's skills were a reflection upon him. She had provided him with a proper home and the ability to increase his possessions. She was valuable to him.

There was more to it than Ellis was able to process through, feelings he couldn't completely understand. He was becoming aware of her physical self as well. In all these long months, they had rarely touched. Yet there he was, sharing a spoon with her. There was something terribly intimate about it, watching the spoon glide from between her full lips, their hands grazing one another in just the hint of a touch, and then putting that same spoon between his own lips. At one point, her knee encountered his leg beneath the table in an innocent nudge, and Ellis felt a flush spread over his face, as if he had been caught doing something taboo in front of his friend, something private and surreptitious.

"I aim to head out to Oklahomie," Forster said, shoving another generous spoonful into his mouth.

The declaration was enough to jog Ellis from his contemplative moment. He stopped mid-chew, considering Forster's announcement. His eyes narrowed. "You foolin'?"

"I ain't," he answered matter-of-factly.

"What for?"

"Met a feller that's got hisself a dairy farm, a big 'un, and he done offered me work. Says he'll pay my way and all."

"What'd your daddy gotta say 'bout that?" Ellis asked.

"Not much. He got four more boys can hep him out with the farm an' all, so's he don't think it a bad notion."

"And your mama?"

"I give her nothin' but trouble since the day I's born. Prob'ly glad to see me go," he joked.

"Oklahomie, huh? Why you wanna go there for?"

"Seems like anywhere's better'n here," Forster said with a shrug. "Got nothin' holdin' me, you know. And I ain't gonna be free to do it for much longer afore I get tied down and got no choice in it."

"Never thought I'd see the day," Ellis replied. "You leavin' Pickett County? Never thought you would."

"Come on, now. You'd prob'ly tag along with if you didn't go on and get yourself a wife." He grinned across the table at Clairey who grew troubled.

Ellis observed that Clairey did not find his jest funny. It was particularly disturbing given the circumstances surrounding their marriage. He sensed that this was probably what she was thinking when Forster made his thoughtless comment. But Forster knew none of this. Still, Ellis felt the need to defend Clairey, to ease her discomfort.

"It don't matter if I got a wife. I still got this here place and my daddy's place too. It's enough, ain't it? I need to get up there and see to my daddy's place soon, make sure it's in order, but I ain't found the time. 'Tween this place and his, I got my hands full. What'd I want with Oklahomie anyhow?"

"I ortta check on my shortenin' bread," Clairey murmured and got up from the table. She took the pan from the oven and set it on a flour-sack towel to cool. "It's done, but it's still too hot to handle. Y'all wanna go rest on the porch some so's I can clean up, and I'll bring it out direc'ly?" she suggested.

The two men took their chairs out onto the porch, where Forster built a hand-rolled cigarette and struck a match to light it. He puffed generously and then offered a drag off of it to Ellis. Ellis shook his head, and with the tips of his fingers, he shooed a fly away. The old dog, Trapper, spotted them and came at a slow trot to curl himself up at Ellis's feet, lazy and sluggish in his old age.

Sitting in the shade of the porch, they watched as the sun lent a concluding magnificent light over the mountains in the distance before it finally slipped beyond their view. They seemed comfortable just to observe, not saying anything.

At last, Forster said, "No foolin' 'bout her cookin'."

Ellis grinned, his lids half concealing his eyes as he leaned on the back two legs of his chair. "No, sir."

"You got that over Furgus's little gal anyways."

"Wish you'd lay off Furgus. You get him all worked up, pester him, get him all riled. What's he ever done to you?" Ellis asked, managing to keep his voice amicable.

"Easy target, I guess."

"I'll give you that, but after while, an easy target ain't no fun no more."

"It ain't seemed to wear off yet." Forster snickered.

"'Sides, how you know what his 'little gal' cooks like anyhow?" Ellis asked.

"Don't know that I know of myself. But his mama goes on 'bout her and don't got much good to say."

"Think on the source," he told Forster with a hint of a suppressed smile. "She'd turn on any hen in the henhouse that aims to cut them apron strings from offen her."

Forster slapped his leg, nearly choking on his cigarette as he howled.

"That poor boy'd yet be sucklin' if she was to have her way 'bout it." The two of them visualized Myrna Bayard's abundant bosom, which made the observation all the more funny.

"You got that right," Forster managed to get out amidst his laughter, having to lean forward to regain his balance on the chair.

"Don't matter who Fergus was to a-brung home, she'd a-found fault with her," Ellis observed.

"And she do find fault," Forster said, beginning to regain his composure. "Goin' round town bellyachin' 'bout she don't cook good, she don't take care with Fergus as she ortta, she be laaazy." He dragged the word lazy out to stress just how lazy she was.

"They come up here just after harvest, Fergus and Elvira. He done tole her she'd only be livin' with his mama for a short time. If he's to have any brains in that there head of his, he'd have had her outta there by now, afore that ole heifer eats her live."

Forster chuckled. "Poor Ellis," he said, his voice dripping with pity.

Ellis drew his brows together in confusion. "You mean poor Fergus," he corrected.

"No, I meant what I say."

"What you feelin' sorry for me for?" Ellis grumbled.

"You just always tryin' to make somethin' right. Always tryin' to fix somethin' or n'other. And I s'pect that's an awful heavy load to carry for one man."

Ellis shook his head, feeling slightly annoyed by his friend's observation. "You don't know nothin'," he said, forcing a laugh. But what Forster had said bothered him more than he wanted to let on.

Forster shrugged. "Maybe not. Maybe not."

Clairey let the screen door slap behind her as she came out onto the porch with two generous hunks of shortening bread for the two men. She handed them each their own slab and then disappeared into the house again. Now that supper was nearly cleaned up, she would be going to bed and leaving the men to their talk. Their bread was still warm when they bit into it, and they relished the taste.

"This here's better'n my mama's shortenin' bread," Forster remarked as he crammed his mouth full.

Ellis couldn't help but mentally gloat over Forster's reaction as he ate the bread. They sat on the porch for a while longer, till it was good and dark, eating and talking.

When Clairey came back out on the porch to check on the men, Forster was sitting by himself. She froze, shy and unsure with this veritable stranger.

"If you're lookin' for Ellis, he done gone to lock up for the night," Forster told her as he gestured toward the barn, where Ellis would be inside, tending to the animals.

"I's just gonna see to it you didn't need nothin' more," she replied.

"Don't s'pose I do."

"Well, I'll leave you-uns alone then."

"Hold up a minute there," he said.

She stopped with her hand on the doorjamb, looking toward him but not directly at him, more off to the side of him. "Yes?"

"You mind me askin' a question or two?" He must have sensed her hesitation because he rushed on. "I mean, I was just wonderin' how Ellis and y'all met up."

"What'd he tell you?" she asked. There was an edge, a certain amount of suspicion in her voice. She didn't know yet if she liked this fellow.

"Well, he done tole me as little as he could get by with," Forster admitted.

"We met up in a snowstorm," she said. "I's walkin' on the road, and he stopped and offered me a lift."

"Don't mean to speak outta my place or nothin', but it come as strange to me that he done run off with you like he done, all a-sudden like he did. Well, 'cause he had hisself a girl he's all moonin' over, and then he done gone and murried you, you know?"

"No," she whispered. "Didn't know none of that."

"She's called Dulcie Mae, she is. And he's all broke up over her for a long time now. He musta thought an awful lot of you to go off and get hitched, 'cause nobody else got his attention. Why, he had eyes for only her, till you."

"Was she purty?" Clairey asked softly.

"Purty don't cover it. She knowed it too."

"What happened with 'em?"

Forster didn't hesitate. "He's hot after her. Boy was he! And she felt the same for him, I s'pose. But her daddy didn't like Ellis none. She's bound to listen to Ole Bill Prewitt. Whatever he's to say was law, you know. So when Ellis asked her to murry him, she done turned him away. On account of her daddy. Done tole him no. And she murried another."

"Why wouldn't he want Ellis for his daughter? Why wouldn't he?"

"Well, now, there's some that don't regard Ellis highly. Don't know as I can say what for, but that boy seems to inspire the worst in 'em. Always been so. There's been talk…Well, but I never saw why it'd cause 'em to turn on him, to dislike him so."

"Talk?"

Forster looked as though he were avoiding the subject. He shrugged and said again, "Don't know. I don't understand it all."

That was strange to Clairey, because from what little she had seen of him, he didn't seem to mince words. She persisted. "But Ellis is a fine man. A good man."

Forster smiled in amusement. She read his expression and thought perhaps he was mocking her. She dropped her eyes and went back into the house without saying anything more, retreating to the bedroom, away from him, away from the both of them.

Forster finally left for home during the late hours of night, with a full moon to light his way. He seemed sad to go. Most likely Ellis wouldn't see his old school friend again in this life. He would leave for Oklahoma, and that was as good as being on the other side of the world. Ellis climbed into bed, dead tired and dreading the morning when he would start all over again in the field.

He lay on his back, staring at the ceiling, listening to Clairey's even breathing next to him. He thought about sharing that spoon with her, and he felt a little thrill that surprised him, made him somehow uncomfortable. He began to contemplate what life would be like if they were to truly be man and wife. He had discovered she was more than a lost girl: she was a good woman who had gained his respect. His daddy had taught him well. He had taught Ellis to treat a woman with reverence. Ellis was beginning to understand how this applied to Clairey.

He rolled to his side and watched her for a time. Really, she wasn't so bad looking. She had lips that were full enough to be almost too plump, but he imagined they might be soft and generous if he ever had a chance to kiss them. Her brown eyes were an exotic almond shape. He thought her freckles were endearing, making her seem genuine and guileless. He had the reckless urge to put his hand to her skin, and then thought himself foolish for it. She was certainly no striking beauty.

If only her dark hair were taken care with. If only she didn't always look so frightened and half wild all the time. She sighed softly in her sleep, and he wondered what she was dreaming of. What was floating around in that brain of hers? He could see in her eyes at times, her mind working, but she didn't talk much, and so he was left to speculate what it was she was thinking or feeling.

It aggravated him how complacent she seemed. He would have liked for once to see her get emotional; he wanted to see her show anger, laughter, annoyance—anything that might be an expression of her true feelings.

He wanted to solve the puzzle because she was such an enigma to him, but instead he was left to speculate about who she really was. It seemed the more he thought on it, the more his thoughts were consumed by her. He blamed her daddy for it. Because the one thing that Ellis *could* read, could see through, was Clairey's fear. Fear of disapproval? Fear of rage? He really couldn't say what it was.

Sometimes it made him angry that she was afraid because it was something he had no control over. He couldn't erase her past mistreatment; that was already a part of her, established long before they had met. Ellis wanted to punish her father for what he had done to her, for how he had scarred her. Even if he could give that man a whipping, it wouldn't change what had happened to Clairey.

A man reaped what he sowed. A seed that was not watered and cared for didn't grow. It was simply the law of the harvest. And it was as his daddy had told him all those years before: a person was just the same as a seed. Those were his thoughts as he drifted to sleep.

CHAPTER 17

Ellis was out in the far pasture for the day, clearing and fencing more acreage in his ambitious way. Shortly after lunch, he left with Katie the mule, the chains to pull logs with, and his ax. As Ellis worked in the field, Clairey stuck to the house, working at her own domestic tasks. The sky was overcast, threatening rain, and in the distance, thunder rumbled and groaned. It was still light enough that Clairey did not need a lamp as she worked to make a pie.

Once the pie was finished and baking in the oven, she went out to the chicken coop to gather some fresh eggs and feed her fowl. The hens were a pleasant sort on the whole, but the rooster was a temperamental thing. He did not like intruders in his yard taking eggs as they pleased. He would threaten her by approaching in a confrontational swagger, making noise and ruffling his feathers to intimidate. Clairey was accustomed to him by now and calmly disregarded him. If he was treated with indifference, he generally backed down.

As she left the chicken yard, she glanced up at the sky. Judging from the looks of it, she would not need to water her garden. If it didn't rain today, it surely would by tomorrow. She checked on it anyhow, setting her bowl of eggs on the ground at the edge of her perfect rows. She began looking for signs of pests by crouching down on all fours, lifting leaves and peering at them closely for signs of anything that threatened to ruin their production come fall. While she was there, she took the time to weed, picking at any little stray green that popped up in the wrong place, making sure she got the roots and all. It was much easier to get them when they were of an insignificant size and before they grew to be a force to reckon with.

Clairey went back up to the house to check on her pie and take it from the oven. Before she mounted the steps, she noticed muddied boot prints upon the once clean porch. Ellis had not come back from the fields; she would have seen him.

She heard the scraping of the kitchen chair against the wood floors from inside the house. Someone was moving about within. A strange, inexplicable fear took root within her breast. Clairey knew. She stood just at the edge of the stairs with that knowledge turning her innards to pudding, desperate to not have to face him. But she couldn't stand there forever, putting off what would inevitably come next. With a budding dread, she dragged her feet up the stairs, her hands gripping the rail to keep herself steady.

She paused outside the screen door, looking into the gloomy interior, again attempting to prolong the confrontation. Although she had expected it, she was startled nonetheless when she saw her father sitting at the table, making short work of her pie. She opened the door and stepped across the threshold and waited.

Joe Davenport turned to his daughter with the spoon in his hand, berry stains on his beard, acting as if it were the most normal thing in the world for him to be there, devouring her pie. Clairey's heart went from a naturally slow rhythm to a fast and furious pounding. The bowl she carried in her arm tipped forward ever so slightly, and a few of her precious eggs rolled out, breaking over the floor.

"Look what you done," he teased. "Ortta be more careful." Joe had begun right off with the sweet-talking angle, his way of ensuring submissive cooperation. This meant nothing to Clairey. He might play nice now, but she knew it was simply a precursor to his rage.

"Yes," she murmured. "I made a mess."

"Well, ain't you got a howdy for your old papa?"

"How is it with you, Daddy?" she replied carefully. She had learned from many years of previous experience to be wary of him.

He didn't seem to hear her inquiry. "Curtis Bowler done tole me you was a murried woman, and I was glad to hear it."

Clairey waited. No point in saying anything. He would make his intentions known soon enough. Pressing him would only anger him. She shifted uneasily, waiting for him to make his next move.

"Fine pie you made. Sure miss the cookin'." He used his spoon in a sweeping motion to include the cabin. "Nice place you got here. Looks like you done real well for yourself. Never thought you'd a-done so well." He then dipped the spoon back into the pie to help himself to another bite.

"S'pose so," she agreed.

"S'pose so?" he repeated with a hint of sarcasm. "Nothin' to it. You got a nice place. You don't gotta s'pose. Just look round and you can see it."

"Well, now, Ellis done worked real hard to make it so."

"Does Ellis got any 'shine layin' 'bout? A body gets awful thirsty, you know."

"Ellis ain't a drinkin' man."

"No? What sort of man be he then?" Joe laughed feebly.

Clairey didn't answer. What she wanted so say, what she thought in her head, was: *He's a man that's nothing like you! That's a-certain!* She watched him with a cautious gaze, guarding her tongue against saying anything that might upset him. She was inexplicably worried that he might have read her thoughts and that he would punish her for them. Despite their separation, she had not forgotten how quickly his anger could grow. *And here it begins*, she thought. *Yes, here begins the erosion of his false motives and counterfeit gaiety. Here begins the crumbling away of his deceit until the serpent's tongue is revealed.* Her silence only proved to irritate him.

"You gonna answer me, girl?" he barked.

"He be a good sort," she whispered.

"The sort that'd hep out his woman's daddy if need be?"

Clairey's brow puckered, her eyes narrowing as she began to understand why he had come. She saw what direction the conversation was taking, and her anxiety flourished. "He ain't got nothin', Daddy."

Joe chuckled. "Hell, he ain't. Curtis Bowler done tole me your man got hisself a dozen or more cattle. Heard it with my own ears. You sayin' Curtis Bowler is a liar?"

"I never said he were."

"So's how'd your man get all them cattle if he ain't got nothin'?"

"Well, but he barra'ed against 'em. He never paid for 'em outright," Clairey explained.

"I see how it is," Joe spat. "I see. Don't think I don't. You got yourself in a good spot, and when your family needs you, you turn your back on us."

"I done tole you, Ellis don't got nothin'. And even if he did, it ain't mine to give. None of it's mine," she reasoned.

"If it wasn't on account of me, you wouldn't have none of this, not none of it, you ole heifer. I seen to it you was murried off good. Nineteen years of age, and not a prospect in sight. If it wasn't on account of me, you'd have none of it. I done right by you, and now you think you're too good for your old papa?"

"I don't," she insisted.

"Where's he keep it?" Joe demanded.

"What?"

"Where's he keep his monies, damn it?" Joe got up from the table and walked toward her.

"He don't got nothin'. He don't," she maintained.

"Don't lie to me," he barked, taking her face in his hand and giving it a brutal squeeze. "I could always tell when you was."

She felt the tears come to her eyes and hated herself for it because she knew that it would give him satisfaction. She was afraid of him still, wilting beneath his strength. And if she was afraid of him, perhaps she would cave. That was something she could not allow herself to do. She would not betray Ellis. Not for this man or any other. "I don't know. I don't know," she lied.

He hauled off and slapped her across the face, stunning her. "You don't know?"

She shook her head no, and he slapped her again. Clairey's tears became a full-on sob.

"You don't know?" he persisted, and gave her another blow with his open hand. "You gonna tell me what I wanna know, girl. Yes, you are, 'cause you a girl that does what she's tole, now, ain't you?"

"No," she said, her voice nothing more than a weak whisper.

Joe's expression was one of surprise, as his mouth hung open and his eyes grew wide. She'd never stood against him before, and she could see that it had caught him off guard. "What'd you say?" he growled, his eyes withering as he popped her in the mouth again.

She was struggling to get the word out, to answer him. She was frightened by her own mutiny, but unwilling to give into him, she endeavored to fight back. Clairey tasted the bile rising up in her throat, could smell the pathetic fear she was giving off, and they were as familiar to her as waking and sleep, as hunger and thirst. In her time of peace there with Ellis, she had nearly forgotten the taste and smell of it, how her joints became liquid and her mouth became sour. That was what violence did to her.

But something else was surging through her body just then too. Clairey felt her own separateness, her own identity that was apart from her father's. A sudden and powerful realization was planted within her. She might have come from his seed, she might have been his flesh and bone, his daughter, but her daddy did not own her. Indeed, Joe had no power over her.

In all of those years that she had been stifled by the dark cover he'd cast over her, she had felt so small, so irrelevant. There had been no ability to extend past the limits he had set for her. Only, Clairey had not been under his thumb for months now. She had experienced freedom for the first time. Her eyes had been opened, and there was no going back.

Why had she never seen how weak this man was, this big man who had brutalized her and her brothers and her mother? Her mind brought to recollection the most traumatic of her childhood memories. Her mama had been big with child when Joe had come home drunk and in a foul mood. Mama had told her to get because she knew what was coming. Although Clairey hadn't wanted to leave her mother, she'd been too afraid to stay, to try to absorb some of the blows herself. She'd only been seven and too small and helpless to stand up to him. She'd run to the other room and hidden beneath the bed. But Clairey had still had a full view as Joe struck her mother over and over. Her mama had been up the rest of the night in labor, and the baby had finally come in the early morning hours, a baby that was stillborn.

What a small man! What a hateful and loathsome man he was! She might have been too frightened at seven to stand against him, but she wouldn't bend any longer. Clairey was willing and able to take what he was dishing out. For the first time in her powerless life, she felt capable of standing up to him.

"I'm talkin' to you!" he roared, hitting her so hard her head bounced back and hit the door frame.

It was slightly louder this time when she found her voice. "No," she said.

"I ortta…" he began, raising his fist as if he might hit her again.

There was a moment of hesitation in which Joe looked into her eyes, and she looked back without flinching. Many a time, he had been at the same game with her, and she had always crumbled, bowing to his will. Now, he must have realized he was looking into the eyes of a stranger. She was someone he could not recognize, a foreigner inhabiting the body of that old Clairey, the girl he had abused, intimidated, and broken. Clairey decided then and there she would no longer cower before him. It was almost as if she were daring him to strike her in their unspoken exchange.

Go ahead and see if I care! she thought.

Chapter 18

Ellis came back to the house at suppertime to a dark, empty place, no lights lit within to beckon him home. He knew immediately something was amiss. The door was ajar, and he nudged it open cautiously to discover a mess of broken crockery and half a dozen smashed eggs scattered across the floorboards.

"Clairey?" he called out.

She did not answer.

He found the oil lamp on the table and lit it carefully, noting how the rooms had been rifled through, pie smashed to pieces against the wall, clothing scattered across the bed. The rooms had been ransacked. Someone had gone through everything, not bothering to shut doors or drawers. He checked for his money in the top dresser drawer in the bedroom and found it gone. Then, he began to panic, wondering what had transpired there. Still, there was no Clairey. He stepped out onto the back porch and called to her again.

Holding the lamp out in front of him, he inspected the yard and then headed for the barn, shouting her name at intervals. Ellis thrust the barn door open, yelling for her one last time. "Clairey!"

He heard her timid voice above him, muffled and emotional in the shadowy darkness. "Ellis?"

He set the lamp down and climbed up to the loft, his upper torso hovering above the floor. "Clairey, come on down from there," he coaxed.

She worked her way out of the hay, hesitating for a moment before she obeyed him and crept over to the ladder to follow him down. He waited until she was safe with her feet upon the ground and then took up the lamp and led her back to the house. She was crying once more, falling to her knees the moment they got through the door, franticly picking up pieces of the broken bowl and eggshells, working to put them into a pile.

Ellis had kept himself in check up to that point. He assumed that Clairey would voluntarily offer up her story. But when she remained silent, he lost his temper. "Mind tellin' me what's gone on here?" he asked, briskly rubbing the back of his neck in irritation.

She continued to cry, avoiding looking at him. "Nothin' come of it," she said. "He come and gone, and nothin' come of it."

"Who?"

"I thought he's gonna kill me, but I runned off. I got away from him."

"Money's gone."

She became still. "He musta took it," she finally groaned.

"Who?" he repeated, more sternly this time. "Who took it?"

Clairey rested her head against her forearm as she squatted next to the mess she had left. "My daddy," she said.

"Your daddy was here?" Ellis asked. The implications of the situation were sinking in, and he was not pleased with any of it. "What'd he want?"

"Said he was in need of hep, but I done tole him you ain't got nothin'. Only, he wouldn't believe it."

Ellis felt his blood boil. He strode across the room and picked Clairey up by the elbow so she was standing again. "He touch you?" Ellis roared, examining her closely. "He lay a hand to you?" He knew before he even asked. The dim light of the lantern revealed the bruising, and the shattered expression in her eyes told the rest.

She was sobbing, trying to catch her breath as she recoiled from his rage. She didn't have to answer him. Her face said it all.

"I'll kill him!" he vowed. "I'll be damned if I don't kill him!"

"Please," she begged. "Please don't."

"No good…sorry…" he sputtered. He was so agitated that he couldn't seem to find the words to express himself.

"Promise me," she said. "Promise you won't do nothin' bad, Ellis."

He paused, surveying the damage to Clairey's face. As angry as he was, he could see the torment in her expression and felt empathy for her. His jaw line relaxed, and his anger diminished as he sought to comfort her. "It's gonna be all right," he said, drawing her near and holding her close.

"Promise," she sobbed, trying to pull away from him. "Promise you ain't gonna do nothin'. I couldn't stand it if you got yourself into trouble or was hurt because of me. I couldn't stand it!"

"I promise," Ellis agreed so that she would calm down. "You all right?" he whispered against her hair.

Clairey wrapped her arms around his waist, nodding her head against his shoulder.

The brush of her body against his made Ellis forget completely about her father, about his desire to go hunt him down and make him pay. Holding her like that was touching on something he had forbidden himself from considering up to that point. He began to berate himself inwardly but stopped, utterly tired of fighting his natural instincts.

He recalled randomly how it had been the warmth of her body that had sustained him that long night in his truck on the side of the road, her body that had kept him from death in the bitter cold. Ellis leaned into Clairey, pressing her between himself and the wall, relishing the feel of her in his arms. Was it his imagination that she was clinging to him too? *I'll touch her face, and she'll stop me,* he thought, *and that will be the end of it.*

He felt the hammering pulse in her neck, fast and insistent. Ellis remembered how he had held a frightened, wild rabbit in his hands when he was a child, and how its heart had beat similarly. *Will she stop me?* he wondered. He felt inhibited by his ignorance of women and by his inability to know what she was thinking.

Clairey could feel the change in him, how the lines of his muscles had seemed to soften and relax. He slid his hands down her arms, his fingers leaving a slow trail, his breath heavy and uneven as he stood before her, face to face. There was something in his eyes that she couldn't read, although it seemed surprisingly like bashfulness. Ellis had always seemed so confident, so sure of himself. It was something she had admired very much about him. Yet there he was, showing vulnerability. She realized he must have been as insecure as she was, and it somehow made her more self-assured.

He leaned down and put his lips to hers, barely touching in an almost kiss, just enough to send goose bumps over her body, so that they were exchanging breaths, his sweet and alluring. Perhaps he was expecting that at that point she would protest, make him stop, but she didn't. She simply stood there perfectly still, trying to get her emotions in check as she struggled to stop crying.

His hands and lips were gentle, uncertain, inquisitively slow and deliberate as he explored her face. He put his fingers to her throat and her collar bone. Now and then he looked into her eyes, as if he were asking her without words if she approved or if she wanted him to stop.

Clairey met his gaze with unabashed frankness, the excitement stirring within her. Since that first night when she had come with him unwillingly, there had been a change in her. Although subtle, it was nonetheless a complete transformation from what she had been. She recognized now that she was in a very different position. For it was given to *her* to choose. Would she become the mistress of that house in word and deed? Would she take her place in the world as a woman or stay forever that frightened little girl she had been brought up to be? She saw what she was doing to Ellis, how his body reacted to hers, and it gave her a sense of power unlike anything else she'd ever experienced.

Clairey let him kiss her neck and touch her with quiet relish until it wasn't enough anymore, and he needed her completely and totally. Ellis clasped her arms in his firm grip, moving her away from the wall and guiding her backward into the bedroom, working his mouth over hers impatiently while he steered her.

The energy surged between them as he knelt before her on the floor while she sat on the edge of the bed, his clumsy fingers working to unbutton her dress with poor results. The buttons didn't seem to want to accommodate him. As he was thus fumbling, again he looked up to meet her gaze, and he hesitated.

She was watching him, her almond-shaped eyes half concealed by her lashes, softly returning his gaze, and for the first time Ellis faltered.

"You prob'ly think I'm nothin' but a fool. A ham-fisted dumb animal…" He pulled away. "If you want, I can stop."

In that moment, Clairey knew that she was nobody's victim anymore. She was in control of her own destiny. She was taking her place in the world. She realized then that this was something she wanted desperately, to belong, to be anchored.

Ellis apparently read her silence as rejection. He took a deep breath and let it out in a ragged sigh. He said again, "I can stop."

"No," she assured him. Clairey took his face in her hands and drew him to her. She let Ellis know that stopping was not at all what she wanted.

He seemed surprised by her uncharacteristically brazen behavior, but he was not displeased by it. After living with one another for months in their peculiar coexistence, they finally lay together, body to body, as husband and wife.

The next morning, Ellis went about his usual business in a drizzling rain, tending the animals then eating the breakfast she had prepared. Not sure if it was the rain or his reluctance to leave their warm bed, her body pressed next to his, he had slept in. Then, without disturbing her, he had crept out to take care of his chores. When he came in out of the rain again and she was there, he hardly knew how to carry himself. Ellis was acutely aware of the change that had transpired between them. He, however, chose to behave as if there were nothing out of the ordinary and today was like any other.

"Where you goin'?" she asked when he put his hat on and took his gun out.

"I aimed on goin' over to my daddy's place. Just wanna check up, look round the house, make sure it's locked up still," he said.

She drew in close to him. "Not today," she enticed. "It's rainin'."

"Been meanin' to do it for a time now. Won't be but a short while," he told her with a winningly persuasive grin. "Can't get much else done in this here rain anyhow. And I'll be back long afore supper."

Her hands rested in his, her palms to his palms, and he inspected them for a brief moment, marveling at how small they seemed. He flipped them over, noting the calluses that lined the pads of her hands just below where her fingers joined. He thought how nice it would be if she had a pair of gloves like the ones the ladies wore in town. He kissed her hands and then her lips with a sense of tenderness. He felt eager anticipation at returning to her when his business was done.

"Don't worry none. Maybe make another one of them pies of yours while I'm gone. That'd be awful nice to come home to."

"I will if you want it," she agreed.

He nodded his head with a smile before he went outside, tossed his rifle in the back of his truck, climbed into the cab, and drove away.

Ellis remembered the way to the shabby little cabin instinctively. And without any hesitation, he drove in the steady rain to the source of his trouble. The route was permanently recorded in his memory from last winter. He pulled off of the main road onto the gravel road and then to a dirt road that led to the hollow.

When he knocked on the front door, Clairey's mother answered. It occurred to him that he was married to this woman's daughter but did not even know her name. Her poor face was marred by a glaringly ugly black eye, swollen to the point that it was nearly shut. She looked alarmed when she saw him. And he knew what she was thinking, how her gut must have been churning right about then.

"What're you doin' here?" she said, looking around in panic to see if her husband, Joe, was aware of the two of them talking. "You need to leave afore there's trouble."

"I come lookin' for trouble," he replied with a hard smile. "Maybe you know where he is?"

She didn't have to be told to whom he was referring. She hesitated for a moment. "The barn" was all she said, and her eyes wandered over in that direction.

Ellis turned to head for the barn.

"Wait," she called in a desperate whisper.

Ellis paused and turned back toward her. He lingered expectantly, staying to hear what she had to say.

The woman's expression was grave. "Clairey," she murmured. "How is it with her?"

Ellis looked at her, pity overcoming him. "She's well. Eatin' good. Got a warm bed and all she needs."

"Would you tell her...tell her her mama sent her love."

Ellis's eyes grew tender, and he seemed remorseful for having to decline her wish. "I can't do that," he apologized. "She don't know I'm here."

"Prob'ly best," the woman agreed with a little nod of her head. "Prob'ly best. Take care with her for me, will you?"

He nodded. He couldn't save her. It was too late for the woman. But he could save Clairey. That was his aim. That was his purpose in going there. "You got my word, ma'am," he assured her.

The interior of the barn was dim in the midmorning gloom of the rain, but he easily spotted the man sitting on a stool, sagging heavily against the wall. He was sleeping, snoring loudly in a stupor brought on from the drink he had likely bought with Ellis's money. Ellis knocked the man's foot roughly, waking him with a start.

He looked up, confused, disoriented, until his eyes eventually focused on Ellis, and he grew angry. "What're you doin' here?" Joe barked.

"You been out to my place, you dog. Did you think I was just gonna let you get away with it?"

"Ain't a man allowed to see his child? His own flesh and blood?" he asked in an innocent tone. "I come to see Clairey. But she's disloyal to me, her own daddy! Well, she never was good for nothin'."

"Don't you talk about her that a-way!"

"Didn't I provide for her all these long years? Didn't I trick a man into havin' her when nobody else woulda looked twice at her? And she won't give me the respect I deserve! No, she never was good for nothin'."

"You wouldn't have her. You turned her out! You don't got no claim on her no more. And when you come to my place, into my home, hurtin' my wife and takin' what's mine, well, sir, you gotta answer for it."

"That right?" he said with a laugh. "What're you gonna do 'bout it?"

"Well, that's up to you, mister. I either come to warn you off or kill you outright." He spoke quietly but with intent.

Joe got up, unsteady on his feet, but he was too drunk to realize how impaired his reflexes really were. "I don't need no feller too big for his britches comin' round tellin' me what for, damn it!" he growled. He launched himself at Ellis, who easily moved out of his path, and Joe crashed to the ground on his stomach.

Ellis waited for him to get up, sickened by the show. "You sorry drunk," he railed. "Good for nothin', sorry drunk."

Joe got to his feet and came at him again, missing completely and falling heavily against the stall gate. Draped there, with no energy left to pick himself up, he did not move.

"I got my gun out in the truck there," Ellis told him. "I ortta go on and get it. I ortta use it on you right here and now, old man. Save a lot of people a lot of trouble. Ain't nobody'd miss you."

"Why don't you then?" Joe taunted. "Why don't you go get it?" As he spoke, his words were slurred, and spittle streamed from his mouth.

He seemed such a pathetic sight that Ellis didn't have the stomach to harm him. He thought of his own daddy, of how he had told him to use his hands for good, and the thought of hitting this man, who was so drunk he couldn't even stand on his own two feet, made him uneasy.

"Can't kill a drunk what can't even pick hisself up from the floor. So let it be a warnin' this time. You come round my place again — you step one foot on my land — and I'll do it. You lay one finger on that girl again — you so much as look at her crooked — and I'll do it. I'll blow your brains out."

He gave Joe a kick in his pants, and Joe grunted loudly as he sprawled forward onto his stomach in the muck of the barn.

"You sorry puke, hurtin' women and children. You ain't nothin'. Ain't even fit to wipe my boot on. Don't worry none 'bout payin' me back that money you stole. I consider it worth the loss if it means I don't never have to see your face again." Ellis watched him for a moment, hating him with such a loathing that he wanted nothing more than to hurt him, to cause him terrible pain.

Growing resolute, Ellis stepped over him and walked back to his truck, leaving the shabby little cabin behind for good. Whether Joe believed him or not, Ellis had no way of knowing, but he never laid eyes on him again.

Part IV: Budding

CHAPTER 19

Spring of 1935

It took some doing, but Ellis and Clairey eventually got the field prepared for setting. It was then just a waiting game until the tobacco was ready. To Ellis, the process seemed to be taking forever. His whole future was riding on that crop, and he wouldn't feel relief until it was stored like dry seaweed in the rafters of his barn. He was fidgety, distracted, nervously thrumming his fingers on the tabletop during meals, checking and rechecking the plants several times a day. As if willing it would make it so.

"For sure it'll be soon now," he told Clairey as she churned butter on the porch, the rhythm of her paddle steady and reassuring.

Her eyes were earnest when she looked up at him. "No need to fret so," she said. "It's comin' long right nice, and we'll have work enough when it comes time." He sat down heavily next to her with a deep sigh. "What troubles you so?" she asked, tucking a piece of hair behind her ear.

"Don't know. Just worried, s'pose. That crop don't do well, and we gonna lose our shirts."

"It's gonna do well. Just you see," she soothed.

"How're you so sure?"

"How's anybody sure? How you know the sun's gonna come up over them mountains in the mornin'? How you know them seeds we planted is gonna turn to terbaccer when you sowed 'em? No way of knowin', really. You just gotta do the best you can and then trust in the good Lord and know he's a-watchin' over you, and things'll be as they ortta be," she answered.

"And what if he ain't?" Ellis asked, staring out over the majestic mountain range far in the distance before their view. It was green and alive, unvarying and constant.

"You know that ain't so, Ellis. You read the Good Book, and you pray to him. I know you knowed he's a-lookin' out for you."

"I s'pose he is. But it ain't all good in this here life. Just like ole Job. All his friends done tole him to curse God and die, he's so bad off. And ole Job, he's a good feller. Never done no wrong to nobody. He's afflicted sore."

"Well, sure that's true. Bad things come to the good just the same. Why, even our Lord Jesus done suffered somethin' terrible. And he ain't never done no wrong to nobody. And then he done got strung up on that there cross on the hill, and he died in a fearful way because of it. Ain't nobody better'n he were. It's like my mama done said over and over. You can't get through this here life without some bumps 'long the way. But now you got nothin' to worry over that there crop. It's a-gonna come out fine," she reassured.

"You miss her ever?" Ellis asked, switching subjects suddenly, because when she had mentioned her mother, his mind went off on a tangent.

She stopped churning for a moment, eyeing him warily. He could see that he had caught her off guard with his question. She began to churn again, more slowly this time, and answered thoughtfully. "'Course I do. She's my mama."

"And your daddy?"

She shrugged, choosing to remain silent instead of dignifying the question with any sort of an answer. He knew some things were better left unsaid. She probably didn't feel the need to verbalize her no when he already knew very well she did not miss him.

After a pause, she said, "I'm grateful to him for givin' me life."

"Takes more than the givin' of life to make a father. Spreadin' seed is the easy part. Any dern fool can do that."

Clairey stopped churning again and met his gaze with widening eyes and a raised eyebrow. He realized that he shouldn't have talked so rough. He had probably deeply offended her, but she didn't seem angry, only mildly surprised.

"I'm gonna tell you somethin' right now. I never will slap, kick, nor beat you round. A man ain't no count that'd do that to a woman; don't care who he is. That ain't never gonna happen to you again. He ain't never gonna knock you in the head or beat on you that a-way no more. I can promise you that." His speech became heated, and then he felt somewhat chagrined by his passionate outburst, got up from his chair, and quickly stalked off with no place in particular to go.

The next morning, after breakfast, Ellis took the scraps from his and Clairey's plates and added them to the slop bucket on the porch, where a few flies swarmed about it. He took the bucket and headed out to feed the pigs.

While he was dumping the slop into the trough, over the fence he saw one of his squealing shoats with its head stuck in a can, running franticly around the pen, trying to dislodge it. The sight amused him, and he laughed to himself as he dropped his slop bucket to the ground and opened the gate. It took him a few laps around the pen before he got hold of the pig, its loud protests growing more fevered by the minute. How that pig managed to get himself in such a predicament was a mystery, but the humor of it left Ellis in a mood of merriment.

He bent down and pulled on the can, finding it was lodged more tightly than he had anticipated. He gave it a good yank, and when it did not budge, he gave it another. The can finally yielded, and he pulled it off the distressed pig's head. The little shoat immediately took off into the shelter, traumatized by the whole episode.

It was at this point, as his attention diverted, that the half-wild hog, Snaggletooth, struck. Like a punishing fiend, he came around the shelter, drawn by the squalling of the shoat, full speed, and hooked his one good cutter right into the meat of Ellis's left leg, knocking him to the ground with his brutal blow.

Ellis was in shock for a split second, lying in the mud of the pig pen, when he saw the boar coming at him again. His brain was heatedly trying to form thoughts, attempting to work out a plan of escape as his body rolled, kept rolling, while the boar rooted after. Snaggletooth caught up to him, vicious with his cutter as he went for another hit, frothy slobber emitting from his snout. Ellis grabbed the projecting lower tusk and gave it a mighty yank that sent the hog's head spiraling sideways, twisting his body and laying him out on the ground.

It gave Ellis a moment to struggle to his feet, ignoring the intense pain that was exploding through his leg, his sense of self-preservation taking over, and he made for the fence, toward safety. The hog wasted no time resuming his pursuit of Ellis; he was not about to lose the match. He worked his body in the mud, squirming until he was back on his feet and back to the attack. His short legs pumping fast and furious, he caught up with Ellis, getting another good hook into his leg — this one not as deep as the other because Ellis was now a moving target — before Ellis staggered frantically to the fence and launched his body over in a limp bundle on the other side. The boar ran himself again and again into the fence, pawing and rooting his nose, bloody spittle flying, trying desperately to still get at Ellis, all the while grunting and squealing and making a terrible noise. Trapper bounded for the fence, barking and growling at the hog. Even the dog did not faze the devil boar.

Ellis lay face down, covered in mud, groaning in agony, unwilling to move right away, listening to that wretched boar's caterwauling and Trapper's reaction. He finally got the strength to pull himself further away from the fence by dragging himself several feet forward on his elbows. As he looked toward the house, he thought that it might as well have been the same distance to the moon; it seemed that far. With a great effort, he managed to get to his feet, keeping his weight off of his left leg. He limped bit by bit through the yard, falling once, then again, moaning from the agony radiating from his lower leg, the warm, wet blood running down into his boot so that his foot sloshed in it when he put his weight on it.

Once he made it to the porch, he endeavored to climb the stairs but collapsed before he made it all the way up. "Clairey," he called out weakly. "Clairey!"

She was inside, cleaning up after breakfast, untouchable within the haven of those walls, oblivious to his plight just beyond that screened door.

His desperation made him panic. He struggled harder to move himself, pulling his body with his arms up the last few stairs, and gasped again, "Clairey!"

She heard him this time and came through the door, alert, searching for him. And when she saw his predicament, she rushed to him, bent down with a little gasp, her eyes fearful. "Ellis, what happened?"

"That devil hog run me through," he told her through clenched teeth as she helped him back to his feet. For a moment, he thought he would lose consciousness. His vision was lost, and there was a ringing in his ears he couldn't account for, but he fought it because he knew that Clairey couldn't move him into the house if he didn't do his part. He leaned on her heavily while she guided him into the house and to the bedroom.

Ellis fell on his stomach across the bed, grunting loudly.

"Is this where he got ahold of you?" she asked.

But he didn't have to answer her. The leg of his overalls, torn and saturated all the way through and dripping with blood, alerted Clairey to where his wound could be found. She rushed over to the chifferobe, fumbling through the contents of her sewing basket, and came back with a pair of scissors to cut the pant leg up the side seam so that she could survey the damage.

She pulled the blue jean flap back gently, and her heart sank. "It don't look good," she said, her voice anxious when she saw the ugly gouges in his leg. One was more shallow than the other, but they were both deep, the more severe one just shy of the bone, jagged and ripped. Without the restrictions of skin, the pale layers of fat and pink muscle tissue swelled from the slashes with a constant issue of blood draining from it. She hurried to the cupboard in the other room, grabbing a few clean dish cloths, and rushed back to press them to his calf in an attempt at stopping the bleeding.

"You're gonna have to clean it," he said between pursed lips as he grimaced.

"There ain't nothin' to clean it with," she replied as she leaned heavily against his leg. She put most of her body weight behind her clenched hands, but the cloths were already drenched.

"Whiskey in the cupboard. You're gonna have to use that."

She had seen the whiskey before, in a tall thin bottle that was nearly full to the top, but she had never seen it used, not once since she had been there. Ellis kept it only as a curative remedy.

She could see the fine sheen of sweat on his brow. He was hurting bad. She couldn't begin to imagine how much pain he was in, and she knew that it would only grow worse if she poured whiskey over it. "I ortta go get the doctor," she protested, reluctant to be the one to inflict more pain upon him.

"Go on and get the whiskey," he ordered her. His tone called for no disputation on the matter.

Clairey went again to the cupboard and retrieved the bottle of whiskey kept there and returned, pale and troubled, as a foreboding filled her breast. "It's gonna hurt," she warned him.

"I know, but it's gotta be done."

She straddled him, facing backward, putting her full weight on his upper thighs, and then took hold of his leg at the bend of his knee, gripping it firmly as she leaned forward. She pulled the cork from the bottle with her teeth, pouring the tawny liquid over the gashes on his leg. The tears came to her eyes when he let out a yell, just once, as he writhed beneath her. It was difficult for her to keep her balance for he was moving so, until he went limp and grew quiet, and she knew he must have passed out.

Clairey searched out a clean sheet, tearing it into thick strips, their edges frayed and shredded; she used them to bind Ellis's leg. When she had finished, she sunk to her knees next to the bed and began to cry. Her heart hammering, her mind strained, she wondered what she should do next. What was the best thing for Ellis at that point? She had cleaned the wounds, but they were still seeping blood, and she knew they would need to be sewn shut. That was something she did not feel she was capable of. Again and again, she settled upon one thought: she had to go get the doctor and bring him back to Ellis. She had to go and get him right away before it was too late. Time was not his friend. But she could not bring herself to leave him. What if he was to wake while she was gone and not know where she had gone?

Before long, Ellis stirred, his voice feeble. "Claire?"

"I'm here," she answered, sliding her hand across to his and touching him lightly. "We gotta get you cleaned up. Can you manage it?"

"I don't reckon I feel up to it," he mumbled. His face was deathly white beneath the smears of mud, and he hardly had the strength to speak.

"I'll hep you," she promised. But when she tried to pull her hand away, he held it tight, refusing to let go.

"Where you goin'?" His words were nearly inaudible.

"I ain't a-gonna leave you," she soothed. "But I gotta get that there bucket of water in the other room there. You just sit here for a spell, an' I'll be back direc'ly."

He unwillingly let go of her fingers, and she went to get the water. She poured from the bucket of well water into the wash basin, dropping a washcloth, and soaked up the liquid.

When she returned, she tenderly set about bathing his face and hair, removing the dirt and grime as if she were working with an infant. "Can you sit up?"

He nodded his head slightly, struggling to position himself upright. Clairey had to assist him, propping the two pillows from the bed behind his back. She unclasped his overalls and unbuttoned his filthy shirt, easing his arms out of it as he grunted and groaned from the strain of it. She pulled his undershirt up over his head and tossed it onto the floor.

His eyes seemed unfocused, and he was disoriented, signs to be alarmed over. She brushed the cool rag over his clammy skin, working in gentle, even strokes until she felt she had done all she could. She then helped him into a clean, fresh undershirt and shirt, buttoning each button carefully.

"The doctor," she began. "I ortta go fetch the doctor, Ellis." Clairey felt the tears welling up in her eyes again because she was afraid, because she felt so alone, but she resisted the urge. "He'd know what to do."

"Ain't no need to do that," he told her. "I'm fine. Just fine."

"If I leave now, I can be back afore nightfall."

"If it's as bad tomorra, we'll fetch him then," he insisted, doing his best to talk her out of it.

"Might be too late tomorra," she protested. "You could lose that leg or worse, Ellis." Clairey was trying to scare him a little so that he would agree to what she was asking for.

"My daddy tole me once that he left my mama to go and get the doctor when she was fixin' to have me. He tole me it was the worst thing he ever done, leavin' her alone like that." He struggled to keep his words even, to keep any emotion from compromising his message. "Didn't matter no how 'cause the doctor weren't nowheres around to come hep. My daddy was the one that brung me into this world after all of it. He tole me if he'd a-knowed she was dyin', he woulda stayed with her. He wouldn't a-wasted the time he had left with her, you know."

She didn't speak for a long while, wondering what she should say to him, what would convince him. She ended up deciding not to try convincing him. "I'm gonna go get the truck," she told him. "I'm gonna bring it right up to the porch, and you're gonna get in so's I can drive you into town, Ellis," Clairey said in a quiet but firm voice. She left no room for argument.

Chapter 20

The doctor swabbed Ellis's leg with cotton soaked in iodine, leaving an orange stain over the back of his calf. He had already administered morphine, and now Ellis was lying upon his stomach, out cold. Clairey leaned eagerly over the doctor's shoulder as she hung on his every word.

"I'm appalled by the amount of damage here," he remarked. "The entry wound is clean, but when that boar pulled upward, he literally ripped the skin and tissue into pieces."

"Can you fix it?" Clairey asked. Her voice was strained, and she was doing her best to keep from losing her composure.

"It isn't the worst I've ever seen, but it certainly isn't good. It'll be difficult to repair; that goes without saying. If all else fails, I may have to take the leg."

Clairey let out a little sob. "Oh, no. No, please…"

"I think it might be best if you waited outside. This is not for the faint of heart," he said rather sternly. "I must be able to work without distractions."

She waited in the parlor with Gilda Fielding, nervously twisting the hem of her old dress while the older woman watched over her. She occasionally glanced over to the closed doors where the examination room was, wondering what was transpiring in that place that was off limits to her. The anxiety and the helplessness of waiting idly were eating her up inside.

"Doctor Fielding knows what he's doing. Your young man will be just fine," Gilda reassured her.

"Thank you, ma'am," she answered.

"What's your name?"

"Clairey, ma'am."

"Well, Clairey, I've known Ellis all his life. I was there when Doctor Fielding delivered him," she confided. "And Doctor Fielding has a special fondness for that boy. He'll take good care of him. I promise you that."

"I tole him I wouldn't leave him."

"You're still here, aren't you?" Gilda Fielding pointed out. "And when he comes around, you'll be there right beside him. We'll see to it."

"Yes, ma'am."

Gilda paused for a moment and then spoke with a soft entreating voice. "I hope you don't take this the wrong way, child, but it looks as if you could benefit from a bath."

Clairey observed her own appearance for the first time since arriving and became painfully aware of how she looked. "I'm right sorry, ma'am," she replied sheepishly, for she knew she must have appeared lowly indeed to this fine woman who smelled of lavender and lemons, with her silver hair pulled back in a neat and tidy bun. She hadn't had a chance to wash before she and Ellis had left the farm, and she still wore Ellis's blood, dried out and dark brown, a smear on her cheek, covering her hands, all over her dress. *The doctor's wife must be feeling such pity for the poor mountain girl,* she thought.

"There's nothing to be sorry over," Gilda assured. "Perhaps you would allow me to draw a bath for you? Might pass the time."

"Do what now?"

"Come along with me, and I'll run some bath water for you," Gilda offered. She showed Clairey up the stairs into her bathroom.

Clairey was slightly in awe when Gilda reached over and twisted the knobs, and water began to pour from the spout. While she knew of running water, she had never witnessed it for herself before, a miracle that seemed an impossibility. She reached across and felt the warm water running over her fingertips with a slight smile upon her lips.

Gilda took a glass bottle of scented Epsom salts from her medicine cabinet and sprinkled some in the tub, watching them disappear as they melted away into the water. "If you'll take off your dress, I'll wash it for you."

Clairey seemed somewhat uneasy, but she unbuttoned the dress.

"Is that your good dress?" she asked.

"It's my only dress, ma'am," she admitted, taking the dress off and handing it over.

If Gilda was surprised by this she didn't show it, but she certainly seemed taken aback by what she saw next. She scrutinized the wool long underwear that Clairey wore with obvious disapproval. "What's this?"

Clairey looked down at herself, feeling her face burn, realizing again what she must look like from Gilda's perspective, and she was ashamed. "Them's my underwears." Her explanation was nearly inaudible.

"Is that all you have?"

"Yes, ma'am."

"Well, they simply won't do," she said, shaking her head. "You use my robe on the back of the door here when you're through, and then we'll figure what to do next," Gilda instructed. She left with Clairey's raggedy old dress, shutting the door behind her.

Once Gilda was gone, Clairey slipped into the warm water, feeling immediate relief to her stressed and frayed nerves, the calming effects much appreciated as she took a sponge and rubbed it up and down her limbs. She had never in her life had a real bath before, always bathing from the water in a wash basin. It was a luxury that left her drowsy, completely sated, and detesting the thought of having to ever end it.

She washed her hair, letting it float in the depths of the bathtub like a cloud drifting around her, running her fingers through the strands that swayed to and fro in the current her body made as it moved in the water. She stayed in until the water grew cold and she was shivering. Then, she did as directed and slipped Gilda Fielding's silky robe over her body, holding it shut tight with her crossed arms. She opened the bathroom door a crack and peeked from one side to the other down the long hallway, searching for Gilda, seeing no one.

"Mrs. Fielding?" she whispered loudly.

Gilda popped her head out of one of the bedroom doors. "I'm in here," she replied. "Come along now. I have something to show you."

Clairey did as she was told, padding quietly down the hall, self-conscious of the fact that she was in nothing but a robe. Gilda let her into a bedroom with a pretty little vanity scattered with powder and perfume and lovely trinkets. There was a heavy, black camelback trunk open next to the bed, and Gilda guided Clairey over to it.

"These were Millie's. My daughter's. They might be a smidge too big on you, and they're a bit out of date, but I think they'd be a sight better than the dress you wore before," she told Clairey, pulling a few of the dresses out and holding them up to examine them.

Clairey watched as Gilda laid a dress out across the bed. She marveled that it was the same color blue as the dress the woman in the grocery store had worn months earlier. It immediately caught her eye as she let out a little gasp, and she touched it tentatively, not willing to believe that it might be hers. "Them's awful purty," she murmured.

"Millie married a doctor out of Chicago. He practices out of a proper hospital there. When they were promised to one another, we got her a brand new trousseau, with all the bells and whistles. You should have seen all of the lovely things. Some of it all the way from Paris, France, if you can imagine. And, well, she didn't have much need for all of this anymore—her old belongings. She's got herself three beautiful children and a fine home just outside of Chicago now." As she talked, she plucked underwear and hosiery from the depths of the old trunk and sorted them in piles on the floor.

"Now, I don't want to make you feel badly, but it's just disgraceful that you're wearing men's underwear. You should be wearing something like this." She held up a pair of one-piece, white, soft-knit underwear trimmed with hand tatted lace, cinched around the neck line with a pale pink ribbon, and a flap that buttoned closed on the bottom. "And then, over that you wear a slip," she tutored, displaying a finely woven, delicate cotton slip that was dainty, to say the least. "Why don't you go and try these on with one of the dresses?"

"I can't take your fine things," Clairey protested.

"Now, shush. I'm giving them to you. They aren't of any use to anyone else. Been sitting here for seven years. May as well throw them out if you won't take them off my hands." She leaned in toward Clairey and picked up a lock of her damp hair. "What to do with this. That's the next question."

Clairey took the underwear and slip from her, chose the blue dress from the bed, and dressed as she had been told to. Then Gilda wrapped a towel around her shoulders and took a pair of shears to her dark brown locks.

When she was done and showed her handy work to Clairey in a full-length mirror, Clairey just stood there dumbly, not recognizing the girl who stared back. Gilda had clipped her hair into a popular bob style just below her jaw line, showing her how to put bobby pins in to create a wave that framed her face. She wore the blue dress and thin stockings with a pair of Millie Fielding's discarded fancy shoes. They were just a bit too large, but Gilda had stuffed the toes with tissue paper to make them fit.

"Don't you look just charming?" Gilda observed from over her shoulder.

"I never had me such a fine dress," Clairey confessed. "I sure am grateful to you, Mrs. Fielding," she squeaked as she ran her eyes over the dress with pleasure.

When Gilda presented Clairey to the doctor, he tried to hide his surprise over her transformation, but Clairey recognized it. She noted, too, when Gilda winked at her husband. This seemed to humor him. He gave his wife a half smile and shook his head just slightly, their unspoken language saying volumes to Clairey. Perhaps she should have felt foolish with the two of them carrying on so, but she was so pleased with the way she looked that she couldn't make herself care.

"What have the two of you been up to, Mrs. Fielding?" he asked.

"Girl things," she replied. "Just girl things."

"Well, Mrs. Hooper. I suppose you can go on in to your husband now. He's still out, but he'll come around soon, I'd guess."

A blush spread across Clairey's face when he called her "Mrs. Hooper." He patted her shoulder and then led her to his examination room. Doctor Fielding had done his work, but so had Mrs. Fielding. She had given a gift to Clairey that was priceless beyond measure: the ability to flourish.

Ellis was lying on a metal table in the middle of the room, his jaw slack, his appendages sprawled, his leg bared to the knee and wrapped tightly with gauze bandaging. She thought he looked dead.

"He's gonna be all right?" she wondered, seeking his assurance.

Doctor Fielding pulled a straight back chair up next to Ellis for her to sit in. "I believe he will. He'll have to take it easy for a while, mind you. But I did the best I could, and barring infection, I believe it will heal."

"When can I take him home?"

"Not for another couple of days. I plan on keeping him on something for the pain and watching him to see he doesn't get gangrene before I let him go off."

"I got the farm to see to," was her mild protest. There were animals that needed feeding, a garden that needed tending, and the tobacco would be ready for setting soon. If she wasn't there to do it, what would happen to the place?

"Don't you worry about that. I'll send for Fergus Bayard. He'll go up and care for things for a few days," the doctor promised. "Seems like Mrs. Fielding has taken to you. I don't think she would mind having you as a guest until Ellis here can be moved."

"That's right good of you, Doctor. It means an awful lot. Don't know what'd become of us if you wasn't here for him."

"Well, Mrs. Hooper, I'm glad I was here."

"Mrs. Fielding says you was there when Ellis was born." She said it as if it were some amusing little piece of information, light and inconsequential.

The doctor hesitated, becoming visibly uncomfortable, perhaps not expecting her random flashback into the past. "Did she now?"

"Yessir." Clairey waited expectantly for some elaboration. She had thought the story Mrs. Fielding had told was strangely inconsistent with the one Ellis had told her, and she was hoping that the doctor would shed some light on the matter.

"Then I suppose I was. I've birthed a lot of babies in my day. Sometimes it's hard to keep track of them all," he said with the slightest hesitation in his voice.

Clairey sensed he was not being totally honest with her. "Ellis's mama, she died when he was born, didn't she?"

"Yes," the doctor answered as he turned away from her and tidied up his tools, putting them carefully back into his black bag one at a time. She thought he might be trying to dodge her questions. "I never knowed her. How was she?"

"Ellis's mother? She was a fine woman. She was kind and friendly. She was a strong lady, so it was a shock. I don't know anyone who didn't like her, though." The doctor finished his task and turned to look at her with something she couldn't read in his eyes. "If there was anything I could have done to save her, I would have done it."

"And Ellis's daddy brung him up?"

"That's right."

"Why didn't he never murry again?" she wondered.

"I couldn't answer that. I don't really know."

"Well, it don't make no sense. He had a child to raise and a farm to run. Seems like he woulda wanted a woman to hep him and such," she pressed.

"Jim Hooper was a good man. He had his faults, to be sure, but a good man. If things had been different…well, maybe…"

"Different how?" She was still struggling to understand, to put the pieces together. Just as she had felt something amiss when she had overheard the clerk talking to the woman in the store those months ago, she knew now that there was something more going on there as well.

Their conversation was interrupted when Ellis stirred, his eyelids appearing heavy, and it was with great effort he focused his eyes as he glanced around the room. He looked confused, most likely not remembering where he was. He shifted slightly, and then his gaze fell upon Clairey who sat next to him, eager to hear him speak.

Ellis looked at her for a long while, studying her intently, and then he said to the doctor, his speech slightly slurred, "Who's that purty girl with the blue dress on?"

Clairey was embarrassed, but the doctor grinned at her pleasantly. "Why, that's your wife, Ellis."

"My wife?" he muttered. He seemed to be thinking hard, searching his brain for the memory of such a wife.

Doctor Fielding spoke to Clairey conspiratorially. "Don't mind anything he might say. He's been given morphine. His head isn't right."

"Clairey, that you?"

"Yes, Ellis," she confirmed.

He reached his hand out and touched her hair. "I ain't never seen you this a-way before. What'd you go and do?"

"Mrs. Fielding done it for me," she explained.

He looked down over his body and beamed. "Looks like my leg's still attached. That's good, ain't it?"

"Sure it is, Ellis. The doctor says he figures you're gonna live so long as you keep away from them pigs. How is it with you?"

"Don't know," he said. "But I feel wrung out."

"Why don't you go on and rest some?"

"Just might." His eyes closed again, and he slept.

Late in the evening, Fergus showed up with Elvira after Doctor Fielding had gotten word to them about what had happened. Clairey had never met either of them before, which made her feel nervous and shy around them. It was not in her nature to ask for help. But it was even more difficult to ask help from strangers.

Doctor Fielding took it upon himself to mediate. "Clairey, this is Fergus Bayard and his wife, Elvira. Fergus here took his schooling with Ellis when they were boys."

"How do," Fergus said with a nod.

"How do," she replied, her eyes looking down and to the side, anywhere but on him.

"How's Ellis fairin'?" he asked.

"He's comin' 'long."

"He acceptin' comp'ny?"

"We've moved him to the bedroom down the hall. He isn't all himself yet, but you can see him if you'd like," the doctor said.

"You-uns go on and sit with Ellis a spell. She and me'll wait here in the parlor and visit some," Elvira informed the two men. "Prob'ly ain't room 'nough for all of us anyhow."

Clairey followed her into the parlor and sat on the edge of the settee.

Elvira took the rocking chair, smiling sweetly as she focused her attention on Clairey. "Ain't this a nice room?"

"Yes, I s'pose it is," Clairey agreed, stroking the velvet settee thoughtfully. She finally got the courage to meet Elvira's eyes and was struck by how beautiful she was — dark, exotic looking, very striking. She felt out of place in such a beautiful room with the beautiful girl. She felt completely inadequate in comparison.

"We was real sorry to hear of your woes."

"Thank you," Clairey responded.

"Now, Fergus, he don't mind none hepin' y'all out."

"It's right good of you. I know it's an awful lot for you. Don't know what we'd a-done without you."

"I been to your place afore. Fergus took me there right close to the time after we was murried, you know. It's a fine place."

"Yes, real fine," Clairey concurred.

"Fergus done promised me a right nice place such as that, a place of my own. So it ain't gonna be much longer now."

Clairey didn't know what an appropriate reply to that would be so she kept quiet.

"We's livin' at his mama's place now, me and him."

"When do you aim to get your own place then?"

Elvira's expression changed. She grew serious, maybe a little troubled. She looked around as if she were making sure no one was around, as if what she was about to say was of a sensitive nature. "Don't rightly know. Truth is Fergus done promised me that for nigh on a year now. It ortta be soon though. 'Least I hope so. Don't know how I can stomach that ole woman much more."

Clairey felt uncomfortable. She hardly knew the girl, and she felt that the information she was sharing was a little more than she maybe wanted to know. "What ole woman?"

"Fergus's mama, of course."

"Oh."

"She's a mean ole sow." Elvira dropped her voice, perhaps afraid that someone might overhear. "Never can do no right by her."

"Sorry to hear it."

"I wouldn't tell it to nobody but you," she went on in a rushed undertone, although Clairey was sure she would have told anyone that would have lent an ear. "But she listens to all that's said. Why, we ain't got nothin' but a little ole curtain for privacy, and she listens through it. Can't get nothin' by her."

Clairey grew wide-eyed at that new bit of information. "She ort not to do that."

"And she says I's worth nothin', and she tells Fergus he ortta put me in my place or put me away. That's what she tells him. But it's none of her business. None of it. She ortta mind her own affairs. That's what she ortta do."

"I'm real sorry to hear it," Clairey replied again.

"It won't be much longer. Not much. There's to be a baby comin' in the winter, and Fergus done promised that afore the baby comes we'd be in our own place—him and me and the baby. 'Cause I done tole him we need our own place to raise a baby."

"Well, that's real nice now. Real nice that you gonna have yourself a baby," Clairey said with a sincere smile.

"I wanna girl. I tole Fergus I just knowed it's a girl. I done seen the signs."

Clairey grew fascinated, far more than she would have liked to have admitted, because it wasn't proper to discuss such things so casually. Her curiosity got the better of her, and she asked eagerly, "How can you tell it?"

"Oh, lotsa ways," Elvira told her with a little shrug of her shoulder.

Clairey's interest piqued. She didn't like herself for it, but she was hanging on the other girl's every word at that point, her curiosity having gotten the better of her. No one had ever told her about such things, and Clairey was eager to know more.

"I don't want no part of the heel of the bread. Now I done gave up on eatin' it afore I even knowed I was with child. And then I done put a wooden spoon and a pair of scissors under the bed I sleep in soon as I found out so's to make certain it'd be a girl. And then I put some thread through a needle, and I hold it like this over my hand." She turned her palm up and held an imaginary needle and thread suspended over it. "And it starts a turnin' and a turnin' in a circle. Now, if it was to be a boy, it woulda gone back and forth and not in a circle like it done."

"That so?" Clairey said, leaning forward, her attention held.

Elvira settled back in the chair, puffed up with self-importance. "It is." She waited to be compelled to tell more.

Clairey hated to feel ignorant. She knew Elvira was much younger than she, and yet Elvira was the more informed of the two of them. "Do you reckon it works that a-way every time?"

"Yes, ma'am," she insisted in a definitive tone. "It worked for my mama. She tole me so. And there's others, too, that says it. It's to be a girl. And I'm gonna call her Bathsheba from the Bible."

Clairey looked confused. "But Bathsheba weren't no good from the Bible. She done bewitched that good ole King David, and she done beguiled him to do some mighty bad things on account of her." She could see right away that her words hadn't set well.

Elvira puckered up her berry-red lips into a pout and grew defensive at Clairey's statement. "I don't care none what she do. And' ain't it more David's doin' than hers anyhow? 'Sides, I done set on that name, and I aim to have it. It's a purty name, ain't it? Purtiest one I ever done heard."

Worried about offending Elvira any further, Clairey nodded her head enthusiastically, trying to set a convincing expression on her face. She figured it was not worth getting into a debate over. So Bathsheba had been a bad woman. So she'd been the cause of David's downfall; it was none of her business if Elvira wanted to name some sweet innocent babe after the woman. So she lied. "'Course it is. Real purty. I think it a fine name."

Elvira relaxed again, the pucker on her lips fading away. It seemed to Clairey that Elvira was not one for a two-way conversation. She liked to hear herself speak, and she liked her company to listen. That was the extent of her communication skills.

"Fergus's mama says if it's to be a boy, we ortta call him after Fergus. I done tole her we was 'cause I knowed it ain't no boy. I knowed it's to be a girl. So it don't matter none to me if she wants to call it after Fergus."

"A girl'd be awful nice. I'm right glad for you."

"You and Ellis'll prob'ly start yourselves a family direc'ly now, won't you?"

Clairey understood what Elvira was doing. She was fishing. She was hoping for some stirring revelation that she could share in her other circles. Ellis and his new bride were probably a hot topic of conversation. There was probably all sorts of speculation revolving around the hasty state in which she and Ellis had married. Likewise, they likely wondered over when their relationship had begun, how they had chanced to meet, why he would take up with the Davenports in the first place.

She could imagine the lot of them saying it was a shotgun wedding. They probably thought she was in a family way. Why else would Ellis marry her but out of duty? Only she knew that half of it was right, that it had been duty that had made him a husband. When there was no talk of a baby and not evidence of one, either, that must have thrown them for a loop.

Clairey suspected Elvira was dying to bring to light what had really transpired, one and all hanging on her every word as she divulged the titillating details to them, and they, in shocked horror, mouths open and eyes wide, would say how they just couldn't believe it, how it was just too wild to be true.

Clairey shrugged. "Don't rightly know." She was hoping that would suffice. It did not.

"You ain't got problems, have you?" Elvira blurted, and it was almost as if she meant to hurt Clairey with her seemingly innocent demeanor as she continued her interrogation. Perhaps it made her feel superior to be the one that could carry a child and Clairey without her own. She was, after all, no more than a child herself, and perhaps living with her mother-in-law had made its mark upon her.

"Problems? I don't reckon so." Clairey felt stung by the question and fought to keep a lump from forming in her throat. It was far too personal a matter to her, and she mentally summarized the girl as silly and mean-spirited, trifling with people's emotions like that.

Elvira wasn't about to give up, however. Whether she couldn't read the reluctance of Clairey's wish not to discuss it or she just didn't care wasn't clear, but she went on. "What d'you mean? You don't know? Maybe you ain't tryin' for one yet? That it?"

"No. Well, I mean to say…how'd I know I got problems or not?"

"You tryin' and you ain't got no baby is how you knowed. Means you're barren."

Clairey's face fell, and she grew misty-eyed, but more than anything, she was just shocked.

Elvira seemed to change her tactics when she saw that she had caused Clairey distress. "I knowed a girl that was barren. Why, her husband done put her away. He done found hisself some other gal that could bear him youngins and put her away," she said. "But I'd not worry none yet, if I's you. You ain't been murried long. There's still time in it. Lotsa time."

"Yes, lotsa time," Clairey agreed absently.

"Maybe it ain't you no how. Maybe Ellis don't know his way round. How is he with you?" she asked slyly, her head tilted and her eyes watching Clairey with intense awareness.

They heard the men's voices in the hallway, and Elvira quickly changed the subject, her whole demeanor changing instantly and completely. "Now don't worry none 'bout that farm, not one little bit. Fergus'll see to it."

"I'm indebted to you. If you ever need a favor returned, why, you just let me know."

Fergus appeared in the doorway, leaning against the frame with his thumbs hooked in his belt loops, the doctor at his elbow. "What you girls been up to?"

Elvira popped out of her seat, approaching Fergus with her most charming and alluring smile. "Nothin', Fergus. Just talkin' is all. Wasn't we, Miss Clairey?"

"Yes," Clairey agreed. She, too, tried to smile, but it ended up being a weak attempt.

"Well, come on, gal. We got to get on up to Ellis's place afore it gets too dark," he said, sliding his arm around her neck.

Doctor Fielding showed them to the door and came back to the parlor. "It's been a long day," he said. "Think I'll turn in for the evening."

"Yessir."

"But you make yourself at home, and if you need anything, give a holler." He drifted up the stairway and was gone.

Clairey went to the bedroom where she and Ellis were to stay and prepared herself for bed, wearing a white nightgown that brushed the tops of her toes from the trunk that had once belonged to Millie Fielding. She climbed under the covers and did something that she normally never would have done, but she knew that Ellis wouldn't know the difference. He was out. And if he did happen to wake, he wouldn't remember her wanton behavior anyhow. She wrapped herself around Ellis's body, pressing close to his side with her hand resting flat on his chest. His heart thumped loud and strong, and the pressure of him against her was solid and reassuring. He was still alive, thanks to the doctor and his wife. She felt gratitude wash over her for the doctor's ability to mend what was broken and for Mrs. Fielding's capacity to cultivate. Through the two of them, the Lord had provided.

"I'm awful glad you ain't dead," she revealed just under her breath. "I'm fond of you, you know. More than I wanna own up to." She lay there in the dark, taking pleasure in the closeness of him. "Nobody ever called me Mrs. Hooper afore," she said, unable to keep a smile from her lips. It left a warm sensation in her body. It brought her pleasure, made her feel as if she mattered. She was somebody. She was Ellis's wife. She was Mrs. Hooper. She belonged.

As she nestled in tight next to Ellis, Clairey was glad the day was over. It seemed to be a day without end. While she was troubled over Ellis's misfortune, it was something else entirely that filled her thoughts as she lay there next to him.

That day, Clairey had learned more about being a woman than she had in her entire life. Mrs. Fielding had taught her how to dress, how to do her hair, how to keep herself clean. But it meant far more to her than just acquiring a new dress. It was the first time Clairey had ever felt pretty. What a lady Mrs. Fielding was. How generous and good. Oh, if only she could tell Gilda Fielding how much those things meant to her. She felt a great desire to be like the doctor's wife, to nurture the best in others, to be strong and confident and true to who she was.

Clairey had never been mothered before. She had never been taught that she could be something better than what she was. Perhaps her own mother would have bestowed those gifts of wisdom upon her if she'd had them to give. But her mother was merely surviving, only trying to endure.

As fondly as she now recalled Mrs. Fielding, she also remembered Elvira and their meeting. Clairey knew enough of human nature to know that Elvira was not someone she could trust. She'd spotted it right away — her mean nature, the manipulative undertones of her every word and gesture. Hadn't Clairey known enough of her father to instinctively recognize those qualities in others? Yes, Elvira was a cat, a prowling, devious cat, whose inborn nature it was to toy with people's emotions as a cat would toy with a mouse.

Was Elvira really going to have a girl? Clairey might not have been fond of Elvira but envied her nonetheless. What would it be like to carry a child, to have a life developing inside of her? How would it feel to have Ellis's baby move within her womb? And what could she hope to give to a child, a daughter? One thing was certain: her daughter would never have to be as empty as she. Clairey would see to that. She would take the things she was discovering for herself, and she would impart that wisdom upon her own girl.

She pondered all that she had discovered that day, things that she had learned, things that she wanted to commit to memory. She had been educated in both the good and bad of being a woman from Gilda and from Elvira, little kernels of knowledge that she would tuck away for later use. Another person, a newer person, a wiser person, lay within the skin of old Clairey. She began to doze, and eventually the steady tempo of Ellis's heartbeat lulled her to sleep.

The next few days passed by slowly, agonizingly for Clairey. She watched Ellis suffer in the worst way. He was feverish and sweaty, out of his mind much of the time. She was diligent in sitting by his side, cleaning his leg twice a day and re-bandaging it with fresh linens. She shuddered at the task, the wounds oozing and resembling raw meat that had been stitched together at the seams.

Doctor Fielding kept him on morphine for the first few days to manage the pain, but he dared not continue that treatment for a prolonged amount of time. He explained to Clairey that he didn't want her husband to develop a taste for it.

Gradually, Ellis grew well enough to sit up on his own, to get out of bed with a great deal of discomfort, and take care of his own basic needs. He talked incessantly of getting back to the farm, fretting over the state it would be in once he returned to it. Clairey could see that he wouldn't rest well until he was back in his own place, surrounded by the hills, trees, and long grass that were familiar to him. She began to understand that he couldn't heal at the doctor's home. He needed to be at his own home.

Chapter 21

Clairey saw to it that Ellis was comfortable in bed before she went out to the barn to hunt out the ax. She found it hanging on the wall and took it down then headed with a single determination for the pig pen, stepping through the gate, holding the handle of the ax with both hands, ready to swing. "Here, piggy," she hollered. "Here, pig!"

Snaggletooth came tearing at her, making his customary racket, snorting and squealing. "That's right, you son of a gun, come to mama! I got somethin' for you," she said, standing her ground.

Clairey braced herself with her feet apart in a semi-squatting position, pulled the ax back, and took a mighty swing with all of her weight in it; holding it so that the blunt side and not the blade was coming down, she bashed the boar on the skull with a loud thwack. The hog's head flew backward, his whole body momentarily leaving the ground until he fell prostrate on his side, motionless. Working a rope around his hind legs, she tied it tight, tugging a few times to make sure it would stay. The hog stirred, ready to attack had it not been bound by rope. She was squatting next to it and was startled by its resurrection, falling back on her bottom, scuttling backward and groping for the ax as it squealed and raged, bent on making some noise and chasing her down with all of its wild wrath. Her hand probed frantically in the grass until it made contact with the ax, and she grabbed hold of the handle with urgency, hitting the animal on the head again just as it was upon her.

She stood over it for a moment, the ax still in her hand, her heart beating wildly, and then she took the loose end of the rope she had secured about its hind legs and tossed it over the tall wooden frame in the yard, pulling with all her weight until the hog was suspended upside down. Then she secured the end of the rope to a stake pounded into the grass. The pig never knew what hit him. She went back into the house, took a knife from the drawer of the cupboard, and then she went back through the door, returning to the pig pen.

Snaggletooth hung limp, swinging slightly in the breeze at the end of the rope. It took some effort to slash through the layers of fat, fat she would cut into chunks and use later to make soap, but she did the work in one quick swipe, the blood spraying out in a fine mist. Clairey cleaned out the innards, leaving them in a messy pile on the ground, and then began scraping the hair from the boar's skin, shaving it clean. She left him there to bleed out for the better part of the day so that the meat wouldn't spoil, before she cut him down and carved him up, putting most of the meat into the smokehouse to cure, leaving the rest to soak in a salt mix in a box on the porch.

Not a bad show for one day's work, she thought as evening set in. That devil pig wouldn't hurt anyone anymore. Vengeance made tasty meat.

Trapper sniffed at the locked box that sat on the porch.

"That ain't for you," she scolded the dog. "Now off with you."

The old dog regarded her with his deep brown eyes and then took off at a trot down the porch steps to find something else to eat.

Clairey went to the back porch, stripping down to her underwear, and gave herself a good cleaning in the barrel of rain water that sat under the eaves, lathering up her arms and face and hands with a chiseled chunk of lye soap. She washed the blood and grime from her body with satisfaction, happy with the outcome of end of Snaggletooth.

That night, as Clairey cleaned Ellis's leg, he noted for the first time that she was wearing a white nightgown, and he hadn't remembered seeing her in it before. He wondered where it had come from. "That a new nightdress you got there?"

She was concentrating intently on her task. "Why, Mrs. Fielding done give it to me."

He watched her move about the room, taking things out, putting things away. His eyes admired her as her hips gracefully swayed. Not having those over-sized boots on made quite a difference in the way she carried herself. She looked like she was floating in the cotton nightgown. He wondered how he hadn't noticed the change until then.

"It's awful nice."

"Yeah," she said. "But them there underwears was a sight warmer."

He chuckled at her admission.

She stopped what she was doing to look at him. "Well, they was," she told him defensively.

"Sure they was," he agreed, stifling his mirth. He didn't want her to think he was poking fun at her. "But you look real fine in it anyhow."

She seemed embarrassed by his remark, growing self-conscious. She went to great lengths to arrange the blankets on the bed, fluffing his pillow before tucking it under his head and keeping her hands busy while trying to avoid his gaze. Clairey climbed into bed next to him, twisting her body to extinguish the kerosene lamp on the table next to the bed.

"Night," he said softly in the darkness.

"Night," she responded. She lay on her back briefly, before she rolled onto her side and went to sleep.

The next morning, Ellis was served fresh bacon for breakfast while Clairey changed his bandaging again. Every morning and every night it was to become their ritual. Slathering a thick coat of salve that the doctor had given her and directed her to use generously on his leg, she took the opportunity to inspect the damage. It looked downright horrible, but the doctor had told her that for the next several days, she wouldn't see much of a visual improvement.

Clairey put a clean bandage back over it and put the salve on the chest of drawers for safekeeping. She then busied herself by picking up the old bandaging to be cleaned and tidied the room a bit as she waited for him to finish eating.

"Looks like Fergus done a good job takin' care of the place," she commented as she pulled his pant leg down and propped a pillow beneath it to make him more comfortable. "You know, he and Elvira is to have a baby come winter. She tole me when we was in town."

"A baby?" he said absentmindedly.

"That's what she says." She noticed that Ellis hadn't eaten much of anything. "Somethin' wrong with the food?"

"No." But he pushed the plate away to indicate he was finished. It had been hard to ignore his somber mood for the last few days they had spent at the Fielding home, but she had hoped that once he was home, his disposition would improve.

"You ain't hungry?"

"Not particularly," he said.

She picked up the plate but didn't leave, studying him closely instead. "You all right?"

"Fine."

He wasn't very convincing, but then she didn't suppose he was trying to be. She knew something was eating at him, but she wasn't sure if she should push it or not. Growing up in a home where she asked as few questions as possible had made her wary. Avoidance was the safest route in her experience. "Can I get you somethin' afore I go on out?"

"No."

"I'll come back to feed you again after a while," she assured. "You need anythin' afore then, you got your walkin' stick there. But the doctor, he don't want you gettin' up too much, you know."

He didn't say anything.

"What's eatin' at you?"

"Don't matter." He wouldn't look at her, shifting to turn himself in the other direction.

She immediately felt sick to her stomach. Was he angry with her? Had she done something to bring his displeasure? "You ain't cross at me, is you?" she asked, nearly holding her breath as she waited for his reply.

"What'd I be cross at you for?" Ellis seemed somewhat put out by her assumption. She could hear the displeasure in his voice. "No, I ain't cross with you, Claire."

She felt some reprieve, but then his tone kept her from feeling totally relieved. She stood with his plate, debating whether she should leave him be or stay and get out of him what his angst was over. She opted to stay. "What is it then?"

"I done tole you, it don't matter."

"Matters to me," she replied. "Why won't you say it?"

He paused. "My leg busted up this a-way, why that terbaccer is gonna rot and die afore I'm up and round. Don't know what I'll do. S'pose I'll have to sell my daddy's place," he grumbled.

She didn't have any words to console him. She thought of the rows and rows of infant plants in their plant beds waiting out near the tree line at the edge of the yard, and she, too, felt the urgency of what he was saying. Ellis had borrowed against that crop, and if he couldn't tend to it, they were in danger of losing their farm, of losing everything. She was prompted, however, from somewhere deep inside herself to give him comfort. "It's all gonna turn out right, Ellis." But even to her, it sounded weak, faltering.

"There's them that have and them that don't have, and we gonna spend the rest of our days with them that don't have. You can fight, claw, tear your way out, and you just gonna get kicked down again. No point in even tryin' 'cause it's all worked out afore you even done had a go at it."

"What 'bout them cattle? They gonna bring a price, ain't they?" she offered.

"Not near enough. Coy Struthers done tole me he wanted my daddy's farm, and I'm gonna have to sell it to him."

"Well, now, it ain't my place to tell you one way or the other what I think of it, but maybe you ortta rest on it afore you decide for sure," she suggested softly. "'Cause it might work out some way." She carried the plate to the other room.

While Clairey washed the dishes, she fretted over what Ellis had said. There had to be some way for him to keep his daddy's farm. All of that work they had done together—the fields they had plowed, the plants they had tended—only to have it end like that. The tobacco plants wouldn't last much longer if they weren't set out, and they would lose all of them.

As she toweled off her hands, her eyes fell on the trunk that Gilda Fielding had sent home with her, and she went to it, opening the lid quietly. Rummaging through it, she found her old dress, tattered and worn to nothing, threadbare and patched, and she pulled it out. When she came out to the barn, she was wearing it again, with determination burning in her chest and a vague game plan rattling around her head. There was no way that she was about to let it all fall apart now, not after all of the work and effort she and Ellis had put into it. She would save that crop, even if it killed her trying.

She took the harness off the peg and opened Katie's stall door. The old mule came without being prompted, and Clairey slipped the harness over her muzzle. Ellis had a long flatbed wagon that she hooked Katie up to, and then she guided the animal out to the plant beds. A plot of about eight feet by forty feet of cleared out earth comprised their beds, enclosed on all sides by logs for protection and then covered with canvas to shield the little fledgling plants from the sun and elements. This, also, was why they had planted them along the tree line, to offer protection from the sun until they were ready to transplant to the field that she and Ellis had plowed up.

Once they had grown six to eight inches, they were more than ready for relocation. Clairey watered them down until the soil was wet and friable, and then she took ahold of the plant, working it out of the soil by the roots. As she went down the line, pulling up plants, she laid them flat, stacked like cords of wood, on burlap sacks, loading as many of them as she could work with at one time onto the flatbed to haul to the field.

All day, she labored to pull up the tobacco plants, haul them, and then go down the rows of the field, poking holes with a wooden stick so that the bright green baby plants could be set into the ground. As they were situated, she pushed the dirt back over their roots and gave them a cup of water for good measure.

When she had cleared off the wagon, she went back to fill it up again, continuing with her task until it was late in the night and the sun had long since gone to bed. It was tedious, physically demanding work, but she kept at it at an almost inhuman pace.

There were only a few times that she broke away, and that was to get Ellis his midday meal and then again to get him his supper. When she went in at lunchtime, he was dozing, and she left the plate next to the bed. Come suppertime, he was sitting up and wanted to visit. She could see he was nearly bored out of his mind. Here was a man that was always about some business, and to be confined with nothing to keep his idle hands busy was nothing short of torture for him. It left him with nothing to do but think, which was not altogether a good thing, because what he thought about was bringing him down, making him sorry for himself, filling his head with worry.

She told him she had to feed and care for the animals. It was true; she did. But when she had finished, she went back to setting. In the glow of moonlight, with the short tobacco plants appearing white against the dark red dirt, she stood over the field and surveyed her work with a mixture of pride and desperation. Despite her best efforts, she had maybe set an eighth of the furrowed rows, just a fraction of what was required to finish the job. On average, three to four people could set maybe half an acre in one day. She had planted a fourth. But then there was still one and three quarters of an acre left to go. Too weary to fret over it, she willed her body to walk the distance back to the barn, where she put Katie away for the night, and headed back to the house for her own bit of rest.

Clairey was up long before the dawn to begin again. Not wanting Ellis to know what she was up to, she was forced to do a bulk of the work while he slept. Her muscles cramped, and moving much more slowly than she had been the day before, she set to pulling the tobacco from the seed beds and replanting by setting them in the field. The one thing that kept her going was a song, and she sang it over and over as her hands instinctively did the work.

"I shall not be, I shall not be moved. I shall not be, I shall not be moved. Just like a tree that's planted by the water, I shall not be moved." The words of the song became her anthem. When she didn't feel that she could go any further, she would sing it through her clenched teeth, and she would go on.

Close to a week after returning home, Ellis began hobbling about the place with his cane. In the beginning, it had taken all of his strength and willpower just to get up from the bed. He was in horrible pain, and he felt so weak, so terribly weak, but gradually he was able to do more. He limped from one room back to the other, sweat pouring from him, muscles shaking from the effort of it. Falling into bed, he dozed in cat naps, regained his strength, and tried again.

Time seemed to crawl with nothing to do and no one about. He thought on his daddy's place and considered what he would ask Coy for it. His mind went over sums, and he added and subtracted and figured out how he would finish in the black next season. The cows, the farm, winter coming on — they tangled themselves in his brain. The more he thought about it, the more his head ached. And yet, he couldn't let it go as he struggled for some resolution.

Several days more went by of puttering around the house, and Ellis was ready for the sunlight on his face. He ventured out on the back porch, limping down the few steps to the yard, panting to get his breath. The laundry was flapping with a slight snapping sound in the breeze as it hung from the clothesline. With nothing better to do, he approached it, eyeing Clairey's newly obtained drawers. If anyone else had been about, he might have gone red. He had never seen women's underwear before, and he was somewhat drawn to them out of curiosity.

He reached his hand out to touch them, to examine them more closely. The cotton was of the finest quality, a material that only grew softer with washing, gauzy and smooth as cream. His fingers ran over it, caressing it, rubbing it between his thumb and fingers, testing it to see how it felt. The flimsy garment slipped from between the clothespins, off of the line, and fluttered gracefully down from its perch there. He grabbed at it frantically, trying to intercept it before it hit the ground, but it seemed to be intentionally avoiding his touch, out of his reach, as it sailed sporadically on the wave of the breeze. He managed to grab it just in time, standing upright and looking around to make sure that no one was there to witness the incident. The last thing he wanted was to get caught handling women's unmentionables.

Ellis quickly replaced the underwear, eager to be rid of the evidence. It took both hands to put it back on the line with the clothespins securing it, and he had to let go of his walking stick. When he bent to pick it back up, trying to keep his weight off of his injured leg, he nearly fell over. He decided that he would go back into the house where he was safe.

Clairey came in for the midday meal looking haggard and gaunt. She was surprised to see him sitting at the table. "You up and round?" she asked.

He shrugged. "Can't lay 'bout doin' nothin' for the rest of my days."

"I's hopin' you'd stay off that leg till we get back to have the doctor take a look at it," she said.

"He don't need to look at it. We can't afford to pay him no more. We can't afford to pay him for what he already done."

"Can or can't, he's gotta. Ain't got but a little salve left. He's gonna have to get us more," she scolded him mildly. "'Sides, he done tole me he'd take eggs and milk for your next visit. So you're not to worry over it none. We got plenty of eggs and milk."

He was just a little taken aback by her assertive stand. He had never really seen her behave in such a manner before. He narrowed his eyes as he studied her then asked, "Where you been?"

"Out yonder in the garden," she replied.

"I's just out there in the back, and I didn't see you."

"Musta been in the barn," she said, avoiding his eyes as she busied herself with making his meal.

"How's the corn a-lookin'?"

"It's lookin' good. Up past my thigh," she informed him.

He enjoyed the reference to her thigh with a little grin.

"We got us a fox round 'bout here somewheres, though."

"You seen him?"

"I ain't. But he got hisself one of them there chicken's last night, poor thing. Heard it too. Them chickens was makin' an awful noise."

"I'm gonna leave the gun by the door there, and if you hear him again, you wake me," he told her.

"Two of them cows seem to be with calves."

"That's good. Extras we wasn't plannin' on. We can sell 'em come next spring for a good price. Whatcha fixin' there?"

"Some biscuits and some ham and some fresh tomaters from the garden. Made them biscuits fresh this mornin'."

She put a plate in front of Ellis and sat down with him. He sprinkled some salt over the top of the tomatoes and cut into them, chewing thoughtfully. There was nothing like a tomato grown ripe on the vine for taste. He tried the ham, and it was good too. But when he bit into the biscuit, he instinctively spit it out without hesitation, complete with retching and scraping his tongue with his spoon to try to get every last crumb. Something was off with it. He thought it tasted bitter. He quickly took a drink to try to wash the taste from his mouth.

Clairey looked at him in surprise. "What's wrong with it?" she asked with a hint of defensiveness.

"Don't know," he replied. "Don't taste like they usually do though."

She tentatively took a bite, testing it on her tongue, and then spit it out too. "I musta put in bakin' soda 'stead of bakin' powder," she lamented. "That's awful stuff."

Her forlorn expression made him smile, and then he started to chuckle. He could see her hesitate, caught between embarrassment and seeing the humor in it. But then her face broke into a grin, and she conceded to the funny side of it.

"Them pigs is gonna have good eatin' today. Come and get it!" he yelled, as if he were calling to the pigs. "Hot biscuits!"

"I don't think it's fit even for pigs."

When she went back to work, he was sad to see her go. She passed him on the way out, and he worried over her and how worn out she seemed. He wanted to tell her to stay, but then he knew that the place would fall apart if not for her. He felt a twinge of guilt over being so helpless and having to rely on her to care for him. She was so frazzled that she had mistaken the baking powder for the baking soda. He hobbled back to bed, propping his leg up to rest it a spell.

One day wore on into another, much the same as the day before. Ellis busied himself with burning the trash in a barrel in the backyard one afternoon. He sat back on the porch in a ladder back chair, a cat running itself along his leg, while he watched the plumes of smoke ascend toward the sky. Clairey found him there at noontime and sat in the empty chair next to his.

Ellis watched her suspiciously. "Why you wearin' that ole dress again? Why ain't you wearin' one of them that was given to you?"

"Didn't wanna get 'em dirty while I's workin'."

"You gettin' sleep?" He studied her closely, waiting to gauge her response.

"Some," she said, not willing to expound. Their silence was easy, comfortable. Somehow, they had grown accustomed to one another, and it wasn't the same discomfited silence that it had been in the beginning. "You're keepin' busy, I see," she observed, motioning to the barrel of burning trash. "That's good."

"Every day it's a little better and a little better," he informed her. "I figure I can start hepin' out now."

"I aim to take you to Doctor Fielding in a day or two. Wait till he sees you and says it's all right to."

"Ain't gonna hurt to water the garden and do some weedin' and feedin' of the animals," he argued.

"You ortta just take it easy, Ellis. No point in ruinin' your health. You want that leg to heal proper, don't you?"

"A man ain't no count that'd let his wife bear all the burden alone. You go round waitin' on me and a-doin' all the chores to boot, and I just lay in that there bed up to nothin'. It ain't right." He stared at the barrel, at the bright orange flames that leaped above the rim and then disappeared again. He didn't want to look at her. He was ashamed, and the thought of meeting her eyes was too much.

"A man can't hep if he done gone and got his leg busted. 'Sides, it says in that there Good Book a wife's to be a hep mate. Ain't that what it says?" Her tone was defensive, as if she were protecting him from himself.

Her speech touched him, although it did little to comfort him. "I'm indebted to you. Don't know what'd have happened if you wasn't willin' to pitch in like you done. Don't know what's gonna become of us come fall, but this place woulda falled apart if it wasn't for you."

He finally looked at her, and what he saw surprised him. Clairey had a small smile on her lips, her eyes tender, full of emotion. "I'm indebted to you for a whole lot more, Ellis Hooper. Don't know that I can, but I s'pose I'll spend the rest of my days tryin' to make it up to you. Maybe I never said it afore, and shame on me for not, but what you done for me…Why, I'm nothin' but grateful. If you was to tell me to foller you to the ends of the earth and back, I'd do it. 'Cause I owe you that much and more." She got up from the chair and went into the house, leaving him there to let what she had said sink in.

Nine long days Clairey worked from before dawn and then continued on until long after the sun had gone down. There was a noticeable change in her appearance—her bloodshot eyes, her worn face. She was a woman on the verge of breaking. On the night that she finished setting, a storm blew in, and she finished her work with the rain coming down on her. She allowed herself the luxury of a good cry, figuring that her tears were mingling with the downpour to soak into the soil. It was relief. It was joy. It was the knowledge that she had overcome, and it spilled out with her tears onto the ground that she had toiled with, to become a part of the crop she had planted with her own hands. It had sought to defeat her, and she had prevailed. Now, she was permanently a part of it.

Somewhere deep inside, she knew that she would never be the same. The weak and frightened Clairey would be tucked away somewhere within, and the new, stronger Clairey was permitted to come out. She was capable of anything. She grasped an understanding that if there were no challenges, there was no growth.

Strange to her, but she felt an unexplained kinship with those tobacco plants, wondering if they had resented being torn up by the roots as much as she had. But now they possessed unlimited possibilities, room to grow, sun to warm in, water to drink, the ability to reach their full potential. Her body felt light as if she were floating as she went back to the house that night in the steady rain, and she sang again, this time in triumph, as she walked.

"Glory hallelujah, I shall not be moved. Anchored in Jehovah, I shall not be moved." Her voice grew louder with conviction so that she could hear herself above the rain. *"Just like a tree that's planted by the water, I shall not be moved."*

Ellis rolled over in the night, roused from a deep sleep with a vague impression that something was amiss. He lay still in the darkness, his senses heightened, aware of the rain as it clattered on the tin roof above him, the sounds of the wood shifting and moaning in the wind. His arm instinctively reached out, but Clairey was not next to him. His fingers groped empty bedding, a vacant pillow. Then, above the drumming of the rain, he heard it, a faint but vaguely perceptible noise that was just audible above the downpour. Had it been this that had awakened him, or Clairey's absence?

He fumbled in the gloom for his overalls and slipped them on, not bothering with his shirt, then proceeded cautiously to the front room, feeling for the rifle he had left next to the door with his stretched out hands. He gripped it tightly as he made for the door and stood on the porch, straining to hear what it was he had heard before. And then it came to him, drifting with the storm. He was confused and on his guard, sensitive to anything that was out of the ordinary. This was certainly out of the ordinary.

It was Clairey's voice he heard, Clairey coming up to the house from the barn, drenched through by the rain. She was singing, and her words were competing with the sound of the rain. "*Though the tempest rages, I shall not be moved. On the rock of ages, I shall not be moved. Just like a tree that's planted by the water, I shall not be moved.*"

He met her on the porch as she was coming up the stairs. "Claire?"

She looked up at him, squinting her eyes against the drizzle, and his confusion grew.

"What in thunder you doin'?"

"Come see it, Ellis," she begged, grabbing his hand and tugging on him.

Ellis resisted. "Come see what?"

"Come see and you'll find out," she persuaded, not letting go of his hand.

He wavered still then carefully set his rifle down on the porch before he allowed her to lead him into the rain. Her pace was quick, urgent. A few times she slipped in the mud and nearly lost her footing, but she continued on toward the field. He struggled to keep up with her, limping and trotting, slowing her down when he couldn't manage it.

Ellis and Clairey came to the edge of the field, the field the two of them had worked together to prepare for the tobacco, and there they were, leaves drooping beneath the raindrops that fell on them: the tobacco plants lined in neat rows, stretching out before them. She turned to him, her expression full of excitement, her eyes seeking his approval.

It was too much for him to fathom. "What...What's this?" he asked.

"The terbaccer," she answered.

"How?"

"I done it. Every last one of 'em is set, and I done it," she cried.

"The terbaccer?" he yelled above the din. "It's planted? All of it?"

She nodded emphatically to all of his questions.

Without thinking, reacting from pure instinct, he picked her up to swing her around, forgetting momentarily his handicapped leg, until it folded under the weight. They both tumbled to the ground, laughing, ecstatic, unable to control the sheer joy they were experiencing in that moment.

"It's done," she said again. "All done."

He sat up and looked over the field. "Shoot, if it ain't the purtiest thing I ever saw!" he cooed. The two sat there for a while, watching the tobacco with wonder and awe.

Part v: Blossoming

Chapter 22

Summer of 1935

Although it was a balmy summer's night, Ellis made a fire to dry their clothes and warm themselves next to. He turned from his task to watch Clairey, who was shivering as she put the kettle on to boil some water. She was soaked clean through, and he allowed his gaze to linger over her clinging dress. There was something about her that he couldn't explain, even to himself. The draw was like two magnets passing close enough to be immediately glued to one another.

During the first six months of their marriage together, Clairey had seemed nothing more than a nuisance to Ellis. He could not say when those feelings had changed. It had been a gradual thing, like roots and stem and leaves sprouting from a germinating seed. Their relationship had begun small and nearly indiscernible at first but gradually grew up and out, stretching toward the light of the sun.

Now, almost a year after he had met her, he was experiencing new feelings. He was surprised by that. He was sure a large part of his reluctance to be close to her came from the fact that he had held on so tightly to his feelings for Dulcie Mae. Ellis had believed there would never be any chance that Clairey could measure up to Dulcie Mae. He could never have imaged he would have developed any sort of an attraction for her. But now, he was feeling like a husband, like a lover. He couldn't help wanting her. He realized it was more than just wanting to satisfy his needs. He desired *her*. He fancied Clairey.

"How'd you manage it?" he wondered in admiration.

She shrugged. "Don't know. Just set my mind to it and done it," she explained as she busied herself with her task. "Didn't wanna get your hopes high if it happened it didn't work out, so I didn't tell you 'bout it."

"Claire," he said, trying to get her attention.

"Huh?"

Ellis didn't respond right away. Instead, he waited for her full consideration.

She stopped what she was doing and turned to him.

"I'm awful proud of you," he complemented. "You done good."

"You won't have to get rid of your daddy's place now."

When she said those words, he realized that Clairey hadn't simply done this to save the farm: she had done it to save him. She had done it so that he wouldn't have to live with selling out to Coy Struthers. It meant so much more when he understood exactly why she had done what she had.

"Come on over here and sit by the fire. Warm yourself," he said, motioning to her.

She did as she was told and came over to the fireplace, holding her hands out tentatively toward the heat, the flames fanning her face, drying her cheeks. Ellis felt the familiar flutter of his stomach as he slid in behind her and wrapped an arm around her waist, pulling her back against his chest. She relaxed a little and dropped her arm to cover his, her hand on his hand.

He put his face to her wet hair and said softly, "You smell good." It was the rain, the earth, and her skin.

She laughed. "I smell like an ole wet dog."

He was goaded on by her light manner. "Claire?"

"Yes?"

"I just wanted to say I grown real fond of you," he told her in a mild, tender voice.

"And I you, Ellis," she replied, with an ease that put his fears to rest. "I's fortunate to have a good man such as you. Your daddy woulda been real proud of you."

"My daddy, I think, woulda liked you."

The kettle began to hiss on the old black stove. "Pero's done," she murmured. "You want some?"

He sighed deeply, annoyed by the interruption. "Sounds good," he said, letting her go. He sat in the rocking chair, and she brought him a mug and poured the dark brown liquid from the kettle spout to fill it. She poured one for herself as well and dragged a chair over to sit down opposite him with a bashful smile.

He looked like a boy, sitting with his mug between his hands, in his undershirt and overalls, with his hair matted down and wet.

"Ellis," she began, but hesitated.

"What is it?"

"Can I ask you somethin'?"

"Yeah."

"Somethin's been eatin' at me. I know it's gonna sound strange, but I was wonderin'…What was your mama's name?" And the secret that had been burning in her for a while now worked its way to the surface. She had never felt comfortable enough to address it before, not until now.

"My mama's name? It was Edith," Ellis answered. He gave the impression that he was thrown by her out-of-the-blue question. "Why you wanna know for?"

"It weren't Lottie Borden?"

Ellis looked truly puzzled now. He watched her sip at her Pero with a troubled frown. "No, it weren't."

"Oh," she said, and decided that she shouldn't say anything more. Ellis was obviously completely unaware of what was being talked about behind his back. She suddenly realized that now was not the time to broach the subject.

"Who's Lottie Borden?"

"Don't know," she responded. "Some name I done heard."

Ellis was scrutinizing her now, and she could feel it, feel his eyes upon her, his suspicion growing. She wished that she hadn't said anything. Why had she brought it up? Maybe she thought that he knew, that he just hadn't told her. Perhaps because it was a mystery and she couldn't let it lay. She wanted a conclusion that made sense, that tied up all the loose ends. But in the back of her mind, she thought maybe he would think she was the one person in the whole world that he could trust to tell him the truth, the one person who hadn't deceived him. Selfish, really, but she hadn't thought that until now, until it was too late.

"Where'd you hear it from?" he pressed.

"Don't know. Round town, I s'pose."

Ellis would not let it rest. He knew that she knew something she wasn't telling him, and he was determined to get it from her. "Who is Lottie Borden?" He was losing his patience, and the tone of his voice made it clear.

"They was talkin' 'bout her in the grocery that day we was in town."

"Who was talkin' 'bout her?"

"That day I was a-standin' and waitin' for you, and they's talkin' and I heard 'em."

"Tell me now what you been goin' on 'bout. I wanna know," he persisted. "I wanna know."

"I'm real sorry I brung it up. It's just that…"

His anger was right at the surface now, and she could tell that she was only agitating him, taunting him by withholding what she knew. "I wanna know right now what happened," he ordered, his shoulders tense, his face expectant.

"That feller at the grocery, he done tole that lady that you was Lottie Borden's. Well, I didn't know your mama's name so I's wonderin', is all. He done messed it up."

"Why'd he think my mama's this gal Lottie Borden? There somethin' you ain't tellin'?"

"I…well, it was somethin' you done tole me when you got your leg run through. You said to me that your daddy brung you into this world."

"So?"

"So when we was a-stayin' with the doctor and his wife, she done tole me that she's there when Doctor Fielding delivered you. And the doctor, when I said it to him, he was behavin' awful strange like."

Ellis seemed completely lost and confused by all that she was saying, his mind unwilling to put the puzzle pieces together. "She don't know what she's talkin' 'bout. That's all. And neither does he."

"You're prob'ly right." She thought perhaps she had agreed too quickly for Ellis's liking.

He scowled at her.

"He even says he can't 'member all them babies he hepped along 'cause there's so many of 'em," Clairey continued, trying to fix the damage she had done. She would have done anything to get out of the mess she'd just made.

"Whatcha gettin' at anyhow?"

She didn't answer, only looked down at her mug, cringing.

Ellis seemed perplexed, his brow wrinkled, his mouth drawn. She recognized his customary habit of rubbing his neck when he was upset or angry. Finally, he spoke up. "You sayin' my daddy gone with some other gal? That what you sayin'? 'Cause he never'd a-done such a thing. My daddy's a God fearin' man. He never." His tone was a mixture of disbelief and defensiveness.

"I never said he weren't," she gasped.

"He weren't like your daddy," Ellis sneered. "He weren't kearn—weren't trash—like that." He saw her reaction, how she looked staggered and hurt all at the same time, and he gave the impression that he was glad for it. "That's right, nothin' but garbage!"

His jaw line was hard, and his lips curled in a jeering small smile. "Don't think I don't know 'bout your daddy and that baby that come from him and your mama's sister. Now you tryin' to ruin my daddy's good name? No sir!" He pushed out of the rocking chair. "I won't have it!" He stomped out in the rain to the barn.

He did not want to believe it, could not fathom it. His daddy had been a good man, a man that never would have done such a thing. He had taught him about God, had read to him from the Good Book.

Clairey was a liar! She was an ignorant good-for-nothing. He never should have taken her in. How dare she throw about such accusations? Edith was his mother! Edith Hooper! His daddy had told him so. Who was he going to believe, her or his father?

In frustration, he kicked the stall door. It flew open and banged loudly. His anger unsatisfied, he looked about for something more to take his rage out on. He took up a shovel and pitched it with all of his strength. It struck the wall and clattered to the floor.

A rage tore loose inside of him, a rage that he had suppressed all those years. It consumed him, and he let it. The memory of his father was pushed aside, and he remembered all of the insults, all of the ill treatment he had received at the hands of those town folks that knew him, had known him since birth, and it suddenly all made sense. They had been aware all along. All along, it had been lurking there, under the surface, and his daddy had kept it from him.

All of those years, he had taken their scorn, their insults. He remembered how the children had taunted him about his mother, and he understood that they must have known too. They hadn't been mocking or making fun of Edith; they'd been talking about this Lottie Borden. And when Dulcie Mae had said her parents would not let her accept his offer of marriage, he had wanted to know what it was they had disapproved of. She had done her best to be vague. She'd told him that they wanted someone with a good reputation. He had assumed that they'd wanted someone who was established. After that, he had done everything he could to make himself respectable, got himself a farm, and worked to make a good living. Every thought he managed to form was proof that he had been deceived. It seemed that every memory he was able to recall pointed to the obvious.

In the back of his mind, he had always wondered why—why they harbored such resentment for him. Now he had the answer, and he felt sick. He felt the bottom dropping out. He lay down on his back in the hay loft with his arm covering his eyes, listening to the rain. He remembered his daddy taking him up on the hill to where Edith was buried. He would talk about her with such tenderness, such love. Ellis had grown to want that more than anything—the joy of finding a woman to cherish, to adore. A woman to spend his life with, to grow old with.

It just didn't seem possible that all that time he'd been lying. Ellis wouldn't believe the man capable of it, if not for the cold hard truth. People were talking, inconsistencies were popping up, and the only reasonable explanation was a terrible reality that he didn't want to face. He should have gone in to bed, but he stayed in the hay loft and eventually fell asleep there. He simply wasn't ready to face her, to face Clairey.

In the early morning hours, he woke with a start and remembered what had transpired with an engulfing dread. He was not ready to confront Clairey. There were still too many questions in his head. He was back to telling himself that his father never would have messed around on his wife. His reasoning skills were shaky at best in his present condition. Every time he felt that, yes, it must be so, he then would argue within his head that he knew Jim Hooper, and Jim Hooper never would have! Seeing Clairey would only complicate things further.

Ellis climbed into the truck and pulled out of the barn. He saw Clairey come out of the house to try to stop him.

"Ellis!" she screamed.

She scrambled down the stairs in pursuit, grabbing the door handle as he sped by. It was the passenger side handle, the one that didn't work. She attempted to jump onto the running board, but Ellis didn't even slow.

He peeled down the drive, hitting the main road, and did not stop until he had reached town. He slowed the truck a bit, not sure really what his plan was. He cruised the streets for a while and then parked and got out to walk. His leg was bothering him some as he limped along the store fronts, lost and troubled, watching people pass him, the faces of strangers seeming to look at him in some knowing way. Across the street, he spotted the grocery store and decided on the spur of the moment to go there. It had all started with the clerk.

He walked past a group of men that were loitering out front, swapping stories and catching up since they'd last seen each other. They paid him no mind. He came through the door and saw the clerk, and he inexplicably wanted to pound him.

The bell jangled, and the clerk looked up from what he was doing, as was his custom, to see who had come in. Immediately, the color drained from his face.

"You been tellin' lies 'bout me to folks round town?" Ellis accused in a menacing voice.

"I don't tell no lies," the clerk replied.

"Don't try to get out of it now. I done heard what you's tellin'." Ellis walked up to the counter, nearly leaning over it as he pointed his finger at the clerk. "You's tellin' lies 'bout me, and I wanna know why!"

"I can't hep you. Best if you just move on 'long."

Ellis glared at the man. "I ain't a-goin' nowheres till you tell me what you done said 'bout me, so's you better start a-talkin', mister."

The clerk pursed his lips as if to say, without saying it, that he wasn't about to talk. He stood where he was with a look of disdain for Ellis.

"I said you tell me what you been sayin' behind my back!"

"I ain't got nothin' to say to you," the clerk spat.

They were in a gridlock, the clerk haughty in his dismissal and Ellis unwilling to let it go.

He opened his mouth to threaten the clerk again, waited for a split second, muttered, "Ah, what the hell," and then reached over the counter and dragged the man to him, pounding his fist again and again into the clerk's smug face.

The man let out a yelp and tried to break away, heading for the door. "He aims to murder me!" he screamed in desperation, blood spouting from his nose.

Ellis held him firm and hit him again. "Shut your mouth!" Ellis commanded, ramming his fist into the clerk's lips.

The group of men out front heard the commotion and peeked their heads in to see what was going on. They saw Ellis beating the store clerk mercilessly, volleying blow after blow upon him. They rushed in to come to the clerk's aid. Three of them attempted to pull Ellis away, but he just kept punching and jabbing at the clerk until they managed to get a good hold on his arms and thrust him to the door.

"I'll kill you, you son of a gun! I'll kill you!" Ellis shouted.

Spectators from other businesses filed out onto the street to see what was happening, but he didn't care. They probably all knew too, he thought. It was clear he wouldn't get another shot in so he shook the men off him that had interceded on the clerk's behalf.

"Get offen a-me!" he growled. "I'm a-goin', so get off!" He walked away, shambling heavily, his leg aching.

His next stop was the doctor's home. He banged on the door, rattling it in its frame, but there was no answer. So he sat on the front steps with his leg stretched out before him, trying to make himself comfortable. He waited for nearly an hour before Doctor Fielding showed. Ellis watched him approach with a guarded expression.

"Good to see you, Ellis. You've finally gotten around to that follow up examination?" Doctor Fielding guessed.

Ellis's black look was not intended to be friendly. He imagined his appearance was not unlike that of his daddy's over twenty-five years ago. A quarter of a century was a long time to hold onto a secret. He wondered how the doctor had managed it. Now, all was about to be revealed. Just as the body worked to expel a foreign object, a thorn, a splinter, this secret had festered until it was now rising to the surface, demanding attention, wanting to be exposed.

Ellis played dumb. "Sure am," he lied.

The doctor squeezed past him and opened the front door. "Well, come on in then," he offered, stepping aside to let Ellis in. Ellis followed him into the examination room and allowed him to remove the bandages from his leg. Doctor Fielding studied it intently, touching it mildly with his fingers, probing it with care. "How's it feeling?"

"It's mendin', I s'pose."

"Yes, well, it looks as if your wife has taken good care of it. It's coming along quite nicely."

"Guess she has."

"Has she ever considered taking up nursing?" he joked.

"Reckon I don't know."

"She seems like a good woman," the doctor commented, looking Ellis in the eye.

"Funny you should mention it. She tells me you and she done had yourselves a visit while we was here." Ellis didn't even blink. He just sat there watching the doctor, trying to gauge his reaction.

"Did she now?"

"Sure did. That ain't all, neither. She says Mrs. Fielding was there when you delivered me." He watched the doctor work over his leg for a moment and then asked, "That so?"

"Like I told Mrs. Hooper, I've delivered quite a few babies in my time. It gets hard to keep track of all of them."

"My daddy always tole me you wasn't round that day. That you was tendin' to somebody else, and you come after my mama done passed on," Ellis said.

The doctor looked as if he were thinking hard, trying to call to mind the events surrounding the incident. "Come to think of it, that sounds about right." The doctor attempted a chuckle, but it didn't sound natural; it was forced. "You know, it's been a lot of years now," he reflected as he worked to re-bandage Ellis's leg. "It's hard to remember the details."

"Where's Mrs. Fielding?"

"I'm sorry, what?"

"Where's Mrs. Fielding? Maybe she 'members," Ellis suggested. He could see the doctor squirm ever so slightly.

"I believe she's quilting over at the church this morning," he replied. "It wouldn't do any good anyhow. Why would she remember if I couldn't?"

"Seems everybody else in town 'members. Seems they done 'membered for you," Ellis retorted. "So you gonna tell me a tale, or you gonna tell me true 'bout my daddy and my mama?"

"Why do you want it from me if you already know?" Doctor Fielding inquired. He suddenly appeared very old, his gray hair magnified, multiplied before Ellis's eyes.

"'Cause I don't know. 'Cause I wanna know the truth. Did my daddy carry on with another woman? Is that what happened?" Ellis barked. "He always tole me my mama died tryin' to have me. But that ain't the real story, now, is it? He's with another woman."

"What are you talking about? Your daddy with another woman? Who told you such a thing?" the doctor demanded.

"If that ain't it, then what is? 'Cause Edith Hooper weren't my mama, now, was she?"

The doctor sat quietly, collecting his thoughts before he proceeded. "Jim Hooper came here looking for me. In a way, I knew that it would come out somehow, that it would come to this. But when I placed you as a tiny babe in Jim Hooper's arms, it seemed unavoidable. Then the years went by, and I grew to believe that the secret was safe, that you would never discover how it had really happened."

"And what really happened?" Ellis encouraged, hanging on his every word.

"It all began when he came to bring me back to help his wife. She was going to have a baby, and it was coming early. But I wasn't here that day. I was out on another call that day."

"So my mama was Edith?" Ellis wondered, growing confused.

"Mrs. Fielding told him that she would have me come as soon as I could. But by the time I got there, Edith was already long gone. There was nothing I could have done for her."

"Who's Lottie Borden then?"

"Let me just finish," the doctor insisted. "Jim was beside himself. He had just lost his wife. He had just lost his baby. A girl."

"A girl?"

The doctor continued, as if he hadn't been interrupted. "A girl. And, well, I suppose he didn't feel he had a reason to go on. I suppose he blamed me—that I hadn't been there when Edith needed me. I can't say as I disagree with that, but he came here one night, intending to kill me."

"My daddy? I don't believe it," Ellis said in mocking disbelief. The man he knew would never have done such a thing. He hadn't been capable of it.

"You must understand, Ellis, he was lost, and he was angry, and he was hurting. He thought that I was responsible for all that had happened, and he wanted to punish me. So he showed up here with a gun and got a little loud, and he woke you up."

"Woke me up?"

"You were sleeping in here, just four days old, and the noise woke you. Someone dies and someone else is born. Strange, isn't it, how that works?"

"What was I doin' here for?" Ellis simply could not connect the dots.

"You were born, and the same day your mother died, Ellis."

"My mother?"

"That's right. Your mother, Lottie Borden."

"Lottie Borden *was* my mama." It was a statement, not a question.

"We were caring for you until the people from the children's home in Nashville could come for you. But Jim came that night, and he saw you and wanted you. He said he'd do right by you, that he could care for you better than they could at the children's home. I knew that to be true, and so...and so I let him take you."

There was a silence that hung between the two of them, thick and suffocating. Ellis felt his insides collapse, his head working hard to understand what the doctor was telling him. "Jim Hooper weren't my daddy?"

"No."

"So this Lottie Borden died, and my real daddy didn't want me?" Ellis asked.

The Doctor cleared his throat. "I don't know about that."

"You said I's to go to the children's home. That's what you said," Ellis reasoned. "So, my daddy, he don't want me?"

"Nobody knew who your real daddy was, Ellis. Your mother was only fourteen, a young girl. If Lottie Borden knew, she never told anyone."

Ellis felt all the energy drain from him. He suddenly understood it now. Before, his mind could not grasp the what and why. But then it all fell together, and he was totally lost. Jim Hooper was not his father. Edith Hooper was not his mother. Everything he had believed to be true up to that point had all been a lie. He was nobody, with no name. It was like he had just disappeared into the crowd of unfamiliar faces and total strangers that he walked among on the street. They meant nothing to him because he did not know them, and now he was one of them, adrift in the crowd. Despair filled him up with darkness.

"Who was she?"

"Lottie Borden?"

"Yes, Lottie Borden," he barked.

"She was Solomon Borden's daughter out of Cole County. I didn't know much of her. She was just a girl that needed a doctor, and I was him."

The front door opened and shut, and they heard Gilda call out. "Doctor Fielding, you home?"

The doctor got up from his stool and yelled back. "In here, Mrs. Fielding."

She appeared in the entrance of the examination room. "Oh, Ellis Hooper. How are you doing? You mending well?" she said with a pleasant smile, surprised to see him.

He was shaking, his hands tremoring, fighting to appear composed. "Fine, thank you, ma'am," he answered with his eyes downcast. If she could sense the tension, she didn't let on.

"Just finishing up in here," the doctor informed her. He plucked a tin of salve from his shelf and handed it to Ellis. "Keep putting this on and you should be fine," he instructed. "You'll still need to be cautious, mind you, but you seem to be healing as you should."

"Yessir," Ellis said, pocketing the tin.

"Is your wife with you?" Gilda asked.

"No, ma'am. She's at home. I come alone today."

"Well, we certainly enjoyed getting to know her better. You have a fine woman," she commented. "You know, she was so worried over you when she brought you in; she'd hardly leave your side. She was just a real sweet girl."

"I'd best be on my way. I done took up 'nough of your time." He got up to leave.

"You'll tell her hello for us, won't you? Give her our best?"

"Sure I will, Mrs. Fielding."

He walked out onto the street, trying to remember where he had parked his truck. His head was in a fog. He just didn't know what to do with himself. As he rambled up and down the streets, he eventually came upon a shop that sold ladies' things. He looked in the window, spotting a pair of white gloves with a scalloped cuff and little pearl buttons. Without thinking, he went in and bought them, perhaps an attempt at appeasing his guilt.

The clerk smiled in a way that made him uncomfortable. "You want them wrapped?" he asked.

Ellis scowled. "No need." He took the gloves and shoved them into his coat pocket and left the store, feeling as if he shouldn't have bought the silly things in the first place.

Once he found the truck, he sat there for a long time, not knowing where to go, feeling like he didn't belong to anyone or anything. Something inside told him to go home, to go to Clairey. He fought that urge. He didn't want to see her now. He was humiliated. It wasn't just what he had said to her, either, although he had regretted the words as soon as they had come out of his mouth. But now, how could he tell her he had no father? How could he tell her about his real mother?

Ellis knew her well enough to know that she wouldn't care. None of it would affect how she felt about him. It wouldn't turn her away from him; he knew this. But having to say the words out loud — to actually speak them, to own up to it all — well, he didn't know if he could do that. He thought the clock would stop and the earth would come to a screeching halt. Life as he knew it would end if he were to admit it to her or to anyone. He felt that he wasn't the same, that he no longer was Ellis Hooper. He didn't know who he was, like his body was disconnected from his head.

All these years he had been so sure of himself, his place in the world. He pictured in his mind his name and traits all written neatly on a chalkboard, columns and columns of information, from his dominant characteristics down to the mundane small details. Then, someone came along and wiped it clean with an eraser, and the only thing that was left was the chalk dust in wide sweeping arc marks. Erased in one moment of time, hardly even requiring any effort to do it. In a flash, it was all just gone. Life would never be the same again.

He really didn't know why, but Ellis, without explanation, decided to visit the Bayard farm. It was not that he craved their company, not that at all. It wasn't until he pulled up to the house that he realized what he was thinking.

Elvira was sitting in the shade of the porch when he came. She stood up and shielded her eyes from the sun with a pleasing smile on her face. "How is it with you?" she asked.

"Fine, thank you."

Myrna Bayard came out the door, squinting to see who had come to visit. "That Ellis Hooper?" she asked Elvira.

Ellis came up the stairs with his hat in his hands. "Good day to you," he said.

"What'd he say?" Myrna had grown hard of hearing in her old age. She had begun to elevate her voice along the way, like a knob being gradually turned up on a radio, because she could not hear the volume of her own speaking.

Elvira put her mouth close to her ear and yelled, "He's just sayin' how do."

"Well, I'll be. What brings you this a-way?" she asked.

"I's hopin' to have a word with Ferg. He round?"

"You say you wanna talk with Fergus?" she shouted.

"Yes, ma'am."

Myrna turned to Elvira, motioning with her finger for her to leave. "Go on and get him, girl."

Elvira did as she was told and took off after Fergus.

Once she was out in the yard, Myrna told Ellis, in what she probably thought was a confidential aside, "She ain't worth shootin'."

It had been plenty loud enough for Elvira to hear. She gave Ellis a look, as if to say, "*See what I'm dealing with?*"

"Well, Ellis Hooper, whatcha want with Fergus?" she questioned, sitting down heavily on a chair with a grunt. She was a large woman, her gray hair swept up in an old-fashioned bun. She wore her dress long—the style that had been popular thirty years ago. Here was a woman who stuck with the old ways, scandalized by the shorter fashion of dresses that girls wore now.

"I's in town, thought I'd stop on by and see how you-uns is doin', is all." He made his voice loud and leaned into her as he spoke so that she could hear.

"You never come by afore, boy," she informed him, her eyes shrewd and penetrating.

"Well, now, I got some empty time, and I thought I'd come on by and let Fergus know I's grateful to him and all for what he done for me. It was good of him."

"Yessir." She nodded. "He's a good boy, that 'un. Always was. Why he'd go and murry up with that gal's a mystery to me. She's got a nice body; I'll give'r that."

"How you been gettin' on?" Ellis asked politely.

"Ah, my arthritis is actin' up on me. Gotta keep my legs up 'cause they vex me sore," she told him, leaning over and rubbing the calves of her plump legs.

"Sorry to hear it."

"When you get as old as I am, things is bound to go bad," she complained. "You know, I's born two years afore the end of the aggression of the northern states." She began to fan herself with her apron. "Never met my daddy. He's killed durin' Antietam in sixty-two without even knowin' I's to be born," she informed him. "Yessir, I done seen it all, and it only gets worse, boy. It only gets worse."

"Ain't that a shame," he said, trying to avoid upsetting her.

"'Course, your kin done fought with 'em yanks," she said with a frown. "Your daddy's daddy took up with Tinker Dave Beaty and his bunch, harassin' and givin' grief to Champ Ferguson and them that follered him. I named my boy for Champ. Poor Feller got strung up, but he died for the cause," she said with conviction. "Couldn't do no better'n that."

Fergus came up to the house, a look of surprise on his face. Likely he didn't have many visitors. "Hey, Mama. Hey, Ellis."

"Fergus," Ellis acknowledged.

"Whatcha up to?"

"Not much." He shrugged.

"How's your leg mendin'?"

"Bothers me some, but I'm gettin' round." They stood, regarding one another for a time, and then Ellis put his hat back on his head and met Fergus on the front lawn. "Mind takin' a walk with me?"

"Sure you up for it?" Fergus asked, observing Ellis's painful limp.

"For a while anyway," Ellis assured him. They walked aimlessly side by side until they were away from the house. "Clairey tells me you're to have a baby," Ellis remarked. "That so?"

"Yeah." Fergus was clearly puzzled by where Ellis was headed with his conversation. "What'd you come for, Ellis?"

"I 'preciate all you done while I's laid up, how you took care of my place and all."

"Weren't nothin'." Fergus waved his hand dismissively.

"Now, don't make light of it," Ellis protested. "It weren't nothin'."

"You're my friend. It's what any friend a-done."

Ellis felt a tug at his conscience. He had always harbored a hint of disdain for Fergus Bayard. He seemed like such a ridiculous character, somewhat pathetic in his looks and manner. But then, when Ellis had needed someone, it had been Fergus that had been there for him. He had said some things he regretted now, had poked some fun and held a certain amount of contempt for him. Ellis didn't want to admit to even himself that he had felt somewhat superior even. He realized now that he had been the inferior of the two all along.

"I come to say thank you and to try and return the favor, if you'll let me."

"What d'you mean?"

"My daddy's place," Ellis answered.

"What of it?"

"Coy Struthers done offered me twelve hundred for it."

"You gonna take it?"

"I come to offer it to you instead. Coy wants it bad, but I's thinkin' on it, how you'd be close to Elvira's daddy. You'd have your own place, and I aim to give it to you for two hundred less than what Coy offered."

Fergus stopped in his tracks, his expression troubled. "Do what?"

"Well, now, you're gonna have to work on the cabin, and it needs a new barn and all, but I figure it'd be a good place for you to start out with," Ellis explained.

"You'd do that?" Fergus asked. "I thought you was of a mind not to sell it at all."

"Changed my mind."

"It's awful nice of you to offer, but I can't afford that," Fergus said, digging his hands into his pockets.

"I was thinkin' you can move on in and pay me half with your first crop, and the next year you can pay me the second half. That way it won't be too much of a burden on you."

"What 'bout Mama? I can't just up and leave her," Fergus debated. "What'll become of her if I leave?"

Ellis studied him closely, perplexed by the reluctant man who stood before him. He had offered him deliverance, and Fergus didn't want it. Either he didn't understand or couldn't see that living with his mother was a bad thing all the way around. Loyalty was one thing, but loyalty to the point of stupidity an entirely different one altogether. He questioned whether Fergus would ever be capable of leaving his mother.

"She got three daughters that live just a stone's throw away, Fergus. They can hep out now and again. And you'd be close enough to come up and hep out too, if you had a mind to."

"Them girls, they don't come round near what they ortta. All Mama gots is me to depend on. She says so many a-time. She ain't gonna be on this here earth much longer. Yessir, her days is numbered. And I can't leave her now that she needs me the most."

"You prob'ly right. It was just an idea. If you ain't gonna take it, I aim to sell to Coy Struthers. Thought I'd give you first choice, is all. But Coy, he wants it awful bad, so I s'pose it'd be best."

"Don't mean to seem ungrateful, Ellis. It was real nice of you to consider me. But Elvira and me, we ain't ready yet to go out on our own. Not with Mama so sick and all. Why, she'd die if we was to leave her."

"I hear what you sayin', but you gotta think of Elvira and the child too, what's best for them. You gotta see to their needs."

Fergus grew defensive. "I'm a-carin' for her. She got a roof over her head, and she ain't hurtin' for nothin'."

"I never said it was any other way, Ferg. I's just sayin' you ortta consider on what she thinks, what she wants. You murried to her and not to your mama."

"Is that what them boys in town is sayin'? Is that what you sayin' 'bout me? 'Cause I won't have it, Ellis. Ain't nothin' wrong with me bein' a good son. She done raised me right, and there ain't nothin' wrong with me carin' for her and makin' her comfortable in her old age. And I'll have words with anybody that says otherwise. You hear?"

"I didn't come to cause no trouble. S'pose I'll be on my way then." He turned around and headed back for the house and his truck.

Fergus yelled out, "Ellis!"

Ellis stopped and turned back to him. "Yeah."

"What you was gonna do, well, I thank you."

"Think nothin' of it," he replied with a forced smile.

"I'll see you round."

"See you round." He went to turn around again, but Fergus called to him once more.

"Ellis?"

"Yeah."

"We still friends, ain't we?"

"Yeah, Fergus. We still friends."

Before he changed his mind, he went up to the old place he and Jim had called home. The cabin was quiet, strangely haunting as he walked through, familiar but foreign all at the same time. There were only a few odds and ends left in the empty rooms. He disassembled the iron bed and loaded it on the truck along with some oil lamps and a clock in a wooden crate. When he came out into the yard, the burnt barn in ruins was a stark reminder of what had befallen the owner.

The barn was reminiscent of his own story, his own identity. All that he had known — his history as he knew it — lay in the dust like the old burnt-out shelter. He himself had not changed, but his story was forever gone, destroyed just as surely as fire had ravaged that place.

He walked through the ash, kicking the ground with the toe of his boot now and again, thinking it was once an impressive building, large and spacious. How could one rebuild something so solid and sturdy? Where would he begin? Ellis knew the answer. Deep down, he knew that the barn would be rebuilt, maybe better than before. It would rise again over the ruins of the old building to be a sturdy and useful place.

CHAPTER 23

Nerves taut, feeling desperate, Clairey was worthless all the day. Since that morning when Ellis had driven away, she had felt her world crumbling down upon her. Out of fear for his safety, because she knew he was in a bad place, she'd tried to stop him. He had to have seen her, heard her call out his name, but he hadn't even acknowledged her. She'd stood helplessly, watching him go with a dread that filled her up. He'd been in no condition to be alone. It was all her fault. All of it. Why hadn't she just kept her mouth shut?

The real torture was in not knowing. Where was he, and what was he doing? She had no need to water the field since it had rained the night before, so she cared for the animals and did a load of wash to keep herself busy. She filled the two wash tubs with water, using one for the soapy work and the other for the rinsing. Clairey vigorously went at the clothing with a bar of lye soap, wrung the garments with her hands, dipped them several times in the rinse water and then processed them through a crank-powered wringer, where they fed through to her basket waiting on the other side. Once she had finished with the actual washing, she hung it on the line to dry. There was something about spotless laundry hanging on the line, clean and crisp as it moved with the wind, that was therapeutic.

Mostly, Clairey simply paced through the house, looking for something that would keep her mind off her current trouble, but finding nothing, she simply sat, her mind going in a hundred different directions. Where had he gone? Would he return or had he left for good? She couldn't believe that of him. That place meant too much for him to abandon it. And she…did she mean anything to him?

The anxiety tore at her, made her stomach feel weak as it churned in her gut. "Oh, Lord, please…please…" she begged with her hands clasped tightly. She didn't have to say anything more. She knew that God knew what she was pleading for.

The shadows grew deeper in the tiny home, and the air cooled as evening set in. She stoked the fire in the cooking stove in preparation to begin a meal. She heard the tires on the drive before she could see the truck. She had strained to hear that sound all day, and now that it was real, she questioned whether she was just imagining it. But the old red truck came over the ridge, and relief flooded her. She rushed down the steps as Ellis climbed out then flung her arms around his waist, pressing her face hard into his chest until she thought she might not be able to breathe.

Ellis did not react, his arms limp, his face carefully blank, which only made her cry harder as she clung to him, sobbing into his shirt. That was when he seemed to respond. She knew Ellis was a good man, and he probably couldn't help but comfort her. That was just the sort of person he was. He wrapped one arm around her shoulders and used his free hand to pet her hair, stroking it tenderly.

She finally fell silent, and they stood there in the yard, embracing for some time. Finally, she pulled away from him to look up into his face. He didn't seem the same somehow; there was something different about him.

"I didn't know if you was comin' back or not," she said.

He gave her a frail smile. "'Course I come back."

"Where was you?"

"Had business in town," he told her.

"I's just puttin' supper on."

"Sounds good. I'm awful tired," he said. "To the bone tired. I gotta unload this here bed. I figured on storin' it in the barn, and then I'll be up to the house."

She nodded and drifted back up the stairs and into the kitchen.

Clairey, who now had a purpose, began busying herself by frying potatoes. She smiled when he came in. "You good and hungry?"

"Yeah. Smells good." He went to the basin to wash, lingering over the task with careful deliberation, drying his hands before he sat down at the table. Clairey put a plate in front of him and loaded it with food. He waited for her to sit next to him and then bowed his head in prayer. "Dear, Lord," he began. "We thank you for the terbaccer, for the farm, and for all you've given us. We thank you for food to fill our bellies and a home to call our own. Amen."

"Amen."

He went about buttering his bread, cutting his meat.

"It ain't much," she apologized. "Couldn't seem to keep my mind on things."

"You ain't had no rest."

"I'm all right," she assured him.

Ellis studied her closely, quietly, with an intensity that made her nervous. "I got somethin' for you."

"For me?" She cocked her head, her eyes widening, and she felt her face grow hot.

"Yep. But you gotta share it with me."

"What is it?" She'd had few gifts in her life, so it was difficult for her to fathom what it might be.

Ellis stuck his hand in his pocket and pulled out a sock with something in the toe. Clairey looked at it, puzzled.

"Go ahead," he encouraged, pushing it toward her. "Open it."

She wavered, her hand slowly hovering above the sock, carefully taking hold. Then, she rolled the sock down until she found, kept in the deepest part, a roll of paper money in a rubber band. Clairey looked back up at Ellis with questions in her eyes. "Where'd you get this from?" she whispered. It almost frightened her to hold that money in her hand. In her whole life, she had handled maybe a penny or two, nothing like this wad of bills. She looked at Ellis with uncertainty, wondering how he had gotten the money, worried that his rash behavior had led to something that might have gotten him into some sort of trouble.

"I sold that there farm," he said, shoveling a large portion of potatoes into his mouth before he had to explain himself any further.

"Your daddy's place?"

"Yep."

"But…Ellis, you wanted to keep it. You tole me so," she protested.

"Weren't doin' us no good just sittin' there."

"But you said you's gonna keep it."

"Went up and offered it to Fergus Bayard. Thought it'd be good for him and Elvira to make a start of it there. But he wouldn't have it. He's worried 'bout leavin' his mama. Coy Struthers was wantin' it anyhow. I just offered it to Fergus as a favor. He don't want it, so's I tole Coy he could have it. Now that's only part of it," he said, pointing to the money. "He aims to pay the rest come harvest time."

"Why'd you sell, Ellis?" she questioned. "Why? You said your daddy wouldn't a-wanted it." After everything she had done to ensure that Ellis could keep the farm, he had sold it. She was confused, yes, but more than anything, her heart hurt. She wondered if nearly killing herself to get the tobacco in had meant anything to him.

Ellis grew just a bit defensive. "My daddy left me that land to do with as I please. I worried 'bout what he'd think of me if I sold. But then, he ain't here no more to tell me one way or the other. And I figured he'd want me to make somethin' of it. Since I can't work it my-self, that money's gonna hep us. And that's what he woulda wanted."

"You thought it through? That's really what you want?"

"Yes." He stopped eating and dropped his eyes, concentrating on his plate. He struggled to find words, pressing his clasped knuckles into his forehead. He didn't look at her when he said it. "That money there, it's for you to start out new some other place."

Her gaze narrowed, and she grew alarmed. "You're sendin' me away then?"

"I ain't sendin' you nowheres," he objected. He knew immediately that he had messed up, that he had somehow said the wrong thing. "I'm lettin' you go," he clarified.

"You don't want me round no more?" There was an agony in her voice that tugged at his heart.

"Ain't that neither." He was trying to collect his thoughts, to remember the words he had rehearsed in his head on his way home in the truck. "You never had no choice in it, and it ain't right. With that money, you could go wherever you pleased, and you could do with yourself whatever you pleased."

"What if I don't wanna leave?" she cried. "You turnin' me out? That it? You makin' me go? What if I don't wanna?"

"I ain't makin' you do nothin'. That's what I'm a-sayin' to you. You shoulda been allowed to say for yourself what you wanted, who you wanted to murry and such. I'm tryin' to make it right, is all." He hesitated. "I ain't fit to be your husband. I ain't fit to be nobody's husband."

"Why are you sayin' such things?"

"I said things 'bout your daddy afore I left. And I didn't have no right to. 'Least you got a daddy. 'Least you knowed who your daddy was. I don't got no family, don't got no mama nor a daddy. I ain't fit to be your husband. Ain't fit to be nobody's husband. Ain't even got a name to give you."

"Ellis—"

"You're a good woman, Claire. Truth is, you deserve somethin' better than this, and I can't give it to you. You ain't the same as you was when you first come here. Why, look at you. You learned to read, and look at all you done. Look at how you got that crop planted. Why, now, you can do anything. And you can do a whole lot better than this. You shoulda had better than this."

"You ain't makin' no sense," she said, confused by his behavior. "What happened to you in town?"

"I went to see Doctor Fielding." He paused. "I tole him all that you said 'bout him bein' there when I's born. He tole me…well, he done tole me 'bout my daddy."

"What?" she pressed. "What'd he say?"

"My daddy weren't my real daddy," Ellis said flatly.

"I don't understand."

"Doctor said my daddy had a wife that died all right, and a baby too. And he come to see the doctor, and I's there. I's just born, and my real mama, she done died in childbirth. Doctor says my mama, she weren't respectable, and they didn't know who my real daddy was. So when my daddy says he wants me 'stead of me goin' to the children's home, the doctor gave me to him."

"Jim Hooper weren't—"

"No," Ellis answered before she could finish. "Now you know it. And I'm lettin' you decide for yourself where you wanna go and what you wanna do with yourself, Claire."

Clairey set the roll of money on the table. "I don't want your money. I don't want nothin' from you. If you want me to leave, then you just say it. I'll leave if that's what you want. But I aim to stay, if it's all the same to you. I aim to stand by you."

"I don't got no daddy. That don't bother you?"

Clairey pursed her lips together. He had seen her make that face before, always when she was determined, when she was hunkering down for something that required all her strength. "Ellis, far as I can see, you got a daddy, and his name is Jim Hooper," she told him. "That man raised you and loved you. He gave you all he had and taught you all he knowed. That's what a daddy does. So you think on it awhile, and you gonna come to see what I'm sayin's true. Ain't no shame in what was done for you. He made a good man outta you and gave you life, and that ortta be what counts in it all. Truth is, flesh and blood don't make for a real daddy."

She pushed her chair out and walked away, out into the night to collect her laundry from the line. Ellis leaned his forehead against his fists again, wishing it had gone better, that he had said it right. He toyed with the roll of money and then shoved it back into the sock, angry that he had messed it up so badly.

He knew that she wouldn't leave, that she would stand by him no matter what. Clairey was not the kind to walk away. It was no good for her, married to the laughing stock of the county. But he would never make her see that. She was not capable of being disloyal. He doubted if she would ever leave him, even if it was the best thing for her.

The fine tobacco stretched out with drooping leaves, beautiful green foliage that raised itself to the sun, patient and obedient in its growth, and now it was ripe, ready for reaping. While Clairey put up bottles and bottles of canned tomatoes, green beans, corn, okra, pickles, and beets from the garden, apples from the trees, and jams from the wild berries, Ellis harvested the tobacco crop. Everywhere was the bounty of the fall. The crop had done well, and the garden had flourished, all thanks to hard work and favorable weather. And the two of them were contentedly busy gathering.

Clairey sometimes paused in her chore of bottling to take water to Ellis. She worried about him out in the sun, single-mindedly committed to bringing the tobacco in. She watched him from the edge of the field, limping along the rows as he cut the stalks of his tobacco plants, threading them on a tobacco spear, and then piling them on the flatbed wagon. Her heart ached for him. She knew that he was still in a good deal of pain, but he kept going. She knew he would always bear the scars. He would forever walk with that limp.

They worked together to thresh the hay field, leaving their bundles in rows as they went. Clairey hated the work; it was backbreaking, hard labor. But worse were the chiggers.

"Them chiggers done near ate me up," she complained as she scratched desperately at her legs.

"Let me see," Ellis said, kneeling down on his good leg next to the bed and lifting the hem of her nightgown up. Her legs were pocked with tiny red bumps. He whistled low. "They got you good, now, didn't they?"

"It itches somethin' awful."

"You ort not to wear a dress when you're workin' in the hay," he advised. "You wear some long stockin's and a pair of britches and they can't get at you this a-way."

"Well, it don't do me no good now," she lamented.

"Hold on now, and we'll get you fixed up good." Ellis got up and went into the other room. He came back directly with a rusted can of kerosene and an old rag. He shook the can over the rag and then brushed it onto her legs, his hands gentle as he worked. "This ortta take care of them things," he told her. "Just don't go standin' too close to the fire."

"Now that'd get rid of 'em for sure," she said with a laugh.

The next day, she came out to the field wearing a pair of his old overalls that were tied around the ankles with string.

A buyer came around to collect the tobacco and paid them a good price for it. With everything gathered in, they were ready for winter.

Clairey felt a pride in the products of their labor that was beyond any feelings of satisfaction that she had ever experienced before. Her bottled goods gleamed like jewels lined up neatly in the cupboard. Ellis had made a box shelf to hang up on the wall, her jars stacked two deep, twelve across. She felt that he, too, took pleasure in her hard work. He told her that he had never had the comfort of canned goods, always relying upon his hand-fashioned root cellar to provide him food in the coldest weather. He had dug the customary root cellar too, though, to ensure they would have plenty to get them through.

Just when the weather was growing cold in mid-November, and the skies were gray and overcast even at midday, they received a visit. Clairey couldn't help but notice how different the two of them were when they pulled up the drive and climbed out of the car. Fergus seemed anxious, troubled as he sat down at the table. Elvira was strained as well, her mouth drawn down at the corners, her beauty still evident but dulled. She held her baby in her arms in an almost careless manner and was quiet. When she did speak, she was cold and emotionless. The last year had changed her from a vibrant girl into a faded, disappointed woman.

They talked for a short while, and then Fergus found some excuse to lure Ellis out of the house, leaving Elvira and Clairey alone.

"You don't look well," Clairey observed.

"Neither'd you if you's up all night with this bawlin' thing," she complained.

"All babies is like that," Clairey consoled. "But look at how fine he is."

Elvira shrugged absently. Apparently she was not in the mood for pleasantries. "Don't hep none that he come early," she grumbled. "Doctor says his stomach is weak on account of it."

"Can I hold him?"

Elvira passed the little bundle gladly over, and he began to fuss. Clairey tried to soothe him by bouncing and walking.

"Thought Fergus's mama was bad, but this 'un here carries on more than she do, the little runt."

Clairey looked down on him with a quiet reverence. She momentarily forgot that Elvira was there, her attention trained completely upon the baby. "My mama tole me they's used to bein' bumped round in the womb, and you hold 'em just right, and shake 'em a little, and they think they be back in the womb again."

"If you know so much 'bout it, why you ain't got one of your own?" Elvira snapped.

Clairey figured Elvira had done what she intended; she had hurt her deeply. Elvira briefly wore a triumphant expression, but then in a flash seemed to crumble. She covered her face with her hands and cried.

"Why, Elvira, what's it that troubles you so?" Clairey asked, moving in behind her and patting her shoulder.

"I didn't want no boy," she sobbed. "I wanted me a girl. And he looks just like him, don't he? Just like him and named for him too, the ole dog."

"Why, he's a dandy, Elvira. Just look at him. He's just a fine little thing." Clairey meant what she said. She could see the resemblance between the baby and his daddy. Although his small potato spud nose was Elvira's, it seemed oddly out of place on the face of a mini Fergus, but he was so little and so helpless. How could Elvira not feel something stir in her heart after holding him, after touching his soft skin and seeing his little mouth pucker up in a precious pout before he let out a yell?

"He promised and promised, and still we's with her. And he lies to me, and she gets after me, and the other bawls after me. I can't stand it no more," she finished with a moan.

"Don't know why he'd tell you such a thing if he don't aim to," Clairey consoled. "Ellis says he tole him he's worried over his mama's health. She can't do without Fergus, is what he says. Maybe she won't be much longer in this world, and she'll leave you to peace soon enough."

"Oh, she'll never die. No, not that a-one. She aims to make me miserable for evermore," Elvira said with a fresh burst of tears. "That baby cries and cries. I done tried everything to hush him up. I put him to the tit and I rock him, and he just cries and cries." She wrung the skirt of her dress with her slender fingers, near hysterics, working herself into a fit. "And you know, she takes hold of him, and he quiets right on down. Don't make a peep for her. And she likes it 'cause she likes to make me look like a fool."

"It's only 'cause she knows how to handle a baby. She done gone through what you're goin' through, Elvira. She prob'ly just wants to give you relief, is all."

"No," Elvira insisted. "No. That ain't it at all. They got it out for me. They all tryin' to make me crazy; that's what they's doin'." Her tears stopped long enough for her to look Clairey in the eyes with a wild sort of stare. "I'm his mama!" she cried. "His mama! Why don't he want me? Why'd he want her over his own mama? And why's Fergus always pickin' her over his own wife?"

"Now, you ain't thinkin' right. You just need a night's sleep to see it all different," Clairey said.

"Won't change nothin'. Won't make it no different. It's all gonna be the same when I wake up."

"Look at this here babe, Elvira. He's a strong and healthy one. Think on that. Think on what you got 'stead of what you ain't." She was grasping at straws at that point because she was beginning to see that regardless of what she said, Elvira would not be comforted.

"You don't know what it's like," she moaned. "You got your own place, and Ellis…well, Ellis is a real man what can take care of his own and give you what you need." She gritted her teeth and shut her eyes tight. "Why'd he go and sell that there farm to Coy Struthers? Why'd he go and do that for?" She turned on Clairey with a malicious scowl. "It woulda suited me right nice, that farm. Woulda been just the thing. And he done give it to Coy Struthers."

Clairey was automatically defensive. "It weren't Ellis's fault."

"Sure it were. Why didn't he give it to Fergus?" Elvira wailed. "Coy Struthers don't need it."

"Ellis wanted Fergus to take it. He didn't want it. For shame you talkin' 'bout Ellis that a-way. What was he to a-done, made him take it offen his hands after Fergus done tole him no he don't want it?"

All at once, Elvira became quiet. She narrowed her eyes as she looked upon Clairey with incredulous rage. "Fergus, that skunk! I hate him! He ain't got no intent to put me in a place of my own. And his mama, why she aims to do me in. That's what she aims to do. She wants my baby just the same as she gots Fergus." She wiped the tears from her eyes in harsh, angry strokes, sniffing her nose and straightening herself up. "For all I care, she can have 'em both. They'll get no more of me!"

It hadn't dawned on Clairey that Elvira knew nothing of Ellis offering his land to Fergus, but she saw the change in Elvira immediately. She went to touch her shoulder again, to soothe her, but Elvira drew away, her jaw line hard and unyielding.

"Gimme," she said, wrenching the baby from Clairey's arms. "I s'pose you want my baby too 'cause you don't got one of your own." There was no ignoring the malice in her words. "You might got your own place, and you might got a man, but you ain't got no baby, now do you?"

Fergus Jr. began to whimper loudly, but Elvira didn't seem to notice.

"No, I ain't," Clairey murmured. She told herself that she should not feel stung by Elvira's hateful words. It was obvious Elvira wasn't in her right mind, that she was hurting. She needed someone to blame for her woes, if not Ellis than Clairey. "I's only tryin' to hep, is all."

Elvira ignored her, stalking to the door and going out into the night to sit in the car. Clairey could hear the baby crying even from inside.

When Fergus and Ellis came back to the house, Fergus looked over the room then asked, "Where'd Elvira get to?"

"She went on outside," Clairey said.

"Did she now?" It was almost like he was trying to let on as if that was nothing out of the ordinary, perfectly normal, a regular occurrence.

"What'd she do that for?" Ellis wondered.

"She's awful mad at me," Clairey admitted. "I sure am sorry for makin' her so mad."

"S'pose it's time we go on home anyhow." Fergus shrugged. "Gettin' late and Mama'll worry." It seemed somewhat pathetic that he was trying to play it off as if it were of no consequence that his wife had stomped out and was waiting in the automobile for him.

Fergus went to leave, but Clairey grabbed at his arm timidly. "Now, I don't wanna poke round in your business, I surely don't, but you ortta take her in to see Doctor Fielding. She ain't right, Fergus."

Fergus looked down at her hand then back to her face, a sheepish expression born in his eyes.

"Mama done tole me some women is like that after havin' a baby. She says Elvira'll come out of it direc'ly."

"Doctor Fielding—"

"My mama done had herself nine children. I s'pose she knowed a thing or two 'bout bearin' babies," he replied. His tone was quiet, sad.

"Well, yes, I s'pose she do," Clairey said, dropping her hand from his sleeve. She knew it was pointless to pursue it any further. He was not willing to listen.

"You-uns take care now," Fergus said in parting.

Ellis and Clairey watched from the porch as they pulled away. Clairey couldn't help but feel apprehensive. "There goes a miserable soul."

"Which one of 'em, Fergus or Elvira?"

"He wouldn't hear me. I was tryin' to tell him she needs hep, and he wouldn't listen."

Ellis sighed. "Well, now, Claire, they's some you can't do nothin' for. If they don't take the hep you offerin', there ain't nothin' you can do 'bout it. Fergus always was that a-way. Never could stand up to nobody. I seen him tonight, and he was that boy I used to know, the one that was always tortured and teased. Don't reckon he ever grew into a man. Hate to say it, but he's a coward. Lettin' everybody act on him 'stead of actin' for hisself. Lord, I hope he can teach that boy to be a man."

Chapter 24

Ellis scratched with his fountain pen, fervently working sums on a scrap of paper. Clairey watched him as she sat next to the fire, piecing a quilt square. It was the gentleman's bow tie pattern, the scraps of fabric stitched together to resemble a bow tie at a diagonal through the center of each square. Now and again, Ellis would slash through a number and start anew with his calculations. It amused her, how diligently he worked at it, how determined he was to find his answer.

"Whatcha workin' on there?" he asked, looking over at her.

"Well, now, I done finished that apron I's workin' on for the doctor's wife. And now I aim to start a quilt." She held up her square. "What d'you think?"

"Right nice."

"And what're you a-workin' on?"

"Sums," he answered.

"How's it comin'?"

"We done right well with what we got from the terbaccer and them cows, and 'course the farm monies."

She knew he felt a great sense of pride in the fact that they had money. Just five months before, they'd thought they were ruined, that they would lose everything. Now they had a small surplus, and she was sure he was very relieved and could breathe for the first time in a long time.

"Sure we did," she agreed.

"I's thinkin' on it," he went on. "If we's to double the head of them cattle come spring, we stand to make out better next year than we done this year, even."

"You'd have to put up more fencin' for more pasture."

"Yeah, I'd have to do that."

"I could hep you, and it'd take no time at all," she offered.

"Now, I knowed it was all 'cause of you that we done so well. I's thinkin' we ortta do somethin' for you, since you's the one who did a piece of the work," he said, not looking up as he continued to write out his figures. "This here money's rightfully yours too. So what d'you want, Mrs. Clairey Hooper?" he asked with a smile. "One of them fine treadle sewin' machines, or how's about a well right outside the door there so's you don't gotta haul it from the spring?"

"I don't need nothin'," she said modestly. She thought those things sounded quite nice, but they were things that she could do without. What she wanted she was afraid to ask for. She had been thinking, and the thing she had been thinking primarily of was something she dreaded to put into words. Yet it lingered on her lips, just waiting to be said, gliding under the surface like a fish—sleek and swift beneath the quiet of the water. It was the thing that she hadn't been able to dispel from her brain for the past few weeks as she'd lain with him in their bed.

"Well, now, I aim to do somethin' for you," he insisted, tossing his fountain pen onto the table and leaning back in his chair to stretch.

Clairey continued to sew, but her face grew troubled. "I don't know. Whatever you see fit to do with it is fine by me."

"None of them things strikes your fancy?" he probed.

"All sounds nice."

"Come on, now, why won't you tell me what you want?" he continued, turning to face her.

"Well, now, Ellis, I'd just as soon not say."

"Maybe you want some cloth to make yourself a dress, or a proper chair to sit in by the fire there," he went on. "One that has a cushion."

"I don't want none of them things."

"I'll keep at you till you tell," he informed her, teasing in his manner. "One way or the other, I'll get it from you."

She could feel him staring at her, but she would not meet his gaze. She finally had enough of his game and proceeded in her most quiet voice to tell him what she was afraid to say. "What if we was to put a room offen the back there," she said, motioning with her eyes to the far wall. Her manner was tentative, hesitant, as if it had taken a great deal for her to speak up.

Ellis's eyes enlarged. He opened his mouth as though he might say something then stopped short. He cleared his throat and tried again. "You wanna add on a room?" he repeated, to make sure he understood her correctly.

She shrugged, unable to understand why Ellis seemed so surprised by her request. "We could build offen the back there and put the porch onto that," she suggested.

"Whatcha need more room for?" he asked, his eyebrows drawn together. "Ain't it big enough for you?"

"It ain't that. I…" She hesitated.

"If it ain't that, then what?"

She could see by the expression on his face that he was working it all out in his head. And then his features registered displeasure or disappointment. She couldn't be sure which. She was immediately sorry she had said anything at all.

"You want your own space," he said, like he suddenly understood.

"No," Clairey insisted, shaking her head. "No. That ain't it at all. I ain't sayin' I don't wanna share your bed!" She gathered what little courage she had left before she continued on, her face in a deep blush. "I wanna make room for a baby," she said.

He didn't answer, so she chanced a glance up at him to measure his reaction. His jaw was slack, his eyebrows raised, seeming completely taken aback by what she had just disclosed to him.

"Your baby," she specified.

"What?" he questioned. His face drained of color, and he was speechless. "You sayin' what I think you're sayin'?"

Clairey swallowed hard, feeling her pulse in her temples. "Well, no. I ain't yet," she stammered. "But I been thinkin' on it," she admitted. "And it wouldn't hurt none to be ready for it, you know. Don't you think?"

"No?" Was he relieved or disappointed? One thing was for sure, he did not want to have that conversation. "No, not yet…" He was rubbing the back of his neck, a tell-tale sign. He ran his fingers through his thick dark hair several times and pursed his lips. He seemed to be looking for something to say.

She sought to fill the quiet by plowing on. "You don't think it's worth plannin' on?"

"Well, I don't know," he answered evasively, and his response was a little too vague for her liking.

"Don't you want a baby?"

"Ain't gave it much thought," he replied.

"Oh," she said simply. She grew quiet and didn't push it any further. It had taken all the nerve she had to even broach the subject, and he didn't seem to be responsive to the idea. Rather than look any more foolish than she already did, she decided to shut her mouth.

Ellis felt remorse when he saw her blank face, how carefully she tried to control her emotions. He had hurt her whether she would admit it or not. If he could have, he would have been anywhere but there having that conversation. It was no secret how a baby came to be, and as his daddy had once told him, it certainly wasn't from the cabbage patch. Although he and Clairey might have had a physical relationship, it wasn't something they'd ever really discussed so candidly before. When they made love, there were no words, just one of them reaching out for the other, finding solace in one another's arms. This was a dangerous conversation to be having in Ellis's estimation because it involved a great deal of responsibility on his part.

For a brief moment, he had thought she was telling him she was with child, and in that moment he felt a strange mixture of panic and thrill. Then the walls were closing in on him, and the air grew hot and stale in an instant. When she had said there was no baby, he experienced a moment of regret, of dashed hope. His moods were so wide and varied that he wondered if there wasn't something the matter with him. Clairey had obviously been let down by his uncertainty.

He could see the hurt in her eyes. In his guilty state, he looked for something to say to comfort her. "It's not like we ain't tryin'. If that's what's goin' to happen, then I s'pose it'll happen of its own accord."

She nodded her head in quick agreement. "You're right, of course," she said. "But…"

"But what?"

"Nothin'. Just Elvira."

"What about her?" Ellis asked.

"She tole me I might could be barren."

"I wouldn't listen to nothin' that gal says."

"What if I am?"

Ellis had no answer to that. She looked as if she might cry. The longer he looked at her, the more he was caving. He could not ignore his sympathy for her.

"Don't reckon addin' a room on there would be such a bad idea," he acknowledged. "Just to be ready, and all." He saw a small smile playing at the corner of her lips as she kept her hands busy with her sewing. "Could use it for extra storage till that time come anyway."

She came to him and put her arms around him. He marveled over how she knew how to touch him, how she knew how to make him feel things that he wasn't even aware he could feel. It wouldn't be such a bad thing, this making a baby. If she truly wanted it, then surely she should have it. And who was he to deny her?

The next week, true to his word, Ellis took Clairey into town to pick up supplies and equipment to build the room they had talked about and agreed upon. As she stood at the counter, paying for a spool of thread, she looked through the front window and spied Ellis outside. She saw his face and an expression that she had never seen him wear before. He had been a sad man since his talk with Doctor Fielding—not as quick to laugh or as willing to smile as he had once been—but his face was downright troubled at that moment. She craned her neck to get a better vantage point and saw he was conversing with two women, one older and one younger. It did not escape her attention that the younger's deep green eyes were carefully focused on Ellis. She was a beautiful woman with a slender face and silky blond hair, delicate in her features.

Clairey asked the woman behind the counter politely, trying not to seem overly curious, "Who's that girl?"

The woman looked up to see who Clairey was referring to. "Why, she was just in here a bit ago," the woman informed her. "Had a sad tale to tell. That there's Dulcie Mae Pond. Used to be a Prewitt, she did."

The air went out of her lungs. That name was one that she couldn't forget. Ellis had loved that girl long before Clairey had come along. "A sad tale?" she prodded.

The woman wrapped the spool of thread in a piece of brown paper with some twine. "Her man passed," the woman said, sliding the small bundle toward Clairey and taking her coin.

"What become of him?"

"They say he's bringin' in a load of hay on his wagon, and the wheel broke. Well, he went to change it, of course. And while he's about it, the jack come out from under the wagon, and the axel come right down on him and crushed him dead. Right there on the spot."

"That's awful," she murmured.

"They only been murried for four years, and no children come of it, so she come on back home to her mama."

Clairey was listening, but her eyes were riveted on Ellis and Dulcie Mae. What was he thinking right in that moment as he looked upon her? She couldn't begin to imagine. What were they saying to one another? Did he know? Had Dulcie Mae told him that she was a widow, that she was free? Was he wishing that he was free too?

"Thank you for the thread," Clairey said, shoving it in her pocket and hurrying outside. When she came out the door, she nearly collided with Ellis. Dulcie Mae and her mother were already crossing the street, but she saw the other woman turn and glance back over her shoulder. Clairey figured she was trying to get a peek at Ellis's wife; she was being summed up. She immediately felt self-conscious, trying to conjure the impression she had left on Dulcie Mae.

"All ready?" he asked.

"Yeah." She waited a moment before asking, "Who was that you was talkin' with?"

"Huh?" He appeared not to know who she was referring to.

But she knew that he had to know, and she wouldn't let it go. "Them women you was talkin' with."

"Uh, that was just a girl I knew from way back," he said with an absent-minded shrug. "Haven't seen her in a couple years now."

He guided her over to the truck and let her slide in across the seat. The ride home was mostly silent. She couldn't guess what he was thinking, but her thoughts were consumed with Dulcie Mae.

Clairey couldn't help but notice that Ellis spent the rest of the day avoiding her, working away from the house out in the pasture and barn. She told herself that perhaps it was merely her imagination, but then he hardly spoke at dinner time, and she knew with a surety that it was no coincidence. And so for the next two days, she lived with the knowledge that Dulcie Mae, Ellis's first and only true love, was free again, free to be pursued, free to be with him.

She could not sleep at night for thinking about it. Was that the reason he had been so reluctant to discuss having a baby? It was impossible for her to dispel the notion that maybe he wouldn't have opposed the idea if it had been green-eyed babies with fair skin that he had been given the option of having. Clairey knew well that it was one thing to occupy his bed, quite another to occupy his heart.

Ellis had never told her that he loved her, had never let on that he felt anything for her but comfortable companionship. All the while had he been pining away for Dulcie Mae, keeping his most inner being for only her? Why wouldn't he? Dulcie Mae was the kind of girl that any man would be lucky to have.

It dawned on Clairey that no matter how happy she tried to make Ellis, he would never really be happy with her. That stupid girl had let him go. She had missed her opportunity. But it didn't matter because she was still the girl he desired. How could he give his heart to someone else and share his life with Clairey? It simply would never work.

It was not only foolish to believe that she could change his heart but futile as well. Dulcie Mae had not been thrust on him, unwanted and undesirable. Clairey was nothing but a discarded, broken thing. She had nothing to offer but what she had already given, and it wasn't enough to keep him. *Let it be me*, she thought. *Let me be the one you want to hold, the one you want to keep.*

After grappling with her desire to be with Ellis and her longing to see him happy, she determined that she would have a frank conversation with him. Sooner rather than later would be best. She worked over in her mind how she would bring up the subject, imagining how he would respond. But, in truth, she really had no idea how it would play out.

It was over dinner, a silent one again, when she said in a quiet tone, "Ellis, I wanna say somethin'."

He paused with his spoon mid-air and looked at her expectantly. "What is it?"

"I aim to leave come warmer weather," she informed him. Just like that. It had come out so much easier than she had anticipated, so much more frank than the coy phrases she had imagined herself saying. This would be his test. Either he would protest or he would agree to it, and she would finally know one way or the other.

His mild surprise was evident in his face and the long pause while he tried to consider what his reply should be. "You ain't leavin'," he finally replied with a skeptical edge to his voice and dismissively finished taking his bite of food.

It stung worse than if he had slapped her full on the face. It was sheer indifference, hardly even a reaction from him. Her cheeks grew red with embarrassment. "I understand better'n you think," she said. "I'm nothin' but simple. Simple in my looks and manners, and I ain't smart neither. I know you coulda done a sight better'n this. And I can't live like this no more with the knowin'."

"Clairey," he began, but she scooted her chair back in a rush and breezed past him.

She wasn't interested in hearing his feeble attempts at appeasing her. When she saw him reach his hand out as if he might stop her, she didn't respond. It didn't even slow her down as she made a beeline for the door, waiting until she was outside before her breath came hard and fast, and tears stung her eyes. She had opened herself up to vulnerability, and she had been humiliated. She paced the length of the porch a few times, still struggling for air.

It was then that she realized that she would really have to leave. She could no longer stay there with him, haunting the place like a ghost, a shadow. It was just too painful to love a man, to want him, to see him day after day, sit down to dinner with him, work side by side, lay down next to him at night, and not be permitted to truly have him.

Gathering what little nerve she had left, she went back into the house. Ellis was on his feet. He gave her a curious look when she came through the door again. He opened his mouth as if to speak, but his voice failed him.

"You ain't gonna stop me," she informed him, not caring that she was crying in front of him. "You aim to try to 'cause I know you enough to know you wanna fix it. You wanna do the right thing. But you can't fix it, Ellis."

"Clairey…"

"Say what you will, but I done made up my mind."

"Ain't I been good to you?" he reasoned.

"You been more than fair. But this ain't the place for me," she told him. "I don't belong here."

"You belong here much as I do. You worked this place just the same as I done. You don't gotta do this, you know."

"Yeah, I do."

"That's what you want?" Ellis was calm.

She wondered how he could be, when she felt her stomach twisting in knots and her legs shaking, her control completely gone. "You're nothin' but kind to me, Ellis. More than I prob'ly deserved. But I don't s'pose it's fair to neither of us a-livin' this a-way."

"What's changed? Why you wanna go now? I's only tryin' to do right by you, you know."

"I know it. And you been real good to me, you have. But I can't go on this a-way. And I'd leave now, if it wasn't for the winter."

"I don't want you to go," Ellis said.

"You don't gotta feel bad over it, Ellis. You done what you could for me. And it's a sight more than most woulda done. But I don't wanna be here no more. And you was the one that tole me I could do what I wanted, didn't you?"

He faltered with an answer then simply said, "Yeah."

"Well, I wanna go," she told him. "It's what I want." Before he could argue any further, she left through the door again, out into the frigid night.

Ellis felt numb. Part of him wanted to follow after her, to coax her back in where it was warm, where she belonged. But then he thought how unfair it would be to her. If she really did want to go, then who was he to stop her? He remembered his solitary life before she had come along, and he dreaded the thought of returning to it. He'd come to depend upon her, to crave her company, to yearn for her tenderness. To him, she was a soft place to fall. And all of those reasons for wanting her to stay—they were all selfish. Completely and totally selfish. All about him and what he wanted, what he needed. And so he didn't follow after her; he didn't try to stop her.

Chapter 25

A fine powder covered the ground in just the faintest sprinkling of snow. It was too cold to do much of anything. Cold outside, cold inside. At times, cold to the marrow of one's bones. The fire was kept going round the clock. Ellis and Clairey chopped wood at a steady pace to keep up fuel for it. Despite the fire, the chill seemed to creep in through every crack and gap the walls, doors, and windows had to offer.

During the night, they huddled under great piles of quilts to keep warm. In the morning, Clairey's nose and ears felt like ice. There were few moments when she wasn't frozen through. It made the task of cooking seem like a blessing. Not only did it give her something to do and keep her mind off of weightier matters, but it also kept her warm, working over the black stove or next to the hearth. That was what kept both of them going — working on a task and avoiding one another.

On a day much like all the others, the doctor broke the monotony of their existence. Trapper barked loudly, and it echoed over the skeletal trees, calling Clairey from the kitchen and Ellis from the barn. They heard the automobile before they saw it coming up the lonely drive.

Doctor Fielding gave a wave as he pulled up. He bent down to retrieve a pan from the floorboard before he came up the steps to the front door.

"How do, Doctor," Clairey greeted.

"Fine, thank you."

Ellis followed him up to the house, his shoulders rounded and his eyes down. He hadn't seen the doctor since his visit months before when he had finally found out the truth of his origins.

Doctor Fielding saw him and nodded a hello. "Ellis," he said.

"Doctor Fielding," Ellis answered with his own quick nod. "What brung you out this a-way?"

"Oh, had someone to tend to, and when Mrs. Fielding got wind that I'd be this close to you all, she made me promise to drop by some of her famous date pudding."

Clairey opened the door to him and ushered him in. "What is it?"

"Date pudding. Dates. They're a fruit. Well, you don't see them in these parts. Every Christmas, I have to send for them special so that she can make her pudding. It was her mother's recipe. A tradition. And, well, it isn't too bad, really, if you like sweets." He held the dish out as an offering to Clairey.

"It's awful good of you," she said as she accepted the pan from him.

"Take a chair there next to the fire," Ellis suggested.

Doctor Fielding smiled. "Don't mind if I do. Gets awful cold driving in this."

"Them roads is dangerous in winter," Ellis added. "Surprised to see you out."

"Duty calls. Doctoring isn't for the faint of heart." He chuckled.

"How's the missus?" Clairey asked.

"Mrs. Fielding is well. She sends her regards. She was anxious that I see how the two of you were getting along." He tugged his gloves off and rubbed his hands together then drew his chair closer to the fire. "I'll be glad to report you both look fine."

"Managin' anyhow," Ellis confirmed.

"Yes, well, that's the best any of us can do. But, now, you're getting around all right, aren't you?" His question was more of an observation than an inquiry.

"The leg's comin' 'long."

"It troubles him some in this here cold weather," Clairey divulged. She knew Ellis was far too modest to tell the truth. "'Specially in the mornin'."

"Give it a good rubdown before you go on about your day, and it should be a little easier for you."

"If I knowed you was a-comin', I woulda made somethin' special for you for supper," Clairey told the doctor.

"Well, it's hard to know from one day to the next where I'll be or what I'll be doing. Just this morning, I didn't have any notion that the Gunney family would have need of me until I got the summons, you see."

Clairey had no idea who the Gunneys were, but Ellis seemed to know them. "The Gunneys? They all right then?"

"Nothing too serious. The children have all come down with the pox. The youngest was having some complications with it. He should pull through, though."

"Glad to hear it ain't nothin' too bad," Ellis said.

"Mrs. Gunney, she had the poor mite sitting out in the yard so that the chickens could fly over him to try and cure him. The poor child ended up with the pox *and* the croup."

"Don't hep none that them birds don't fly," Ellis observed with an edge of humor.

"No, I suppose it didn't." Doctor Fielding sniggered.

"What news from town?" Clairey asked.

"There's not much to report. Now I'm up on all the church gossip, thanks to Mrs. Fielding, but I don't count that as news."

"I...I know it ain't none of my business," Clairey began.

"What is it?"

"Now, we got a visit prob'ly four or five weeks ago or so from Fergus and Elvira, and ever since, I worried over 'em. I tole Fergus he ortta visit with you over it, 'cause I thought you might could hep 'em out, you know."

"It's been a month, you say?"

"Weren't it, Ellis?" she asked.

"Nigh on that long," Ellis affirmed. "Ferg, he didn't say much, but he didn't gotta for me to see somethin' was up."

"You hadn't heard then?" Doctor Fielding said. He looked from Ellis to Clairey questioningly. "I'm afraid she left...Fergus and the baby. Left them both and went on back home."

Clairey pursed her lips and shook her head, doing her best not to become emotional. "I knowed she weren't right. I done tole Fergus she needed hep."

"When was it? When she take off?" Ellis asked.

"Just close to that. It was four or more weeks ago."

"Well, I'll be," Ellis said.

"Ain't there nothin' nobody can do for her?" Clairey pressed. "Somebody ortta go and reason with her."

"Fergus went over to her daddy's place, trying his best to get her to come back with him, but she wouldn't even consider it. Elvira said there wasn't a place for her there. She said it didn't look as though Fergus was willing to leave his mother and get them their own place. She told him his mother wanted the both of them. So she could have them."

"She don't even want her baby? Her own flesh and blood? She don't even want *him?*" Clairey could not imagine it. She thought of how her arms had ached when Elvira had taken him from her that night. How empty she felt when she allowed herself to think on how Ellis had reacted to her suggesting they have a child of their own. How could a woman do such a thing? How could a woman walk away from her own child like that?

Ellis didn't have to be told what she was thinking. He knew. It was no coincidence that Clairey had turned to talk of babies after Fergus and Elvira's visit. He had sensed an immediate transformation in her after they had left that day. It didn't seem at all fair. Clairey was a woman who would make a good mother. She should have the one thing she wanted, the only thing she had ever asked for.

"Unfortunately, motherhood doesn't always come naturally to every woman," the doctor commented.

"But her own child," Clairey muttered.

"Yes, well, it's a shame; I won't argue that. Some people stick, and some people run."

"How's Fergus?" Ellis inquired.

"He's taken it hard, I suppose. Don't know anyone that wouldn't."

"I ortta go visit with him."

"That would be a nice gesture." The doctor slipped his gloves back on his hands. "I shouldn't linger," he said. "Tempting to sit next to this fire and not move, but I need to be getting back. You never know when someone else will call needing help."

"I got somethin' for you to take back to Mrs. Fielding," Clairey informed him. "It ain't much, but I done made her somethin'."

"How thoughtful."

"I got some fresh eggs for you too." She plucked a crock bowl from one of the shelves in the cupboard. "I'll hurry on out and collect 'em afore you leave."

"I can get 'em for you," Ellis offered.

"Would you go on into the other room there and get that apron I been workin' on?" she asked. "It's in my sewin' basket." She slipped through the door to get some fresh eggs.

Ellis went into the bedroom, rummaging through the chifferobe in search of Clairey's sewing basket. He found it right away — the apron she had made neatly folded with the quilt squares she had been working on. He took it out and was ready to close the door when he noticed something. Nestled next to her sewing things was a cigar box that he had never seen before. Out of curiosity, he lifted the lid and peeked in.

It housed an odd assortment of things: a variety of pressed wild flowers; a robin's egg, pale blue and speckled; an arrowhead; and a scrap of paper torn from a catalog with a picture of a woman wearing a cloche hat. But the thing that caught his eye was the handkerchief folded carefully and tucked thoughtfully among the simple treasures. It was nothing special — a dingy white square with no frills to it — but he recognized it right away. On a snowy day, he had offered it to a girl who had been caught in a terrible storm.

He heard Clairey in the other room, returning from her errand. "Did you find it, Ellis?" she called.

He brought the apron back and handed it to her. "This it?"

"Yeah, that's it. Be sure and tell Mrs. Fielding we said thank you for the puddin'," Clairey told Doctor Fielding. "And give her this for me."

"Will do," he promised. "I'm sure she'll like it very much."

Ellis followed the doctor out onto the porch to say goodbye.

The older man paused before he headed down the steps. "How are you holding up, Ellis?" he asked reluctantly.

Ellis shrugged. "Leg's tolerable."

The doctor couldn't help but smile. "You're more like him than you will ever know," he said off-handedly.

"Who?" Ellis asked.

"Your father," he replied.

Ellis shook his head slowly as his gaze dropped to the ground.

"You think anyone would have done what you did for that girl in there? You learned it from him. You saved her, just like he saved you. Think on it and see if I'm not right," he challenged, and then he walked down the steps to his car and went on his way.

The next morning, Ellis left. Equipped with a pail of milk and a bowl of brown and white eggs, he went after his morning chores were completed.

"I'll stop and see Fergus, and then I'll check in on Aunt Sissy on the way home. Won't be home till late," he advised Clairey. "No need to wait up."

As promised, Ellis was still gone when it grew dark. She hadn't expected him to be back until late, but she had hoped that he would surprise her. The day wore from early evening into night. Clairey felt a loneliness that she had never experienced before. Her mind wandered from her current state to her soon-to-be future state, and she felt a deep sadness that Ellis had not asked her to stay. She remembered the day that she had told him she was leaving, and she regretted those hasty words. Where would she go? What would she do with herself?

The doubts washed over her, and she had to compel herself to be calm. The only thing she felt certain of was that she would not go back to her father's house. Not that he would have her. And in a moment of deep sorrow, she wondered how the world could go on with her life in shambles such as it was. She had let down her guard long enough to fall in love with a man. She had dared to believe that she might have a future with him, and she had lost at the venture. What had made her think she would be any different than the scores of others who had been hurt by the same game? She *was* no different. She was perfectly common, just as they were. Maybe if she had been special, if she had been exceptional, maybe he would have loved her then. Clairey supposed there was no point in wondering over it; the fact remained that life would never be the same for her. Mulling over how it could have been would not get her to where she wanted to be.

Clairey was startled out of her contemplative mood by the faint sounds of the chickens cackling and squawking from their hen's house. She knew immediately it must be the fox. Spurred by their urgent calls, Clairey grabbed Ellis's rifle and flew through the door, barefoot and heart pounding. It took a moment for her eyes to adjust to the darkness, but she instinctively ran across the porch and down the stairs. The light from the cabin window was spilling over the yard with an eerie glow, barely enough light to illuminate her path. Just before she made it to the hen house, she saw it, stealthily squeezing out of the hole it had dug under the fence. She could see, too, that it had gotten a prize—a chicken whose free wing flapped frantically as it struggled to escape the jaws of its predator.

Clairey stopped where she was, pulled the butt of the rifle to her shoulder with a quick, decisive motion, and took precise aim. There was no hesitation as she squeezed the trigger. The sound of the shot spread and echoed as the bullet went true to its mark. The fox dropped the chicken and scrambled to escape, injured but still capable of running. Clairey aimed again, this time killing the fox dead. She waited, making sure that the fox did not get up. When it lay still, she walked over to it, peering at its corpse with a morbid curiosity. She watched the fox to see if it would move, if it was just playing dead and would try to get up and run again. It remained still, its mouth slightly agape, its teeth pink with the chicken's blood.

The chicken continued to flail with its good wing, clucking in desperation on the ground nearby as its life began to slip away, its white feathers blemished red with its own blood. It was immediately clear to her that the chicken was in a bad way.

"My best egg layer," she said in despair, bending to pick it up. "Shh," Clairey soothed, holding it gently in her hands. The chicken would not be consoled. It continued to struggle in her arms.

There was no help for it, she knew. Her chicken was dying. In an act of mercy, Clairey gathered her resolve, took the chicken in a firm grip, and wrenched its neck. The bird grew still, hanging limp from her hands. Her best egg layer would be dinner tomorrow, their full bellies a reminder of the cruelties of life. Would she serve it with potatoes or bottled beans? Perhaps cook it slow as it dangled from twine spinning on a hook over the open fire, or in a roasting pan in the oven?

Ellis returned to find Clairey furiously plucking the feathers from a dead chicken. "Killed that fox," she said, not looking up from her task.

He watched her at a careful distance, propped against the porch railing with his arms crossed tight against his chest. The tension between them for the past few weeks had kept them from saying much to each other, but for some reason, tonight was different. It was as it had been before; they were familiar and at ease with one another. Looking at her now, he realized how much he wanted her. He hadn't had her in some time, so many long, long days. What he wouldn't do to embrace her now.

"You got him, and he got the chicken?" He chuckled, trying to push the thought from his mind.

"My best egg layer."

"Sorry 'bout that," he consoled.

"Sure hope your day was a sight better," she said, resting her elbow on her leg and wiping her brow with her other arm. The chicken dangled fleshy peach and naked between her spread legs.

"Not much. I'm feelin' a lot like that there chicken," he said with a grin.

"You talk to Fergus?"

"Nope." He rubbed his chin thoughtfully. "His mama tole me he don't want nobody comin' round. She sent me off with my tail 'tween my legs."

"Well, now, you tried, Ellis," she told him, cocking her head and looking up at him.

"S'pose so." He was disappointed, even troubled by his failure.

"How's Aunt Sissy?"

"Spent most of the day with her. Did some work round her place. Ate supper with her. She wanted to know where you was."

"Don't know that I believe that," she said wryly.

"I wouldn't lie to you," he assured her when she gave him an all-knowing look.

"Gonna just have to trust you then." She held the chicken up. "So, how you want your chicken for supper tomarra? Roasted, baked, or fried?"

"Don't matter none to me. I always did like what'er you cooked up."

There was a lull in the conversation. He had something that he wanted to say but did not know how. Finally, he just spoke up. "I got you somethin' on my way through town."

She stopped what she was doing to look at him, her eyes cautious. "You did?"

Ellis went back to the truck to get a brown paper bag that was rolled shut. He held it out to her. "It ain't much," he apologized.

She wiped her free hand on her apron. "I need to go wash up afore I touch it."

"Well, go on then," he said.

She took the chicken into the house, and he followed after her with the mysterious paper bag. She went to the washstand and scrubbed her hands and then took the bag and peeked in. She looked from him to the contents of the bag and back again. He wasn't sure if she was pleased or unhappy. She was too hard to read.

"Time you had a dress of your own," he said.

Clairey put her hand in the bag and drew out an ivory dress with small blue polka dots and short sleeves with wide cuffs. It buttoned down the front of the bodice with a simple cut. She held it out in front of her and let the skirt fall down so that she might inspect it. A little gasp escaped her lips.

"It ain't much, nothin' more than a house dress. But it belongs to you."

"It's beautiful," she whispered, clutching it to her.

"A lady deserves to have a dress all her own." Ellis became confused when she frowned and grew troubled.

"You shouldn't a-done it."

"Why not?"

She didn't answer.

"Look, it's yours to do with as you will. No strings attached."

"I ain't got no way of payin' you back for it."

"You don't owe me nothin'." Why did it make him so angry that she even considered paying him back? Couldn't he do something nice for her?

"I owe you everythin', Ellis. I know it. I know what you done for me."

"I changed my mind," he said.

"What?"

"I changed my mind. You have somethin' I want. I wanna trade. You give me what I want, and you can have that dress free and clear. Never have to think about owin' nothin' to me again."

She eyed him warily. "I done tole you, I ain't got nothin' to give," she said firmly.

Ellis stalked into the bedroom and returned shortly with the faded cotton dress she had been wearing when he'd met her. It was now no more than a rag. He held it up and said, "I'll switch this 'un for that 'un."

Clairey looked at him as if he were crazy. "That ain't a fair trade."

"Don't care. You say I can have it, and I'll give you the other free and clear." He waited for her to answer.

Finally, she shrugged and nodded her head.

Ellis went over to the fireplace and cast the old dress into the fire, watching the flames consume it before he stormed out of the house without looking back.

In the aftermath of that night, they were reduced to polite conversation and coexisting once again. The many months of intimacy erased, they tolerated their circumstances.

Chapter 26

It would be morning in just a few short hours; it wasn't easily discernible. The sun was far from showing itself in the dead of winter, when dawn came dark, cold, and uninviting. Ellis was awakened during the night by an urgent pounding upon the door. He jerked violently as his hand reached out instinctively for his rifle. Clairey sat up, disoriented and groggy, scrambling for the quilts that had fallen away.

"What is it?" she whispered.

"Don't know." He slipped out of bed, rummaging in the dark for his trousers, and pulled them on, jumping up and down to wiggle into them. Clairey was just behind him as he went to the door, their bare feet padding on frigid floorboards. Ellis pushed her behind him protectively as he clutched his rifle in front of him. When he opened the door, he was surprised to see Clifton Davies at the threshold. It had been some time since he had seen him. Not for nearly two years, after that night at the barn dance.

The confusion must have registered on his face because he saw Clifton smile faintly in amusement. "Ain't you up yet?" he joked.

Clairey peeked around Ellis's shoulder to see who their midnight visitor was. Ellis realized that she had never met Clifton before. Clifton was apparently not worried over formalities. He was studying her in a candidly frank inspection, eyeing her in open curiosity. Ellis sensed Clairey's embarrassment as she fell back behind him again.

"You ain't gone done and did it." Clifton chuckled. "You gone off and got murried."

Ellis was thrown. He couldn't figure what this was all about. "What the devil you comin' round in the night for?" he growled, his normal good humor gone.

"It's awful cold out here. You gonna have me in?"

Ellis thought it over and then he stepped aside and let Clifton in, more for curiosity's sake than because he felt sorry for him.

He stoked the fire, putting some fresh logs on, and the three of them huddled next to it, eager for warmth. Clifton took his time, in no hurry to tell them what he was up to, which was just like him. Ellis was watching him expectantly, eager to discover what his purpose was.

"Can't tell me you come up here for to see my new bride, what's been murried to me for well over a year now," Ellis finally said.

"Nope," Clifton agreed. "But looks like you done real fine for yourself." He let his eyes roam over Clairey again.

His unabashed bad manners and obvious lack of respect made Ellis angry. He didn't care for the way Clifton was looking at his wife one bit. In fact, it triggered a jealousy Ellis wasn't aware he even possessed. "Claire, you ortta go on back to bed. Ain't no use in you losin' sleep on account of Clifton here."

"Let me just get dressed, and I'll put some Pero on for you," she offered. "It ortta warm you some." She drifted off to the bedroom, pulling the curtain shut that separated the two rooms.

When she came out again, she went to work filling the kettle. She had to break the icy crust over the top of the water in the bucket before she could access the unfrozen portion. She put the kettle directly over the fire to heat and moved around the room, collecting mugs, pulling out the Pero, sitting them on the table. Clairey went and stood faithfully behind Ellis, resting her hand on his shoulder with all the natural ease of two people who knew each other well and were comfortable with one another.

Ellis forgot for a moment that he was waiting to hear why Clifton had come. He was instead thinking how nice it was when Clairey let her guard down and momentarily failed to remember that she wanted no part of him. How pleasant it was that she occasionally reverted back to the camaraderie they experienced before she had decided to leave him.

Ellis cleared his throat and turned his attention back to Clifton. "What's this all about? You ain't come before. Now it's winter, and I don't see you gettin' the gumption to risk life and limb to see my woman," Ellis reasoned.

"Don't get all bent outta shape with me. Ain't my idea of a good time, runnin' round freezin' my rear off in the middle of the night."

"Whose idea were it then?"

"I come to get you for that ole gal Myrna Bayard. It was she that sent me."

Ellis was annoyed. First off, Clifton had come into his home, disrespecting his wife, and now he was beating around the bush, prolonging the delivery of his news, making them suffer for as long as he possibly could by keeping it from them.

"What's Myrna Bayard gotta do with anythin'?"

"She got the whole of the county up and out lookin' for that fool of a boy a-hers."

"Ferg?"

"Yeah, Ferg. He done took off, and she's worried over him. Done got everybody out lookin' for him."

"He took off?"

"Yessir. She says he's all broke up on 'count of that there woman leavin' him, and he took his youngin and runned off. Now she afeared he'll do somethin' desperate, and she got everybody out a-searchin' for him."

"Fergus took off with the baby?"

"Yessir." Clifton nodded emphatically. "Just as I tole you."

"Dear, Lord, what's he up to?" Clairey murmured.

Ellis turned to look at her and saw the fear in her eyes. "Now, prob'ly it's nothin'," he soothed. "Let me just get dressed, and I'll come on 'long with you to look for him."

He went into the bedroom and took out his warmest flannel shirt then pulled on several pairs of socks before he eased his feet into his boots, lacing them up and tying them in a double knot. He came back through to the main room and shrugged into his coat, wrapping his scarf around his throat. Securing his cap on his head, he pulled the flaps down over his ears and tugged his woolen mittens over his hands.

"Ellis," Clairey said.

He paused in his preparations and gave her his attention.

"Ellis, please don't go on out there."

"I gotta," was his simple reply.

"Ellis, please don't go on out there."

He continued to get himself ready.

"Likely he just gonna show up in the mornin'. He just needin' some time on his own, you know. And then you done gone for nothin'."

"She prob'ly right," Clifton said with irritation. "Fool prob'ly warm in some bed somewheres while we out lookin' for him."

"I'm a-goin' just the same," Ellis insisted.

"Why don't you wait for some Pero?" Clairey enticed. "Get somethin' hot in you afore you go on out?"

"Keep the kettle on, and I'll be home direc'ly." Ellis grabbed his rifle and waited at the door. "You comin'?" he asked Clifton.

Clifton hesitated. "Yeah, I'm a-comin'." He got up and stomped through the door like a pouting child.

Ellis went to follow him, but Clairey stopped him with a hand on his arm. She looked as if she might cry. "Please," she begged. "Please, Ellis. Please take care."

He looked at her for a long moment, thinking he might say something to reassure her, but then he couldn't think of a thing to say, so he nodded his head as if to say, *I will.* He left her there at the door, watching as he went.

"Think I'll head back toward town," Clifton said, as he and Ellis stood with their backs to the wind. "Likely where he'd be, wouldn't you say?"

"Don't know. Don't know where he'd a-gone on a night like this."

"Well, if you wanna head toward town with me, you're welcome to."

"I'm gonna head out yonder to the ole place. Maybe he gone to see after Elvira."

"We part here 'en," Clifton said, shaking Ellis's hand. "Don't get yourself into no trouble, hear? Not on account of that slow wit Fergus." Clifton climbed into his car and drove away.

Ellis headed down the drive in his old Red Baby pick-up, the headlights shining eerily on the naked branches of trees as the trail twisted and turned, until he hit the main road. He knew the way with his eyes closed. His childhood home was like a beacon, like a lighthouse to a wandering sailor. It wasn't far, but the entire twenty-some minutes, he kept his mind carefully blank. He didn't want to think, didn't want to speculate what Fergus might be doing right then.

It was nearly dawn when he came to Purvis Little's house, quiet and dark. So dark he fumbled on the stairs. He knew when he saw the place that Fergus was not there, but he went and knocked on the door anyhow.

It took some time before Purvis answered the door. He looked considerably older than he had since the last time Ellis had seen him. Ellis understood that his circumstances had changed drastically, and that he had good reason to seem older. He had a daughter that was the talk of the county, a girl so cold-hearted she had abandoned her own child.

"Ellis Hooper?" He was confused, disoriented, and Ellis thought about how, just a short while ago, Clifton had awoken him from a deep sleep too.

"Mr. Little. Sorry to wake you, truly am."

"Well, what is it, boy?" he asked, with a deep frown creasing his brow. The circumstances of their meeting must have put him in a bad mood. After all, who would want to be woken from a deep sleep on a winter's morning such as that one?

"I'm lookin' for Fergus. You ain't seen him, have you?"

"Fergus? What'd he be doin' here?"

"I's thinkin' maybe he done come for Elvira. Did he come for her?"

"No. And if he had, I'd a-sent him away, just like I done before and just like I'm a-gonna do with you too, boy." He went to shut the door, but Ellis wedged his boot in the door frame and wouldn't let him.

"Now, I don't mean to be a bother, I sure don't, Mr. Little, but we got some trouble."

Purvis grunted and gave Ellis a withering stare. "Your trouble ain't mine, boy. Now move your foot afore I take it off. You hear?"

"Fergus, he done took off with the baby, and nobody knows where he got to. His mama's worried sick, and they got men out and about all over a-lookin' for him."

"Elvira!" Purvis bellowed. "Elvira, get on out here!"

Elvira materialized within minutes, hugging a quilt that was wrapped around her body. She saw Ellis, and her eyes narrowed, her pretty full lips that were prone to a natural pout becoming more pronounced. "Yes, Daddy?"

"One way or the other, I aim to get some shut-eye, you hear? So you go on and take care of this, 'cause I had 'bout all I can stand of it." He disappeared back into the bedroom, leaving Elvira and Ellis alone.

Ellis could see small heads peeking out from behind her, hidden but aware and listening to everything that was going on. It made him significantly more nervous. He stuck his hands in his pockets and discovered something balled up in one of them. He pulled it out to see what it was. The white was bright in the dimness of the doorway. It was the felt gloves that he had bought for Clairey but had never given to her. Clairey. She was at home waiting for him right then. But for how much longer? How much longer before he would return to an empty home?

"Whatcha want with me?" she said, breaking into his thoughts.

"You heard from Ferg?"

"I sent him off. I ain't talked with him since. And I tole him I wouldn't. Why don't he leave me be?"

"He ain't come up here last night?"

"No. I tole you no. Why you keep on it?" She glared at Ellis with open contempt.

"Leave off on givin' me the stink eye, girl. I'd put you over my knee and give you a whoopin', only you ain't fit for even that."

"You're lettin' the cold in, Ellis Hooper. So you tell me or you don't. I don't care one way or the other, but I ain't standin' here waitin' for you to decide."

"He took off last night. He done took off with the baby, and his mama's got a whole bunch out a-lookin' for him. Now what you got to say?" Ellis snarled.

"Where'd he go?"

"Don't know. But she's worried of the state he's in."

"He ain't come here. Check with them sisters of his."

Ellis rolled his eyes. "You really think he's gonna go to his sister's place? Now think on it and tell me someplace he's likely to be."

"I done tole you, I don't know. I'm free of him. Understand? I got nothin' to do with him no more. Now go on and get, 'cause I ain't got no more time for you." She slammed the door in his face.

Before he got back into his truck, he stood there for a time, waiting. He wondered what he should do next or where he should go. Where would Fergus go? Where? But Ellis already knew. He would go there. That's where Fergus would have gone.

The sky had turned a deep shade of gray, just light enough that Ellis could make out shapes. He could make out the barn and the fences on Purvis Little's property. It seemed unearthly quiet to him. He wondered if he was going to get himself shot as he moved slowly away from the truck and began an investigation of the area.

First, he went through the barn, the smell of musty hay and cow dung assaulting his nose when he opened the door. Cows were dozing, standing in their stalls, unaware of their visitor. It was considerably warmer in the barn, with all the animals giving off heat within the cramped confines of the walls. It was tempting to think about staying there, letting the heat circulate over him.

Finding nothing amiss, he went back out, walking around the perimeter of the yard. Again, there was nothing out of the ordinary. Surely something would have caught his eye. Hesitantly, he decided before he got into any more trouble, he should leave. Fergus must not have gone there after all.

Maybe Elvira was right. Maybe he had gone to visit one of his sisters. Maybe he, too, had had enough of his meddling mother and had decided to seek asylum somewhere else. But the nagging feeling that had plagued him from the time Clifton had woken him would not leave him in peace. He started down the drive in his truck, working his way back from where he had come.

That's when he saw it, sitting in a lonely patch of trees, just off to the side of the drive about halfway down to the road, positioned haphazardly facing toward him. He supposed he must have missed it because it had been so dark when he had come up. The car that had been given to Fergus by Purvis Little was parked there, silent and still as the grave.

Ellis parked his truck right there in the middle of the gravel drive and got out. How strangely peaceful the scene was, how utterly quiet, as if no one else existed, no life apart from him. It must have snowed sometime after Fergus had parked there, for the tire tracks that should have been evident were filled in, and the car sat in a vast sea of flawless white.

As he approached, leaving a trail of footprints behind, he could make out the figure of Fergus sitting in the driver's side, but it was as if through a fog. The windows were frosted over just slightly, just enough that Ellis couldn't see clearly.

"Ferg!" he called out.

There was no movement from inside. He came up to the passenger side and raked the frost away with his mittened hand, peering in through the strip he had cleared. The baby lay on the seat, bundled in an old quilt, his little head just barely visible, while Fergus sat up in the driver's side, leaning back against the seat, sleeping.

Ellis rapped on the window. "Fergus!" he called again.

Fergus did not stir a bit.

Ellis went around the front of the car to open the door. Lucky if they hadn't frozen to death in this cold, he thought to himself, somewhat irritated by Fergus's dramatics. That's when he saw it—a rubber hose that was attached to the exhaust pipe snaked through the back window. A heavy sense of dread crept over Ellis, his heart pounding brutally within the cavity of his chest. "Ah no," he mumbled. "No, Fergus. No."

He grabbed ahold of the latch and ripped the door wide open, struck by the smell of exhaust smoke as it drained out of the battered old car.

"Fergus!" he yelled. "No, Fergus!"

Fergus was slumped there, just as if he had dozed off. Just as if he would open his eyes any moment and ask Ellis what all the fuss was over. The only thing that was amiss with the picture was Fergus's dull blue face, lesions beginning to form on his skin.

Ellis clutched the front of Fergus's coat in his fists and hauled him out of the car, dragging him out and laying him on the frozen ground. His limbs and joints were already stiffening, rigor mortis settling in. He rested there as if he were still sitting in his seat, his legs bent, his head slightly reclined.

Ellis turned back to the car, to the baby bundled there, but he couldn't bring himself to touch the little fellow, to check him. He knew. He already knew that the baby would be no different. The poor thing had probably gone before his father had.

Ellis's legs gave way, and he fell to his knees, quaking, a shudder running through him as he gagged and heaved next to the back tire. He hunched there with his back against the car for support, keeping his eyes away from Fergus's lifeless form.

Fergus was dead. And his little son named for him too. He had taken his own life. How hopeless and filled with despair he must have been. Ellis pictured him driving to Purvis's farm with the knowledge of what he would do. How he'd parked the car, hooked the tube to the exhaust pipe. And then how he had let the car run as he breathed in the deadly fumes. There he'd sat until he fell asleep, never to wake again. The car must have idled there until it had run out of gasoline.

How could he do such a thing? Ellis thought of his baby, and it made him angry. It made him so terribly angry that Fergus would have taken the life of his child. He simply couldn't fathom it. What had he been thinking?

Fergus had been such a weak man. Had he thought that taking his own life would make him strong? He'd had no control over his mother, over his foolish young wife. Was this the one and only thing he did have control over? But, surely, he would have thought that taking the life of his own child was nothing but wrong. Perhaps he did not want to die alone. Perhaps he knew that child's fate would have been just as sorry as his. Elvira didn't want the boy. That would've left him to be raised by the same mother that had ruined Fergus's own life.

Eventually, the rage Ellis felt calmed and left a hollow place that filled with regret. Ellis had told himself all along that he had done everything he could for Fergus, and Fergus had simply not wanted his help. But now, in the cold and quiet of the morning, with Fergus upon the ground just beyond his reach, Ellis was overwhelmed with guilt. Where had he failed? What should he have done? What could he have done to save Fergus?

Time passed, but Ellis was unaware of it. He sat hunched against the car for a long time, his suffering complete. He could feel himself crumbling, caving in, collapsing like an old tin can being crushed beneath a shoe. His daddy's death, the discovery of his real mother and her questionable character, Clairey leaving, and now Fergus and the baby. He felt as if his life were falling apart.

Amidst his chaotic thoughts, Ellis thought of Clairey's face, and he clung to that image. He conjured the radiant glow of her eyes when she was pleased with something, and the small, bashful smile that was fleeting but infinitely more priceless because of its rarity. Clairey's memory was the light that came on the heels of a black and starless night. She was the most beautiful woman he had ever known. It was more than her looks that drew him to this conclusion; it was her kindness, her strength, her spirit. Somehow, the thought of her tethered him to sanity.

Ellis began to believe that perhaps there was a chance that things might be good again. He could collect his life back if he could only get Clairey to stay. He felt crushed, yes, and dangerously close to being defeated, but there was a moment when hope began to formulate, weak but persistent. It was possible that Ellis could salvage and build his life back if he could only change her mind, if she would only build it with him.

Ellis was not a runner, and neither was Clairey. If the two of them could stand together, there was a chance. Once his mind settled upon her, he knew that he couldn't give into the darkness he felt, the darkness that threatened to overcome him.

It was the sudden fluttering of a raven's wings that startled him from his thoughts, unaware of how much time had passed while he sat there. He blinked rapidly and looked about him in surprise, made aware all over again of what had happened in that place.

When the horror finally subsided, and he felt his wobbling legs could carry his weight, he made the conscious effort to get up from the ground. He began to walk back up the gravel drive, unwilling to confine himself to his truck. He wanted to breathe. He needed open space and the cold to remind him that he was still in the land of the living, not yet too numb to feel something. He walked back up the drive and knocked on the door again, this time with answers instead of questions.

Chapter 27

She worried over him. When would he return? When would he drive up in the old red truck and tell her there was nothing to be troubled over? She didn't know why, but Clairey kept thinking of the day he had gone into town alone. How he had come back changed, a different man. There was no real reason for her to assume the worst, but she did. It ate at her with dogged persistence. She was aware only of the slow passage of time. How ironic, she thought, that most of her life was spent waiting and not actually living.

Close to noon, Ellis came home. She was making her midday meal, not really sure if she should or shouldn't. His breakfast had gone uneaten, but she had hoped that by preparing it for him, it would somehow draw him home. Clairey had waited until it was good and cold before she'd cleared the plate away. Now, she wiped the flour from her hands with her apron as he came through the door.

He paused there in the door frame, clutching his fists in his pockets, his broad shoulders hunched, blocking out much of the light coming in from outside. When she saw him, she knew that something was terribly wrong from the look of ill-concealed despair that he wore upon his countenance. But she couldn't find the courage to ask. The possibilities terrified her.

"Ellis," she whispered. "You look like you done seen a ghost."

He walked deliberately to her, taking his hands from his pockets and gripping the sides of her face, gentle but firm. She had no choice but to look into his eyes, and his gaze was direct and intense, haunting really.

"I'm your man, ain't I?" he asked. "Ain't I your man?"

"Ellis what happened?" She talked low, betraying her emotions with the fear in her voice. "You're so cold."

"Ain't I your man?" he persisted.

"Yeah, Ellis, you're my man." Her lips quaked as she said it.

He saw this, and his eyes changed from an intense severity to tender and compassionate. He felt sorry for her in that moment, for all that she had been through. It hurt his heart to think on it. If he could have, he would have changed it all, made it right for her. But he was only a man. He did not possess those powers.

"Why you wanna go and leave?" he asked. All the time it had been between them, and they had never discussed it. He had never had the courage to find out until then. Maybe it was him. Maybe he was the reason that she did not want to stay. It could have been that she merely didn't want to be his wife. That she had discovered what everyone else already knew: that he was not worthy of being loved, that he was not capable of being cherished. In which case, Ellis's bruised and weakened ego could not bear that truth. His mind, which had earlier felt as if it might collapse, would surely not survive that bit of knowledge.

"Ellis? Tell me what troubles you," she entreated.

Because of her lack of an answer to his direct questioning, his shoulders seemed to drop, and he felt that his fears were confirmed. At that point, he should have let her go, should have walked away, but there was still so much that needed saying. He attempted to fight back his feelings, working over what he had just seen with Fergus and now what he was feeling with Clairey, and his voice cracked when he said, "I'm worn out, Claire. I'm just so worn out." He sighed deeply, a ragged, painful sound.

Ellis pressed his forehead to hers, the thought of his handkerchief tucked away with her things making him brave. "I'm tired of carryin' on like I don't want you. Like I don't feel nothin' when I see you." When he said it, there was a great relief that flooded over him, a weight that was lifted. A release of all the pain and anguish he was feeling. Good or bad, come what may, he had managed to say what he was thinking. He had at least made the effort.

Tears spilled from her eyes. "Ellis, what're you sayin'?" she cried, resting her hands against the front of his coat and pushing away from him so that she could see his face clearly.

"I don't wanna make you stay if you don't wanna. But I don't want you to go if you feel the same as me. It'd be foolish to do that." He paused, watching her to see if what he was saying was sinking in. "I love you is what I'm sayin', Claire. I don't wanna go on without you. You talk of leavin', and I just can't stand to think on it. There ain't nothin' I wouldn't do to have you." He leaned in against her and whispered against her skin, "I love you. I do."

"You don't mean it." She shook her head in disbelief.

"It's true. I wanna be what you need. I wanna give you all that you want. And I want you to feel the same. If you wasn't here, I don't got no reason to call it home."

She was crying, trembling in his arms, all her strength gone. He held her firmly, keeping her legs from giving way beneath her as she sagged against him. "Shh," he breathed. "Don't cry, Claire. Don't go and cry. I don't want you to never cry again."

"I saw her. I saw her with my own eyes, that girl you woulda had if it wasn't for me. You was talkin' to her. I saw."

"There ain't nobody else. Nobody but you," he insisted.

He thought of Dulcie Mae, of the fire he had felt when he was with her, of how it had burned itself out and became ash, leaving him nearly spent. But then Clairey had come into his life. She had been constant. She had been devoted and true to him—the flame that burned long and low, warming him even through the coldest night. She had stood by him even after she had discovered who his mother was, how he had no father. Would Dulcie Mae have done the same? The answer was in her rejection of him when he had offered her marriage. His journey to loving Clairey had been slower, but it had grown deeper and more endearing than he'd ever imagined.

"Why are you sayin' all this to me now?" She sobbed. "Why?"

Ellis cleared his throat, trying to dispel the emotion he was feeling, and hoped that his voice would be steady, that it wouldn't break. "Fergus is dead," he said.

"What?" she gasped. Her eyes grew wide in shock.

"Died at his own hand." He paused for a moment, the terrible visions of Fergus lying prostrate on the snow flooding his mind. "I s'pose he figured ain't life worth livin' if he don't have the woman he loved. And I ain't of a mind to make the same mistake," he said. "I ain't gonna let the woman I love walk away without a-tellin' her how I feel." He cupped her face in his hand, his eyes studying her intently. "So here it is, Claire. You're the only one ever really knew me, and I'd be nothin' if you's gone."

"Ellis," Clairey cried. "If you mean it, I won't go nowheres. If you really mean all that you done said, I'd be so pleased." She wrapped her arms around his neck and drew herself up to him, kissing him hard on his mouth, letting her emotions pass from her lips to his.

"I do mean it," he promised.

"Ellis," she whispered. "I love you. I do. Heart and soul, you got me."

Ellis was overcome by emotion as he sighed. He put his lips to hers, brushing them again and again, holding her as close to him as he could, wanting nothing more than for their bodies to dissolve into one another. "I'm your man, and you're my woman, Claire. And I'll never want for nothin' with you by me."

Part vi: Reaping the Harvest

Chapter 28

Fall of 1939

When he was born, he came out with his eyes wide open, looking like he was in shock or wonder, or maybe both. He didn't cry right away like most babies. Ellis said it seemed as if he were trying to take everything in, awed by his new world, not wanting to miss a moment of it. The boy was very much like Ellis had been, sober and intent from the beginning. They called him Jimmy. Jimmy didn't look a bit like his pappy, Jim Hooper, but he was named for him.

As he grew, he was told stories of his pappy, of the life he'd lived, of the man he had been. Ellis would sing the same songs—the one of the pony and the cart, and others his father had sung to him—and Jimmy would beg for him to sing them again. Although he would never meet his pappy, he knew him just the same. Everything that Jim had taught Ellis would be passed onto Jimmy. And, in time, Jimmy would pass that knowledge onto his children. In that way, Jim Hooper would live on forever.

There were times when Ellis thought on it, and then he would grow melancholy and ponder over his life and what it all meant, who he was and where he was going. There would always be some part of him that was incomplete. One thing was certain in his mind, though, Jim had saved him. Jim had loved him, just as a father should. He understood that more than ever now that he had a child of his own. Sure, Jim had made mistakes, had been very human, but Ellis hoped that he might do as well at raising his own boy.

It didn't fully dawn on him what Jim had done for him until one day when he was in town. Clairey was looking through the window of a shop that displayed bolts of fabric in the front of their store. Ellis liked to pamper her, mostly because she still was not used to it, and her reaction was always one of genuine pleasure.

He whispered in her ear, "Why don't you go on in and have a look, maybe get yourself somethin'."

She smiled and shrugged. "I shouldn't."

"Why not?"

"I don't know."

"I'll take Jimmy to the truck, and you go on in for a look-see. If you find somethin' you fancy, why, you go on and get it."

"You don't care?" she asked, touching his face with a brush of her fingertips.

"No, I don't mind. Come on, Jimmy," he said, taking the boy by the hand. "You and me'll go for a walk."

The boy trustingly slipped his small hand into his father's big one while clutching in his other hand a wooden horse Ellis had whittled for him.

They were walking along the storefronts, peeking in the windows occasionally, when the three-year-old tripped on his shoelace and fell. He cried some as Ellis bent down to pick him up and dust him off.

"We need to tie your lace," Ellis informed him, already busy at the task. He wiped Jimmy's eyes. "All better now. No more cryin'."

He hoisted the boy onto his shoulders, which delighted Jimmy, who seemed to forget all about his banged knee. He was too happy with the prospect of riding so high to be concerned over recent misfortunes.

The two of them came up to the grocery. Ellis hadn't stepped foot in the place since he had given the clerk a beating. He heard the bell jingle over the door, and out came a woman that had troubled his mind for several years now.

She looked very much the same — the sad expression, the broken look in her eyes. She wore an old calico dress with her graying hair done up in a bun. It seemed everything about her was faded, the color washed away, leaving her drab, leaving her dreary and worn. Her handbag dangled from her forearm as her free hand pumped a fan stamped with a voting advertisement. She stood just beyond the door, waiting.

Ellis stopped in his tracks, working over whether he should approach her or if he should alter his route and avoid her altogether. It had been she, that night at the barn dance, that had taken his face in her hand, that had examined him with an intensity he still could not forget. It wasn't that he thought on it often. Quite the opposite. She was an unsolved mystery but inconsequential enough to be put out of mind. Only sometimes he thought on it, but just long enough to think it was odd, and then dispel the memory to the back of his brain.

The woman did not notice him as she stood there, trying to cool herself with her fan. She seemed distant from him, in her own world, functioning apart from the here and now. And as Ellis stood there observing her, he thought on who she was and what she had seen in her lifetime. Had she been pretty when she was young? Did she grow up on a farm or in town? Did she have both a father and a mother, or was she, like him, an orphan? For a moment, the mystery deepened. He thought maybe he should approach her after all, try to start up a conversation that might eventually lead to how she knew him, why she had spoken to him at the dance.

He watched her there until a man came out of the store to claim her. It must have been her husband from the familiar way they interacted. He took her by the arm with the distinct attitude of ownership. They belonged to one another. She looked up at him, and Ellis couldn't tell what she might be thinking. Was it a smile or a grimace?

Just as he was ready to walk away, he caught sight of the man. The stranger had finally turned toward him, and Ellis felt the blood drain from his face. Like looking into a crystal ball that foresaw the future, Ellis was looking at a man that could have been him in thirty years. The same face, weathered by time, the same hair, peppered with gray — the man was a duplicate copy but for the aging he had undergone over his lifetime. The goose bumps rose on Ellis's skin, and he got a sudden chill. It was then, as he stood there dumbly with his mouth slightly open, that the woman caught his eye.

When she made eye contact, he understood. She had known all that long time. She had known that Ellis was more than a stranger. Ellis was seeing his father for the first time. No longer some abstract notion, some no-name, no-face specter that haunted his dreams in waking and sleep. It was a man of flesh and bones. His *real* father. She saw that he'd seen, and she looked hopelessly lost, utterly devastated.

There was a pleading in those eyes that made him feel something—he didn't know what—but something that was deep and agonizing.

They were very close then, just ready to pass him by as he stood with his feet rooted to the spot. The tug of war going on in his head prevented him from any action. Just as he was ready to turn and run and get out of that place, Jimmy dropped his horse, and it fell to the ground just in front of Ellis. Like a fool, he could not move. Like an imbecile, he could not make his limbs work in their proper fashion.

The stranger—his father—stopped and thoughtfully bent over to retrieve the horse. He straightened upright with the slow careful movements of an older man.

As they exchanged glances, an understanding, a spark of recognition, passed between them. Ellis knew that he knew too.

The older man handed the horse back to Jimmy. "There you are, son," he said, addressing Jimmy.

Jimmy accepted the horse with a "Thank you, mister," and the man moved on.

Ellis stared after him until he had gone several feet. When he found his voice, it sounded strange even in his own ears. "What's your name?" he called out, a ring of desperation in his voice.

The man paused and slowly turned around to face him once again. He didn't answer right away, perhaps contemplating whether he should or not. Then he hollered back, "Artie. Artie Brown." He watched Ellis briefly with a look of longing and sorrow and remorse all in one. He had lived a long time with this knowledge, and there hadn't been a day that hadn't passed with the thought of it somewhere in the back of his mind; it was all on his face, and Ellis saw it, recognized it for what it was. Then he ducked his head down before he spun back around and continued on walking with a slow, deliberate shuffle, walking away in the opposite direction. Ellis never saw him again.

What makes a father? A name? A face? The genetic code which he bestows upon his offspring? All that he is, all that he will ever be, is a direct result of how he has been raised.

Ellis had become what Jim had trained him up to be. It was simply the law of the harvest. He remembered faintly Jim Hooper's tender voice in his head admonishing him: "You reap what you sow, boy. You sow good, you reap good. You sow bad, and by and by, you gonna reap it too."

Special Thanks

Thank you so much to all of those who have helped make this book possible: my parents; my wonderful husband, without whom nothing would be possible; my friends who willingly read early drafts; Kathy Summers for extensive edits and talk fests; my book group gal pals for reading and feedbacks. I am grateful as well to everyone involved from Omnific Publishing: Lisa O'Hara, Alicia Stevens, Traci Olsen, and everyone else behind the scenes! I would not be who I am without all of you.

About the Author

Born and raised on the flatlands of Central Indiana, Tracy moved to the highlands of Utah at the age of nineteen. She quickly discovered that her brand new, top-of-the-line hiking boots were a waste of good money because she was never quite able to acclimate to the altitude in the Rockies. Tracy claims to suffer from a type of disorientation she attributes to altitude sickness to this day. It seems to be a permanent affliction.

Her husband Benjamin cohabitates in a home with Tracy and the four beautiful but precocious children they lovingly created together. Although to others, their home may seem alarmingly chaotic, it is an insanity of their own making.

⟵—➤Erotic Romance⟵—➤

Becoming sage by Kasi Alexander
Saving sunni by Kasi & Reggie Alexander
The Winemaker's Dinner: Appetizers and *Entrée* by Dr. Ivan Rusilko &
Everly Drummond
The Winemaker's Dinner: Dessert by Dr. Ivan Rusilko

⟵—➤Paranormal Romance⟵—➤

The Light Series: Seers of Light, Whisper of Light, and *Circle of Light*
by Jennifer DeLucy
The Hanaford Park Series: Eve of Samhain & *Pleasures Untold* by Lisa Sanchez
Immortal Awakening by KC Randall
Crushed Seraphim and *Bittersweet Seraphim* by Debra Anastasia
The Guardian's Wild Child by Feather Stone
Grave Refrain by Sarah M. Glover
Divinity by Patricia Leever
Blood Vine and *Blood Entangled* by Amber Belldene
Divine Temptation by Nicki Elson

⟵—➤Historical Romance⟵—➤

Cat O' Nine Tails by Patricia Leever
Burning Embers by Hannah Fielding
Good Ground by Tracy Winegar

⟵—➤Romantic Suspense⟵—➤

Whirlwind by Robin DeJarnett
The CONduct Series: With Good Behavior & *Bad Behavior* by Jennifer Lane
Indivisible by Jessica McQuinn
Between the Lies by Alison Oburia

⟵—➤Anthologies⟵—➤

A Valentine Anthology including short stories by Alice Clayton,
Jennifer DeLucy, Nicki Elson, Jessica McQuinn, Victoria Michaels,
and Alison Oburia